SURESH KOHLI was a poet, literary critic, editor, translator, film historian and documentary filmmaker. With 33 published works (including a novel) to his credit, he had also made 100 short films on literature and culture. Apart from India, his films have been screened in Australia, France, Germany, Spain, Nepal and the UK.

RUCHI KOHLI VADEHRA divided her growing-up years between Delhi, Bhopal and Dehradun, with an enviable library and master storytellers for constant company. A voracious reader, she has nurtured a deep love for nature, literature and travel. A juggler of words, Ruchi's penchant for writing culminated in her debut novel, *Great Texpectations*, which was published in May 2018.

MODERN INDIAN SHORT STORIES

Edited by

Suresh Kohli & Ruchi Kohli Vadehra

Om Books International

First published in 2021 by

Om Books International

Corporate & Editorial Office
A-12, Sector 64, Noida 201 301
Uttar Pradesh, India
Phone: +91 120 477 4100
Email: editorial@ombooks.com
Website: www.ombooksinternational.com

Sales Office
107, Ansari Road, Darya Ganj,
New Delhi 110 002, India
Phone: +91 11 4000 9000
Fax: +91 11 2327 8091
Email: sales@ombooks.com
Website: www.ombooks.com

ISBN: 978-93-52766-21-5

Printed in India

10 9 8 7 6 5 4 3 2 1

CONTENTS

INTRODUCTION

My father, Suresh Kohli, lived and breathed stories. Whether in the literary circles of Delhi and Mumbai, or at home, this argumentative Indian's calling card was 'poet, literary critic, editor, translator, film historian and documentary filmmaker'. He would spend hours in his study, glasses perched on nose tip, sifting through mounds of material for the next collection he had promised a publishing house. This series on modern Indian short stories for Om Books International too started on one such day when my father, sitting in the peace and quiet of his study, found the idea worth revisiting.

The first volume, *Stories from Modern India,* was published on 1 January 2013. With its sterling line-up, it became a best-seller. Two years later, on 1 January 2015, *Great Stories from Modern India* was published. It became an instant hit. Going by pendulum regularity, the third volume, *Modern Indian Short Stories*, was to be published on 1 January 2017. But on 23 March 2016, my father, frail of health, yet undaunted in spirit, unexpectedly called it a day.

Since the first quarter of 2015, my father started to sit me down regularly, and discuss the stories that were to be part of the present collection. There was nothing unusual about that. Nicknamed the home bard, he had always regaled us with countless tales. Little did I know he had sensed he was winding down, and had decided to groom me for a new role. In fact, he had already charted out a road map I could follow in case he was recalled to the wings before he could see the collection through.

On 23 September 2016, my mother Chetana Kohli and I picked up the threads. The process, albeit therapeutic, wasn't easy. We felt like interlopers digging into my father's correspondence. My father, of course, would not have wished it any other way. Amidst a flurry of emails and phone calls with the contributors, at times with their literary estates and translators, some already known to my mother, one thing emerged clearly—each one would honour the commitment they had made to their friend, Suresh Kohli. We pressed on, encouraged by such warmth.

We reread each story, each translation, and understood anew the reasons my father had picked them. Each intricately woven tale endeavours to make visible the invisible and articulate voices that are often marginalised. These stories, written in different Indian languages and English, evoke myriad emotions and are more socially relevant than ever in our turbulent times.

Varsha Adalja's 'Breaking Free' explores the complex themes of crime, punishment and redemption. It takes a hard look at the Indian criminal justice system and the horrors of domestic violence.

Ajeet Cour's 'Happy New Year' is an in-depth portrayal of the bureaucratic machine in India and its inner workings. It is also a sensitive portrayal of people caught between the pull and push of living.

Kamala Das's 'Velutha Babu' provokes the reader with its shocking, unpredictable climax that is bound to keep the reader thinking about the true nature of the 'self'.

'Precaution!' by Vijaydan Detha is an interesting tale about life in India through the clever use of animal imagery. Mythology and elements of the folk tale blend seamlessly to provide an engaging read and throw light on human relationships.

'Dalia' lays bare the machinations of feudalism. Gulzar sensitively traces the trajectory of the lives of the powerless as they grapple with power structures that have flourished in India for centuries.

With its spectacular imagery, 'The Ship of Butterflies' by Thomas Joseph takes the readers on an exhilarating voyage of the high seas and the human heart, melding fantasy, myth, romance and fairy-tale.

When my father had asked me to go through Pritish Nandy's *Ma and Other Short Stories* to take my pick, 'Ma' had immediately touched a chord. In this poetic story, faith and family take centre stage. Nandy highlights the role familial bonds and religion play in human interactions in India.

Amin Kamil's hard-hitting 'The Enigma' focuses on the plight of the common man in Kashmir, tracing the insidious ways in which geo-politics impacts individual lives.

My maternal grandfather Prabhakar Machwe's beautifully crafted story, 'Gul,' resurrects memories of the struggle for independence and India's fight against colonialism.

Sukhbir's captivating 'A Sealed Bottle of Wine' poignantly delves into an episode that salvages the remnants of empathy and rehabilitates the lapsed benevolence of human nature.

The stories in this collection represent the diversity of India. Grappling with captivating and socially relevant themes, they cover the entire spectrum: spiritual, philosophical, political, carnal, romantic, and more. These Indian stories celebrate the universality of humanism, horror, pathos and brutality.

I am deeply grateful to Ajay Mago, Publisher, Om Books International, Dipa Chaudhuri, Chief Editor and Vineetha Mokkil, my editor, for holding this collection dear to their hearts, and for trusting me to do right by it.

Chetana Kohli, and Kanchi Kohli and Nupur Bery, my sisters, thank you for undertaking this journey with me. The weight of Father's mantle felt so much the lighter for it.

Suresh Kohli, as I humbly try to take forward your legacy, I hope wherever you are, you have that unfathomable nod of approval that was quintessentially you.

Ruchi Kohli Vadehra
2020

BREAKING FREE

Varsha Adalja

The doors of the prison opened and Avni stepped out. The doors clanged shut behind her, pushing her out in a new world. She walked a few steps—oh, the beautiful sunshine, the incessantly blowing wind, the tree leaves rustling, the dogs barking somewhere. Taking it all in, she just choked up. She couldn't take a step further—oh freedom! She sat down under a tree, putting aside her small bag with her clothes and a few knick-knacks—the very same clothes she had worn on that fateful night that she had entered the high walls of the prison for the first time.

She recalled how on that night too, with just one step in, she had been instantly thrown into the strange new world of a prison. She couldn't believe that she was facing several small cells, with prisoners staring at her questioningly. She had started shivering with shock, so much so that she had to lean on the jailor's table to remain steady, or she would have collapsed. Surely, it was all a nightmare! She had no idea what the jailor asked her and what replies she gave. The nightmare continued as she was thrown into a large room full of women prisoners—some working, some lying down, and some even with small children.

Then she started to panic. She could feel the bile in her mouth. She sat down in a corner, holding her head between her knees. Some prisoners came to her and asked if she was okay, but she just sat very still, trying to stem her panic. They were miffed at her silence. "Let her be, the bloody bitch is a murderer—a murderer no less, and acting pricey!"

Oh God, "murderer?" The word hit her solar plexus like a bolt from the blue. 'Am I a murderer? Yes, of course. Last night, I had plunged a long sharp knife into Kedar with all my might.' He couldn't believe either that it had happened. "Avni, what have you done?" But in her state of mind, she was in no position to hear anything. In her frenzy, she had stabbed Kedar again and again. It was an out-of-body experience. She had came to her senses with a start as the blood flowing from Kedar's body had almost touched her feet.

Avni started screaming loudly as she went back in time,. Frightened by her own screams, she curled up in a foetal position, striving to protect herself from this horror.

A woman prisoner came to her and asked, "Why did you murder him?"

Avni again felt the bile rising in her mouth and put up her hands to suppress it.

"Was he your lover? I also killed my husband. The bastard would drink all day and then assault me. He was even having sex with prostitutes." The woman took a drag on her beedi and continued, "He was a real son of a bitch—*saala* guttersnipe outright," and she spat out. "It doesn't matter to anyone that he assaulted me every day, but when I killed him, and good riddance to the bloody scoundrel, I was sentenced to five years."

Hearing the word "sentence," Avni came out of her stupor—no, no, I won't get a sentence. I am a good, decent, educated person. Then the reality hit her and she started sobbing.

The woman said, "Don't cry silly. Even I had cried a lot, but I still got five years in prison. Never mind, when I complete my term and get out, I'll get married again, to his brother. He is a good sort."

Avni felt like she was caught in a surrealistic web, and its vice-like grip was choking her. She wanted to scream out loud that she was actually not a vicious person. She was a highly educated, idealistic woman and she wouldn't get a prison term. She would be released; she would be set free. How in the world would she be able to live with these scum-of-the-earth criminals?

The woman blew smoke rings and then threw away the butt. "Don't get scared! Initially, everyone panics, but then the prison grows on you, and you actually begin to like it better inside. Do you understand?"

Avni started fuming within. Why was she even talking to this woman? She leaned against the wall and closed her eyes, ending the dialogue.

What a world of difference between yesterday and today! Yesterday, she had been a happy housewife and a free bird. Today, she was a murderer, sitting with another murderer in prison. She swallowed hard and thought of Paritosh, her husband. He will come any moment now and take her in his arms and all her bitter troubles and misfortunes will disappear. Paritosh, so loving, so caring, smart, intelligent—he will deal with all the court and legal hassles and take her away from this god awful prison to her happy homestead. A long time ago, he had done something similar. He had taken her away from her lonely existence in an orphanage into another world and married her. Today too, he will be her Saviour. Then why worry?

"Your advocate has come to meet you." A tense voice broke her sweet reverie. The other prisoner left in a huff. Avni got up and went into the visitor's room.

It was Umesh, her brother-in-law. "Avni Bhabhi, don't worry at all. But what happened? How come?"

Avni began to relive those moments of the murder scene—Kedar's corpse at her feet, his eyes staring at her in shock and surprise. She was standing over him with a long sharp knife in her blood-soaked hands. She started sobbing as if her heart would break.

"Please Bhabhi, don't cry."

"Umesh, I still can't believe that I have killed—I am a murderer!"

"Don't worry Bhabhi, things will be all right. Where is Paritosh? Wasn't he with you?" The very mention of Paritosh began to soothe her nerves.

"God, I am also waiting for Paritosh. He has gone to Delhi for office work. I was alone at home. I am sure he must have got the message by now."

"You mean, he doesn't know? I am really surprised at the turn of events. Kedar is such a close friend of ours!"

Avni wondered what she should tell Umesh and how much! Should she tell him the gory details—that Kedar had tried to rape her! Tomorrow, it would be on the front pages of all the newspapers, with her picture alongside—a housewife from a rich family involved in rape and murder! No, no, never.

"I am sorry, Bhabhi. I know you must be in a shock and totally traumatised, but as your lawyer, I need to know all the details to prepare the case. Just tell me now if you really murdered Kedar, and if so, why, how?"

Avni flopped down on a bench and sighed. Now she would have to narrate the details over and over—not only to Umesh, but to others too and must also face many unspoken questions.

"Yes, Umesh. I killed Kedar. Day before, he returned suddenly from Bangalore and came to our house. He was in a great mood because he had finally got his divorce after a long wait. Paritosh was in Delhi, so Kedar took me out for dinner to celebrate. I rang you up to join us, but you and Heena were not at home. So finally, the two of us went out for dinner. Kedar kept drinking all through dinner. Though I dissuaded him, he paid no heed. We came home quite late."

Avni steeled herself to relive the incident once again. Kedar had ignored her pleas to not drink so much through dinner. He had become totally inebriated. On reaching home, she had started to get worried; her womanly instinct had sensed something wrong, something amiss, as if the air was heavy with lust and treachery. Kedar had then asked for some lime juice. The moment she had gone to the kitchen, he had come from behind her and tried to molest her. In the scuffle that ensued, trying to save herself from the lech, she had not even realised that she had killed him. It was as if she had been functioning on autopilot. It was much later when she regained her senses that she realised that Kedar was lying at her feet, soaked in his own blood.

Umesh consoled her—"Don't worry, Bhabhi, you were trapped. What you did was due to the circumstances. We will get hold of the best lawyers in town. When Paritosh arrives, tell him to meet me. By the way, what did you tell the police?"

"I told them everything. I was in no condition to lie."

Umesh left. Avni then returned to the prison room which was full of women prisoners. She sat down in a corner and closed her eyes. She saw Paritosh smiling at her and held on to the image to preserve her sanity. Maybe, she dozed off for a bit.

All of a sudden, she woke up as her hands and feet were cramping and heard someone telling her that Paritosh had come. Avni jumped up and almost ran into the visitor's room. Paritosh was standing there, a picture of dejection—head down, hands across his chest. Avni went and stood very close to him. He looked up. "Avni what happened? I don't understand."

"Even I don't understand how it happened," she said. "But Paritosh, now that you have come, I know I need not worry."

"Ya, right—but Kedar was murdered!"

"Even I can't believe that I have killed Kedar. You have no idea how horrendous it was for me last night. God alone knows I tried calling your Delhi hotel again and again, but the lines were down—just my luck."

"But how could Kedar do this?"

"It is beyond me. I cannot imagine, Paritosh. He was your close friend. When he came home, he was so happy about getting his divorce and then at dinner, he just kept drinking."

"But why did you go alone with him? Couldn't you have taken someone else with you?"

"I did call Umesh, but he had gone out with Heena, and thereafter, Kedar didn't allow me to call anyone else. Oh Paritosh! It's all so horrible."

Avni put her head on his chest and started weeping. "I told the police to inform you, and they immediately informed Delhi police."

Paritosh turned away and murmured, "That bum came and informed me while the Board of Director's meeting was in progress—'Mr. Paritosh, your wife has been arrested for the murder of your friend Kedar'—stupid, idiot. Anu, I felt so ashamed. Everyone in the meeting stared at me as if I were some strange creature and that rascal Inspector Chauhan, he started questioning me. God, I felt so humiliated."

"The inspector informed you in front of everyone?"

"Yes, everyone relished the scandal—rape, murder and my wife involved." Paritosh loosened the tie from round his neck.

Avni felt a great weight crushing her inside. She was dying by inches; each word uttered by Paritosh was slicing up her heart. She was slowly dying—no, she already felt dead. She whispered, "Paritosh, I thought all my worries would be over when you come."

"Oh yes, sure—money is not the issue. I will give Umesh free rein. The best of lawyers will be engaged to fight your case. But do you see how bad I feel to face the society now—it's so terrible for me, for you."

"But Paritosh, I haven't done anything wrong. Any other woman in my place would also have defended herself." Avni started steadying herself.

"True, but rape, murder and your arrest—everything is grist for the newspapers."

"Are you saying that I should have succumbed to Kedar?"

"No, no, Anu, but some solution, some via media would have been possible—anything at all to safeguard our reputation, to save face, some compromise could have been found."

Avni slowly sat down on the bench, totally broken at this heartlessness. Paritosh stood in front of her, irritated, agitated, thinking only about his loss of face.

Avni had never felt so alone in her life. She asked, "What do you mean by compromise? The man was drunk and hell-bent on raping me. Do you think he would have responded to reason or tears? He was beyond it all. I never thought about killing him—it just happened in a flash."

Paritosh sat down next to her, dejected and despairing, "We have to face the reality of whatever has happened. It's my duty now to fight your case."

"Duty? You will fight my case because it's your duty? Reputation, duty, facing society—is that all you can think of? All you think about is yourself. What about me? Have you even thought about my anguish and the trauma I have undergone? Don't you want to know? Won't you ask me?"

"Anu, please get things in perspective—this whole incident is just a horrible nightmare. You are arrested for murder. When the case proceeds, people will indulge in gossip. I am in a predicament and I don't know what to do."

Avni kept staring silently at Paritosh from the depths of her despair. Was this the same person she had been eagerly awaiting all this while...who was to be her saviour? Had she lived with this person for so many years, giving him her body and soul, and not known him at all? All he cared about was his reputation and standing in society. He had no idea about her mental and physical trauma, nor did he care! For the first time in her life, she asked herself whether she really knew him.

Paritosh rambled on, "Anu, I was to be the president of the company this year. All my hard work over the years has gone down the drain. I had no idea all my dreams would come crashing down one day."

"True, Paritosh. Even I had no idea all my dreams would come crashing down like this one day."

Wallowing in his misfortune, Paritosh added, "Do you know Anu, what would have been my salary then, along with a car, house rent and a foreign business trip every two to three months? Now my career is finished."

"You can only think of your career and your future! What about me? What's going to happen to me now?" she blurted out although she did not want to.

"That's what I mean—people will doubt your character. Why would Kedar attempt to rape you? Oh Anu, you are so naïve! The prosecution will doubt only you. They will tear you apart during the cross-examination. Your honour will be at stake."

Avni screamed at Paritosh, "Stop it at once. Not only are you selfish, but you are a coward too."

"Anu—?"

"Are you shocked? Today, when I see the ugly truth about you, do you know that I am shocked to my core? You have no idea!"

"You call me selfish? What have I not given you? I left my home, I severed all ties with my mother, father, elder brother, my whole family for you—all for you, Anu."

Avni stepped aside, wondering how such straightforward statements could also be lies in disguise.

"I used to think so too, Paritosh, but not anymore. I know now that even if you had not married me, you would have still left home, your family, as you couldn't get along with your hot-tempered, stubborn father. Marriage was only a catalyst."

Avni realised that suddenly she was looking at things anew, especially her past life. Her eyes had finally opened and everything, every little detail was crystal clear now.

After marriage, Paritosh had received one promotion after another, courtesy her efforts and support. He would say that his boss enjoyed the parties she threw or that the boss's wife appreciated the decor of their house, done up by Avni. She had continued with her bits of favours, and Paritosh had continued to climb the corporate ladder.

Paritosh said, "Anu, you are doing an injustice to me by not trying to understand my point of view."

"No Paritosh, you have done a grave injustice to me. You have not treated me as a person, as an individual with my own identity. I have lived in your shadow and I was supposed to be happy about it. You showed me off as your trophy wife—a beautiful, smart wife, and as her owner, your prestige and position were enhanced."

Paritosh strode around the room twice. He had reached the end of his tether. He could not think anymore. He was at a loss. "Anu, you are not thinking straight now, but once this blows over, and we are together again, I will do everything to make you happy again. I promise I will engage the best of lawyers and I will not rest till you are set free."

"Yes, but you will do all this for your own sake, not for mine. If I am declared innocent and released, you will get back your position in the company and your prestige in society. Please leave now." Avni turned around and began to walk out of the room.

Paritosh grabbed her hand and stopped her. "Anu, Anu, have you gone mad? We will overcome this and settle back into our life as though nothing had happened."

Avni shook her hand free and continued to walk away. Once at the door, she stopped, looked back at him and calmly said, "Whatever happened has happened, Paritosh. Please don't bother about me. Don't do anything for me. I don't want to fight this case. I will admit a guilty plea and I will stay here in prison."

Paritosh couldn't believe his ears. "Anu, you have gone completely nuts. Don't you do anything so insane!" He started hyperventilating and grabbed her arm again, "Swear on me you will not do anything so stupid—you want to be here, in prison?"

"This is not a prison, Paritosh. Actually, this is a world where I will be breaking free from your world. There is no sham, no hypocrisy, no false prestige and no reputation to be saved. Nor will I be Avni—in this new world, I will just be a number."

"How will I live without you, Anu?"

"Once, even I thought that way, but now, I just want to discover myself, my real true self."

"Here, in prison? As a prisoner?"

"You are also a prisoner of the societal rules and hypocrisy. Your pretentious acts, false beliefs and ritualistic social practices are indeed more rigid than prison bars. Your world is free only in name; it is but an imprisoned freedom. Let me go, Paritosh." She left and reentered the prison—a world free of the sham and hypocrisy of the outside world as she knew it.

Clutching the small bag with her belongings in her lap, Avni sat there, resting her head on her bag. Her tumultuous prison term had scorched her beauty and youth, but her spirit was still intact—it was her *rebirth.* Avni picked up her bag and started walking on the long desolate road.

(Translated from the Gujarati by Yasmin Dhorda)

MADAMMA IN THE VILLAGE

Chandrika Balan

The day Madamma arrived, the entire village of Devigramam, presided over by the goddess, was in a celebratory mood. The village was literally upside down with enthusiasm and the monotony of routine life washed away.

Madamma came as Krishnan's wife. There are seven Krishnans in the village, so, let us be more specific. This Krishnan is known by his family name—Ambalakkadu Krishnan.

A day before Madamma's arrival, Appu Nair, the only shopkeeper of the village had declared the next day a holiday for the shop. "Please buy all that you need today itself," he told the villagers. "Don't come and knock at the shop door tomorrow and yell '100 grams of oil please' or 'Give me 10 chilies.' Whatever happens, I won't open the shop tomorrow."

"Why are you talking this way, Appu Nair? It is Ambalakkadu Krishnan who is bringing home his wife." Some villagers were irritated.

They never knew that Appu Nair had a prestigious duty on that day. Bullock carts were popular vehicles in the village, but Ambalakkadu Ammini Amma felt that she should not allow her son to come home with the foreign bride in a bullock cart. There was only one taxi in the village, painted yellow and black. She had hired it and asked Appu Nair to go to the railway station to receive her son and daughter-in-law.

Not only Appu Nair, but the entire village excitedly waited for Madamma. On the previous day, men had stood in queue in front of the only one barber shop to make themselves presentable. The girls and women had bought multicoloured bangles and ribbons from the bangle vendor to adorn themselves. When Krishnan had sent a telegram that he had married a Madamma, Ammini Amma had wailed loudly, beating her chest. But now, she dressed up in golden-laced saree and red blouse, combed her hair neat, and stood waiting with a fixed smile on her lips. The villagers gathered in her yard. Expectantly and slowly the crowd spilled over to the road too.

"How will Krishnan talk to Madamma?" one villager asked. "He had failed thrice in the tenth standard."

"Do you think he talks to foreigners in Malayalam?" Ammini Amma asked in anger. "You don't know, my son is so fluent in English. I had stood gaping, listening to him speaking in English."

"How can you say that? You don't know English."

"Why should I know English? Look here, one doesn't have to go to school or college to know these basics. What you do every day becomes your education."

The villagers thought that she had a point there. By profession, Krishnan was a tourist guide. They had heard of him roaming around with foreigners in renowned temples like Sree Padmanabhaswamy temple in Trivandrum, Suchindram temple and Kanyakumari temple in Tamil Nadu, etc. It was in the hands of Krishnan that the villagers had seen dollars for the first time. Also, Krishnan had the historical honour of introducing to the village pocket radios and goggles. When they took leave, the foreigners used to gift him with all the things they did not want to take back—like hats, slippers, trousers, shirts. Now he has got a Madamma!

"Just his luck!" A villager heaved a sigh. "Now he can go with her to some foreign country and settle down there."

"Aha!" Ammini Amma turned belligerent. "No one need dream like that. Krishnan is my only child. I will not allow any Madamma to take him away from me. If he flies, I will be flying with him."

And then they came. When the car was spotted with its dust trail, the village held its breath. Madamma arrived, sitting in the back seat of the car, nestling close to Krishnan. Appu Nair jumped out from the front seat and shouted like a police officer to the crowd to move away. The couple got out of the car. Those who were expecting Madamma to wear only minimal clothes were terribly disappointed. For, Madamma had clad herself in a cotton saree and blouse, had sandal and vermilion on the forehead and white jasmine flowers on the hair. When she smiled through her thickly painted lips and revealed her teeth like lightning, the village stopped breathing. Her blue eyes, ochre-shaded hair and the golden hairs on the fair arms put the villagers in a trance.

Madamma moved forward with firm steps and bent down to touch Ammini Amma's feet. Krishnan just stood there with a shy smile.

The villagers saw a thousand suns rising on the face of Ammini Amma. She blessed and embraced the daughter-in-law and turned to her son: "You naughty boy, come here. After doing all this mischief, you are standing aside!"

The villagers pushed Krishnan forward. Madamma stood with a pleasant expression on her face, watching the mother holding the son in a tight embrace. The villagers stood watching Madamma with open mouths.

One man whispered—"Did you see, her nose and cheeks have turned red. Unusual colour. Wonder why."

"It is her body getting used to our sun."

"Krishnan is really lucky! Wonder from where he got her!"

"What is her name, Krishna?" Ammini Amma asked.

"Radha," Krishnan told her.

"Radha?"

"Yes, Amma. She has changed to our religion, changed the name too."

"Okay. But what is her real name?"

"It will be difficult for you to pronounce."

"Says who? Don't forget that I too have whatever English you have."

"Her name is," said Krishnan, "Noela Miriam D'mello."

Ammini Amma and the villagers stood paralysed. Madamma opened her mouth and spoke in a nasal tone: "Yeah, I was Noela Miriam D'mello. But now I'm Radha. Radha Krishna. May I know your name, please?" she looked at Ammini Amma.

Ammini Amma and the villagers swallowed hard.

"She is asking for your name," Krishnan told his mother.

"If she calls me by my name, I will cut her tongue into two."

Krishnan told Madamma, "Her name is Ammini Amma. You call her Amma. It means Mother."

"Ammini? Oh, how nice! What does Ammini* mean?"

---

* Child's term for breasts in the local dialect.

"Krishna, what is she asking?" A man asked Krishnan who was standing with a reddened face.

"Asking for the meaning of the name."

"Oh, no!" Ammini Amma made sure that her saree was in place while the villagers suppressed smiles.

For the next few days, the villagers were over-curious to know what was happening in Ambalakkadu house and strayed about in the vicinity. They had heard of foreign ladies lying in the sun half naked to tan their bodies. They wandered like restless souls to be blessed with the rare sight in the village. But Radha, the Madamma, never obliged them.

"Will she be doing it in the night?" Somebody raised a doubt.

"You dunce, where is sun in the night?" Someone else silenced him.

The toilet of all the houses in the village were built outside the house, often with their walls and thatched roof made of leaves of the coconut trees. The Ambalakkadu toilet was no exception to this general rule. But one of the first things Krishnan did was remove it and build a new toilet, with walls around and a concrete roof overhead. The villagers thought it was because he did not want to let them know that Madamma used toilet paper. But Madamma surprised them by behaving like any village woman—drawing water from the well in the iron bucket and walking to the toilet with it.

"Then she is not a real Madamma," the villagers came to the conclusion. "Not really foreign, but hybrid. I have heard that in some parts of India, such people exist."

Ammini Amma was really irritated by the villagers staring rudely at her house. She wanted to build strong walls around the house, but Madamma did not agree to it. She said she was coming from a place where good fences did not make good neighbours and so wanted to enjoy the unlimited freedom of the village.

When she lay reading a book on the hammock tied to coconut trees, the villagers feasted their eyes on her. But soon, there were rumblings. Some people claimed that on a moonlit night, they had seen Ambalakkadu Krishnan lying by the lakeside, with his head on Madamma's lap. Madamma was stroking his hair and talking in a low tone to him. That was more than the freedom allowed by the village code to couples.

"What a shame! Why can't they lie somewhere inside the house?" The villagers became indignant. "Appu Nair, you are the only one to whom they will listen. Why don't you give them some advice?"

But Appu Nair did not know how to advise in English.

Once, some schoolchildren playing truant found Krishnan and Radha in the paddy field, sitting among the paddy grass, engrossed in a lip-lock kiss. After that, schoolboys started inviting schoolgirls—"Come, let us play Radha and Krishnan."

"This Madamma will ruin our village!" cried the villagers.

The elders of the village found the problem to be serious, but they were at a loss as to how to tackle it. Only the elders. The young generation was all for Madamma and used to frequent Krishnan's house to sit under the trees and talk to Madamma. The elders, after much speculation, came to the conclusion that it was because the young ones enjoyed Madamma's habit of shaking hands and patting on the back while talking that they visited her and liked her. They found that though her Malayalam was only on the tottering stage, Madamma was using it to lead the womenfolk of the village astray.

The women of the village were a disciplined lot and used to go near their husbands only at night. But now, influenced by Madamma, they wanted to be in the company of their husbands even at daytime. This was a big blow to the mothers-in-law of the village.

It seemed Madhavan's wife told Madhavan, "Today is full moon. Come Madhavetta, let us go, sit on the haystack. Don't you want to enjoy the moonlight?" It was only the previous day that some villagers had found Madamma and Krishnan lying in each other's embrace on the haystack in the back of their house. Madhavan has gone berserk at the shock and now he spends his day and night in the toddy shop, afraid to go home.

"She is misleading both the men and women," the elders said with a sigh. "Something has to be done."

They went to Ammini Amma with their complaint, but Ammini Amma jumped at their throats. "Have you people ever enquired how my son and I lived in the past? I worked in the paddy fields, helped with harvesting, worked as domestic help, washing dirty clothes and eating leftover food. But I sent my son to school till the tenth standard. Now luck has turned in our favour. Her father is a multimillionaire; do you know that? Do you know how many ships Lord D'mello has? She is our Devi's blessing to us. Today, we can cook rice by burning dollar notes. She will do whatever she likes. If you can put up with it, well and good. If not, it is your problem."

"That lady was always haughty and incorrigible. Now she is blinded by her sudden windfall. Appu Nair, you are the only one they are close to. Can't you talk to Krishnan at least?"

"How can I tell him not to be free with his own wife? That too from another country and culture? After all, he is of my son's age only."

Appu Nair cleverly dodged. Devigramam started fuming.

The young generation who used to visit Madamma in spite of all the warnings became the headache of almost every house. Some villagers spread the rumour that Madamma was addicted to drinks and drugs. But they were countered by the young generation who pointed out that Madamma went regularly to the Devi temple to pray. Madamma, they said, had come to Kerala as part of her spiritual quest.

The village of Devigramam had only one public library in the market square. It was used only by men. Some men used it for drinking and playing cards by daytime and at night, they used to bring whores there for enjoyment.

One fine morning, Madamma walked into the library, thus acquiring the historical importance of being the first woman to enter the library by daytime. She had come to have a look at the few English books that were reportedly there.

The card-playing gang—some of them sitting on platforms of heaped books—as well as Madamma, froze at the sight of each other.

"Wish I had the whip that Christ had when he threw out of the place of worship all those who were misusing it! A library is a holy place for reading, discussing and widening the horizon of knowledge. How can you even think of doing these shameful deeds here? You start a separate club for passive sports; I too will become a member. Leave the library for books and readers."

The trespassers stared at her, unable to understand her words till the retired schoolmaster who had come there to read the newspapers, translated them into Malayalam. Strangely, the men left the place in haste.

Appu Nair's youngest daughter said, "I want to go to the library. I want to read."

"Go to the library? Read? You are a girl. Stay indoors obediently or I will beat you to death," Appu Nair shouted at her.

"What is wrong with going to the library?" Appu Nair's wife asked. "Do you think only men are allowed to read?"

Appu Nair was literally jolted. Here was the woman who had obediently shared his life for 24 years! Every evening, as he came home from the shop, she used to wait with *dhanwantharam kuzhampu* to rub on his body and then warm the water for his bath. She who had never opposed anything he had said!

"Saudamini," he asked in a faltering voice, "do you also want to go to the library?"

"No, I don't. You don't have to send our daughter either. But going to the library is not a sin, but using it as a place for games and drinks is really sinful. No one had any complaint when the place that should have been held sacred was misused. How many times had I told you about the scoundrels there who were teasing women, passing obscene comments! Do you remember the day when our elder daughter came home crying because they had insulted her? You told her to close her eyes and ears and live. But you can't close your eyes and ears against Madamma, for she says and does only good things."

From that day on, Appu Nair was gripped by headache and depression. The villagers were horrified to see Appu Nair sitting silently inside the shop and selling things mechanically. They saw it as portending worse calamities that Madamma would be bringing to the village. They were scared that she would transform them too into wooden dolls with mechanical movements.

Strict injunctions were passed that those men who returned home after twilight were not to use the shortcut via Ambalakkadu house. Grandmothers taught grandchildren that Madamma was possessed by the devil, that her blue eyes were that of Kalliyankaatu Neeli, (the legendary demon who was brutally killed by her husband, rose from death to take revenge on him and then roamed around, killing people), that they should chant the names of God whenever they went by that house. The old generation of the village bowed at the feet of the Devi and prayed to her to save the children from Madamma's clutches.

Oh, omniscient Mother, nothing is impossible for you. Please save our village.

And thus, one day the wonder of wonders happened. Madamma, with a stern face, walked out of Ambalakkadu house with two bags bulging with her belongings, crossed the paddy fields to the temple road, oblivious of the numerous eyes staring at her, and got into the yellow-and-black painted taxi. The taxi zoomed away, leaving a trail of black smoke.

The villagers, totally confused, rushed to Ambalakkadu house. Krishnan was sitting on the verandah, leaning against the pillar, his eyes red and cheeks bearing fresh tear-marks. They heard Ammini Amma crying aloud and lamenting in incoherent words from inside the house.

"She left me," Krishnan told the villagers in a voice weighed down with emotion. "She says there is no mental compatibility between us."

The villagers were hearing of such compatibility for the first time. They stood bewildered, looking at each other. Since Krishnan walked into the house and closed the doors, they could not solve their doubts.

As usual, one villager came forward with an opinion: "They may not have matched the horoscopes. Maybe they are talking of planetary incompatibility."

"Don't talk nonsense," another one said. "Do you think foreigners have horoscopes?"

One of the senior villagers said, "Now who will say our goddess is not powerful? She has listened to our prayers."

"That is true!"

The villagers cried aloud, "*Thank you, oh Devi, the omniscient, the omnipotent one!*"

Naturally, the story has to come to an end here. But something interesting happened in the village after a few days. How can the story end without sharing with the readers that news too?

Appu Nair's elder daughter came back home with her two children. She told her father, "I can't live with him. There is no mental compatibility between us."

The number of girls who return from their husbands' homes due to mental incompatibility is on the rise in the village. The library has been reclaimed by the card-players, womanisers and other anti-socials. The goddess sits in the temple after *madhupuja*, satiated with offerings of palm wine. The helpless villagers throng before her with the cry, "Oh Mother, save us, oh, our Devi!!"

(Translated by the author from the Malayalam)

HAPPY NEW YEAR

Ajeet Cour

After years of hammering away on typewriters, Kapoor's fate came to be linked with that of an Honourable Minister of the Central Government. Overnight, his status was elevated from a plain and simple Kapoor to Kapoor Sahib: Personal Assistant to the HM (Honourable Minister).

In those few hours, his chest expanded visibly by a couple of inches. When he strutted down the office corridors, his chest puffed out like that of a crested bantam cock; it seemed as if the corridors were not broad enough for him. Peons, who usually sat on their stools, chewing betel leaf or nodding off, would spring to attention and salute him as he passed.

The metamorphosis took place a few days before the year was to end. In the long years that Kapoor had been a clerk, he had never as much as thought of such trifles as New Year's eve or New Year's day. It had never occurred to him that the year which had been young a little while ago had aged and would soon give up the ghost.

The 31st of December was no different from the 30th or 31st of other months—days of penury. The 1st of January was like the

1st of any other month when he received his month's salary, paid off his debtors, fulfilled his children's oft-postponed demands for new exercise books, new textbooks, new pairs of socks to replace the old ones riddled with holes, school uniforms, pencils, etc.

While doing all those things, he experienced a strange mix of sensations—an imperious feeling of lording over other people's destinies as well as a diminution of stature which came with the realisation that before half the day was over, more than half his salary would be eaten up.

After Kapoor was transformed to Kapoor Sahib, his lifestyle changed.

How the transformation came about was very simple. A businessman—to be more exact, an industrialist—who, had some business with Kapoor's Minister, arrived at the ministerial residence armed with a New Year's gift.

The date: December 31.

The time: 8 am.

Kapoor was ensconced in a room in the outer verandah and seated in the chair of the personal assistant to the Hon'ble Minister.

The Minister took one look at the packet and remarked, "Sorry, I have given up drinks. You must know what the Prime Minister's views on the subject are. She has ordered..."

The industrialist muttered a curse under his breath which referred to the Minister's shady relations with his own mother. At the same time, he felt apprehensive that the bugger might be trying to slip out of his grasp.

However, he bared his dentures and replied, "Not at all, Sir, I'll bring something else tomorrow or the day after. But this is New Year's eve and I mustn't leave without an offering for you." He opened his briefcase, took out a diary and placed it on the table before the Minister. It was a miserable little specimen printed at the government press. However, tucked between its pages was a wad of other papers also bearing the imprint, 'Government of India'. The Minister opened the diary, felt the thickness of the wad of notes and remarked, "You needn't have taken the trouble! It wasn't really all that necessary for you to go out of your way to do all that."

"No trouble at all, Sir," sniggered the industrialist. "This is only to buy sweets for the children."

It can be established that as a person rises in stature, his children's appetite for sweets and candies also increases. The candy box in the diary was worth more than a confectioner's shop crammed with goodies.

The Minister gave a wan smile, baring two-and-a-half of his dentures, and quietly slipped the diary inside the drawer of his table.

The industrialist sighed with relief. It had been a touch-and-go affair.

As he stepped out of the Minister's office, he handed the parcel he had brought for the Minister to Kapoor. The Personal Assistant to the Minister too had to be kept happy. All this happened so quickly that Kapoor was neither able to protest nor as much as utter a word of thanks. It was the first time in his life that someone had considered him worthy of a gift of any kind.

He was somewhat ill at ease but the industrialist's voice, as he left with a triumphant smile, was most reassuring, "It's a small gift for the New Year." Kapoor's hands shook as he put the bottle inside the drawer of his table. He felt hot all over.

Vashisht, the typist, shared the room with Kapoor. He had been the Minister's typist and had sat in the same corner for many years. On the very first day when Kapoor came to occupy his new chair, Vashisht had introduced himself with a reassuring smile, "Don't you worry, Sir, I will show you the ropes. Ministers come and go; their jobs are not permanent. But your humble servant has been confirmed in his post for years and is quite familiar with the goings-on that take place in this room. I will see to it that no trouble comes near you."

Vashisht sensed Kapoor's predicament and casually walked up to him as he took a betel leaf out of a wrapper. "Congratulations, Kapoor Sahib! The first gift is like the ceremony of removing the nose-ring of a bride. You must entertain your humble servants with this bottle and thus ensure the grace of God. We will always pray for your health."

Kapoor was a novice at the game. He immediately realised he could not drink a whole bottle of Scotch all by himself and was relieved that now someone was there to share it with him. "Sure! Why not?" he replied.

"Fine! This evening, we'll welcome the New Year at your home as all the *burra sahibs* do in big hotels. Singing and embracing each other's wives at the midnight hour. If you don't mind, may I invite Gupta on your behalf?"

Gupta was the second typist. He sat in another room which he shared with some other clerks. Besides typing, Gupta's duty was to receive and sort out the mail, which was then passed on to someone else for despatch.

"Sure!" replied Kapoor, expansively.

Kapoor came home a little earlier than usual, carrying the bottle of Scotch in his briefcase. Not anticipating what the reaction of his wife would be, he was not prepared for the tongue-lashing she gave him. "Did you have to bring this destroyer of families into your home? And drink the evil stuff in the presence of the children! New Year? What the hell is this New Year? Today is the 31st—and there is neither a vegetable nor a scrap of biscuit or anything else to eat in the house. I am ashamed of asking the grocer for another loan. Only yesterday I told him I would not be buying anything more this month and asked him to make our bill so that I could clear it by the 1st. We already owe him Rs. 983. If we take another loan, your guests will eat it up. They will go back merrily to their homes, but what will we live on? You want us to eat at the free kitchen at the gurudwara all of next month? New Year indeed! These fads are for the idle rich; people who frequent five-star hotels. We have barely enough to fill our bellies and never a paisa to spare. Only I know how I count every paisa and stretch it out over 30 days!"

What was poor Kapoor to do? If you put your head between the jaws of a crocodile, you cannot hope to escape without a scratch! He tried to explain in his softest tone, "My good woman, this New Year is an English festival, exactly like our Baisakhi or Diwali." But the good woman was beyond reason and refused.

Exactly at 7.45 pm, the two men arrived, accompanied by their wives and their brood of children. The women and children went into the inner room. Normally, children could be expected to create an uproar, but being clerks' offspring, they clung to their mothers' aprons and whimpered like little pups. In any case, it was a very cold evening, and their mothers could not get rid of them by ordering them to go out to play.

Men gathered around the bottle of Scotch and started nibbling on salted peanuts with their drinks. Sitting in another room, the womenfolk compared the prices of potatoes.

"In any event, Kapoor Sahib owed us a treat for his promotion," remarked Vashisht. Kapoor expanded like an inflated balloon. However, he pulled a long face and replied, "What kind of a promotion, *yaar*! Promotion means increase in one's salary. All I have got is more work. I used to get to office at 10.30 in the morning and leave at 4.30 in the evening. Now I have to report at the Minister's residence at 7.45 am and stay up to 8 or 9 pm. I'm sure I don't have to tell you all this!"

"To hell with the work, Mr. Kapoor! Your sphere of influence has expanded; your status has risen to new heights!" remarked Gupta.

"Lots of things happen to people who occupy your chair. You recall that fellow called Sood? Narinder Sood was his full name. He used to sit in the same chair. It must have been about eight years ago when a licence applied for by a Bombay firm got stuck somewhere in the files of the ministry. The firm's chaps had been going round and round for weeks but the Minister was like a duck which would not let a drop of water stay on its back. Utterly defeated, these Bombay Johnnies came to Sood's house and fell at his feet. This Sood fellow performed such jugglery that before the month was over, the licence was cleared. It was entirely Sood's handiwork. The Bombay people worked out that each visit to Delhi cost them Rs. 10,000 to 20,000. So why not employ Sood to do the work for them? They persuaded him to resign from his job, and made him their Resident Executive Director in Delhi. They gave him an air-conditioned office and a spacious apartment. Now Sood and his pretty Private Secretary travel in a chauffeur-driven car. They make the rounds of different offices, handing out invitation cards for dinners. He dines out every night with officials at swanky hotels like the Oberoi, the Taj or the Maurya. Every month, lakhs of rupees pass through his hands; every day, he wears a new suit made of imported material," Vashisht narrated the story of Sood's achievements as though they were blood brothers.

"And *banda parwar* (protector of the poor), you must know that every currency note has a little glue stuck to it. As they are passed along from one hand to another, some get stuck to one hand, some to the other. You are a man of the world, you must know all this," said Gupta.

Kapoor's third eye was beginning to catch a glimmer of light.

"My good friend, all I know is one basic fact. These 84 lakh forms of existence that our holy books talk of are in fact one—that of a clerk. A clerk goes through all the incarnations—cat, dog, scorpion, turtle, jackal, pig, and everything else. And just as a person goes through the 84 lakh incarnations before taking birth as a human being to rule the world, so once in a millennium, a clerk is fortunate enough to be appointed Personal Assistant to a Minister," Vashisht was well versed in the holy texts.

"That may well be so," conceded Kapoor with a half-hearted laugh, "but there is no escaping the fact that the workload becomes much heavier. Your sister-in-law (my wife) has been scolding me for the last 10 days."

"She shouldn't treat a man of your standing like that?" sniggered Gupta.

"Why don't you put some sense in her head? Tell the good lady that by the grace of the chair you occupy, all the four horizons will soon light up. Then, she will prepare *halwa* full of dry fruits and glasses of milk laced with almonds before she sends you to your office," Vashisht roared happily.

"This bottle of Scotch is the first ritual—the sort of gift you give a bride when she first unveils her face," added Gupta.

The two men treated Kapoor like a neophyte about to have his ears pierced before he is accepted by a guru as his disciple.

"When my wife looked at this bottle, it seemed all hell would break loose," said the new convert Kapoor.

Vashisht interrupted him by pleading in a mewling voice, "Please, please, explain all this to our Bhabi. Put some divine wisdom into her head."

Gupta lent his voice in support, "Tell her how everyone in the Customs is eager to be posted at Palam or Sahar Airport and get all sorts of influential people to speak for them. Every traffic constable and sales-tax officer does his level best to be posted in Chandni Chowk, Sadar or Chawri Bazar. How many shoes do they have to polish with butter before they get these postings! What's more, in these big hospitals, when a doctor is put in charge of the wing reserved for VIPs, his colleagues burn with envy. The workload is undoubtedly doubled. But just think—the bigger the head, the bigger the headache."

"Now, take the case of the Prime Minister," said Vashisht. "The poor thing works 18–19 hours a day. During the elections, she runs from one village to another. What prizes does she get for all this trouble?"

"Quite right! All these ministers and leaders of political parties do not run around for the heck of it. With time, all your troubles will be over," said Gupta, laughing.

The bottle was nearly empty. The peanuts had been nibbled away. Gupta glanced at his watch. "Friends, it is almost 9.30. Let us have something to eat. We will not get any buses after 10.30. And we are not ministers who can order our cars..."

Kapoor got up and went inside. A little later, Kapoor's children trooped in, carrying bowls full of lentils cooked in onions and potato curry. The three men were in the outer room; their wives, and children in the other room inside.

Kapoor's wife was busy baking *chapatis*. Her children ran up and down the two rooms serving the guests hot *chapatis*.

By 10.15, the guests departed.

Kapoor felt like a criminal. He started making the beds in the two rooms. He could hear his wife grumbling away as she rinsed the cooking pots and plates. "New Year indeed! To hell with such festivals in this biting cold. They may suit white people. We have our own Diwali and Baisakhi, both in fair seasons. Only Lohri is in winter and people light bonfires to warm themselves. And here I am, rinsing all this garbage with icy cold water. To hell with this New Year."

At long last, the lights were switched off. The children were fast asleep. But Kapoor's wife went on nagging and grumbling. After a while she said, "New Year be damned! Why doesn't it fall on the 2nd of January? By then, you would have drawn your salary."

His wife's voice flitted about in the dark like a bat going round and round the room, and then found a perch on a wall.

At midnight, when the lights in all the five-star hotels were dimmed so that men could embrace and kiss other men's wives and burst into singing 'Auld Lang Syne' to usher in the New Year, the Kapoors were fast asleep with their backs to each other.

(Translated from the Punjabi by Khushwant Singh)

DOORS

Keki N. Daruwalla

A minute had gone by since she had knocked, rather hard and long. She had used all her knuckles and later the palm. It sounded like rain hammering away—rain backed by wind. She was damned if good manners were to come between her and what she wanted. Perhaps, no one was in, she thought. Ringing the bell when there was no one in the house was like knocking on the doors of the Lord, she thought. Absence could be another name for the Lord. She came down the three steps that led to the ground floor apartment and waited. All of a sudden, the door was pulled ajar, and a woman stood there—a silhouette. Brown face to go with her brown hair, dark slacks and a face painted in dark moods.

The woman who had knocked was in the habit of talking to herself. "Brown and aggressive," she said, but a bit too loudly.

"What? What did you say?" asked the silhouette, Bimla.

"I didn't say anything to you," answered Devaki.

"But you did say something now, didn't you?"

"You were not meant to hear it. But now I want you to hear what I have to say. Leave my husband alone!"

She had got it off her chest at last, and said it as vehemently, almost exactly as she had rehearsed the lines in her imagination dozens of times. The other woman now understood who she was. She took in her over six-month-pregnant belly and the slightly ravaged but still beautiful face. Could have been crying, the poor bitch, she thought. So this was the wife he had talked so often about. And that was the belly he had whined about. These frigging Indian males can whine about anything once they are with another woman.

"Why don't you ask your husband to leave me alone?"

Devaki was stunned. Such brazen audacity! "Brassy" was the term a friend had used for Bimla and how right the friend was!

"Don't act smart. You led him on—spread your net like a fisherman…sorry fisherwoman. Even if he were chasing you, couldn't you bang the door in his face?"

She had waited for this standoff for months. It was Bimla who banged the door shut now and the woman with the half balloon of a belly just stared in disbelief. The door opened again. Perhaps, she'll apologise, thought Devaki. Instead, the woman said, "Why did you come here? You could have rung up."

"I wanted to see your face."

"And now that you've seen it, are you satisfied?"

"The issue is your satisfaction. My husband could never have satisfied you. You're the kind of woman who needs six men a week."

"Why not seven? You think I keep Sabbath?" and she laughed. Neither of them was speaking loudly. They didn't want windows in other apartments to start opening.

"Lay off my husband!" said Devaki, desperately.

"Did you say lay your husband or lay off?" the silhouette asked, innocently.

Devaki couldn't believe it. The shameless whore, she said to herself, but quietly this time. She didn't want a street brawl on her hands. The other woman held the door ajar, inviting her to come in, as it were. Devaki walked up to the threshold but wouldn't cross it. Imagine setting foot in *her* house. She looked straight into a corridor dividing the apartment in two and leading to a staircase. A woman called out from the floor above, "Bimla."

Devaki looked at her, enquiringly.

"That's my mother," Bimla explained.

"Oh! With your mother in the house you still manage to do all this?"

"Yes, all this and that. If someone wins your heart, what can you do?"

"And how did he win your heart? Not through wine and roses, I bet."

"How would you know?" she answered. "Just because he didn't give you any."

The wife remained silent.

"Come now, he didn't give you any roses or wine, did he? He just fucked you into pregnancy, your second or is it your third?"

She was shocked into silence for a while—wives often are if the mistress is brazen enough. *How could one bandy words with this woman,* she thought. *Why did it have to come to this? Why did I have to come here at all?* But she couldn't leave it at that. She had to have the last word.

"Well?" asked the other, pretending to be bored.

"I've some advice for you. Keep your thighs together, it'll be good for your health," she said and walked off.

Her shoulders were drooping as she waddled back to her car. She felt she had come out of the slanging match with dirt smeared all over her. She would need a mouthwash. Someone had slapped the side mirror of the car askew, and she saw her own face in it, the patina of grief and dry sweat clearly visible. She straightened the mirror, shut her car door quietly and made it a point to drive off slowly. She wasn't going to give any satisfaction to the woman. Her anger would be the other's triumph. She wouldn't want her to see the gravel spurting behind the rear tyres as she drove off in a temper.

By the time she had showered, her resolve had returned. One couldn't just sit around and let this sort of nonsense go on. She would meet Bimla's boss. She fixed an appointment and was told to come at seven next evening.

"What can I do for you, Ji?" said the boss in an accent thick enough to serve as mortar to patch up a damaged wall. She felt demeaned, talking ill of Bimla. She hummed and hawed her way through the story of her husband's infidelity.

"Very sad, Ji, very sad" said the boss shaking his head. Before half her halting narrative was over, he came and sat next to her on the sofa. For a while, he held her hand in his. Is the fellow genuine or is all this *dikhawa*, she thought. Then, he put his hands on her belly. Is the fellow mad, she said to herself and a bit too loudly?

"The child is not mad," said the boss, still keeping his hands on her distended belly. She was debating whether this could be described as sympathy or empathy when the fellow's hands started moving upwards.

"Good God! You bastard," she exclaimed, disentangling herself from his hairy arms. She kicked him in his shins and walked off just as the peon entered with the tea tray.

How was she going to break this to her husband? She started fantasising. Doesn't take much to imagine or invent a dialogue.

"You went to Bimla! And you said all that! Poor girl!"

"I don't want your bloody sympathy, Yash."

"I meant Bimla!"

"Poor girl, Bimla?"

"Who else?"

How would she proceed further, tell him she even went to her boss and the fellow made a pass at her? Suppose he turned around and said, "You deserved it." She decided to keep things to herself.

Next morning, when Bimla went to the office, her boss cornered her. "What is this I hear, Bimlaji? You are spoiling the fairr name of our furrm." His 'r's rolled like tractor wheels over a dirty road. "I have no time to talk to you in thee office. But you must come home this evening and explain the materr to me. Thee complaintt is verry serious."

"Your wife has gone off to Moga, hasn't she?" asked Bimla.

"You mean Ferozepur."

"Wherever. In that case, whatever you have to discuss had better be in the office."

The boss got genuinely angry. "Thee good name of our office has been spoilt."

"It will be spoilt further if I come to your house in your wife's absence."

And that was that or so I thought. But the boss, Mr. Arora persisted in talking to me in the office the next day. Before he could start in his usual ponderous manner in his Bannu (or was it Kohat?) accent (I've never known the difference between the frigging places), I thought I'd clear the air with him.

"I can guess who came to you yesterday, Arora Sahib. It was Devaki, the wife of Yashpal—you know of Yash Travels. I've tried to keep this quiet merely because a rival travel agency is involved. Otherwise, what I do in the evenings is my own bloody business and no one else's, as you can well imagine, Sir. Well, we had met, Yash and I, at one of those meetings organised by that Tourism Minister, you know the lady who squeezed the balls of a Sub Inspector and flattened him—the poor fellow had to be rushed to hospital in an ambulance..."

"*Chee chee,* Miss Bimlaji, what words you using!" said Aroraji.

"Are you objecting to the ambulance, Sir," I asked feigning innocence.

"No, no, I object to that squeezing part, Bimlaji."

I first wanted to wriggle out of it by saying I had used that merely as a metaphor. Then it struck me that Arora Sahib of Bannu wouldn't know what a metaphor is. My thoughts turned to mischief. "Arora Sahib, have you never in your virtue-stuffed life, never, shall we say, squeezed..."

"*Rab da na lauji*. What a thing to say, Ji! I am amazed Bimlaji."

Rab da na lau, take the name of the Lord, was his favourite expression. If he used it even once in the morning, we girls in the office would start our lunch break with, "*Grub da na lau ji.*"

I mollified him with an insincere apology, though Nathu, the chaiwala had told me first thing in the morning that a Memsahib had kicked Arora in the shins even as Nathu had opened the door to bring the tea in. I could imagine what he had been up to.

I spent the afternoon in the office attending to all the calls, the shifts in the plans of travellers, reading out flight scheds to them, making hotel bookings on the phone. It is not easy for the mind to freewheel when you are in that kind of a job, yet a silent digital printout was going in circles across the back of my mind. What was keeping me here? We had a power breakdown at five. That meant trouble—telling callers that the computers were down. By six, things had eased out and I called it a day. Driving back, even during rush hour, my mind started freewheeling. Why should I work for this bastard? Why, why, why? Any other travel agency would pick me up. I could start one on my own. I was the nearest thing to a hot cake in the travel business. I knew flight schedules by heart—Lufthansa, British Airways, Emirates, even Air India. I knew hotel tariffs by heart. Lufthansa had even given me air miles. *"Sehr geehrter Herr Bimla,"* their letter began (the poor sods mistook me for a man—hence the (*'Herr'*) *"wir freuen uns uber ihre Teilnahme an Luftansa Miles & More."* And it ended with *"Mit freundlichen GruBen"* by which I suppose the Teutons mean, "with kind regards" or things of that sort.

It doesn't take long to know someone closely. When we started getting closer, I noticed that his past was getting all the space. I wanted to interrupt (I don't know if that's the word) but I held myself in check. He might think I was snubbing him. I didn't realise then that far from keeping us apart, his past was bringing us closer.

I had noticed Yash for the first time at the Habitat Centre Bar. Neera and I were sitting at one table and he had his back to us. He was alone and I noticed his gaze roaming left to right constantly like a roving lighthouse beam. It would linger on women, their faces mostly, cheekbones, jawlines, as if he was painting them with his eyes, with the light from his eyes. (Months later, I was to tell him that). Men, who sit alone at a bar, instantly win some sympathy from women. Even something as self-evident as this, I was to realise only later. He asked for another drink and having taken a sip, walked off. Apropos nothing I said, "This man has left his drink and walked off."

"How does it bother us?" Neera asked, rather dismissively.

"Just that he needn't have asked for a drink which he was barely going to touch."

Neera just shrugged her shoulders.

The waiter didn't pick up his glass. He could have gone to the loo, it suddenly struck me. I told Neera so. He walked back and I looked in triumph at Neera.

"How did you know he went to the loo?" she giggled. "Did you see him fiddling with his fly?"

We laughed. He gave us a quick semi-startled look. People instinctively know when they are being laughed at. I put on an unconcerned look as if nothing was the matter. But Neera covered her mouth with her hand and her eyes gleamed with mischief. My ears burned with embarrassment. A foreign lady, British most probably, who was sitting on the settee, raised her eyebrows. The Brits are good at that sort of thing. How expressive can a raised eyebrow be? It told us we were churlish, immature uncivilised bums. It was a put-down. It also said that we didn't belong to her class.

He had a square jaw and a wart under one eye. His shoes were unpolished and his shirt a drab grey that didn't go well with his walnut-brown pigment. Nobody seems to bother about his dress, I thought.

"This man has a thoughtless wife," I said to Neera.

She too raised her eyebrows (this was eyebrow-elevation season) as if to ask, "How does it bother you?" After a while, she asked, "Are you on the lookout for a man?"

My ears burned again though I tried to look nonchalant. "He has a shapely nose," I said to Neera.

"He has an indistinct nose." Neera seemed irritated.

"That's the sign of a shapely nose, its indistinctness. Once a nose gets prominent, it takes over the face." I thought I had said something clever but Neera looked distastefully at him and me.

The Brit woman was now eyeing us carefully. She was tall and muscular and was wearing a red T- shirt and a pair of corduroy trousers. She had long sandy hair knotted in a ponytail. Her sharp nose stood out as did her diamond studs.

Neera asked again if I was on the lookout for a man. "You haven't been near one for ages."

"I am on a freight train to nowhere," I told her.

"Did you pick up that phrase from a novel?" she asked.

"No, it's my own—genuine stuff. But if I repeat it at the right places, say the IHC bar, some novelist is gonna pick it up."

Neera laughed, uninhibitedly. People who can laugh like that are decent people. Neera is decent. I poured some soda in my vodka. Tonic water makes it too sweet, the bitterness is cosmetic—you may as well pour your vodka in a glass of sweetened nimbu-pani.

Mr. Square Jaw finally left. As he was walking off, I noticed a bunch of keys on his table.

"Hey," I called out on an impulse, "you left your keys."

He came back, picked up the keys, walked off (rude bum I thought) then stood there and came back to us. Shy, was he, I asked myself—couldn't have guessed it from his square jaw. He walked up to our table, a little haltingly. "I almost didn't thank you."

"Almost," Neera agreed. "Was it a memory lapse?"

"No, I was just hesitating."

"Don't hesitate," I said. "You won't come to much good if you do."

It was a remark I was to rue for the next few months.

"Thanks for the advice. May I buy you ladies a drink?"

"No," Neera said, "but you can join us for one if you are feeling lonely. It's on us."

He pulled up a chair and sat down.

"Oh, so you admit you are lonely." I could see he was uncomfortable at my remark. Men don't like admitting they are lonely. Buggers think they are a host in themselves. They don't like appearing vulnerable—unless they are trying to trap a woman. Then of course, they play the *lonely-life* card, the *rustic-wife* card, the *soulless-evenings* card—the whole damn pack.

"She liked your nose," Neera said, giggling.

I could have killed her. I had to set matters right. "But, not your square jaw," I said.

"I didn't know ladies discuss men."

"Are you that innocent?" *Kis dehath sey aye ho*? I almost asked, but I didn't want to break into Hindustani. Lowers one's image. "You a country bumpkin or what?"

He didn't understand the bumpkin bit, I think. Neera gave me a half-startled, angry glare.

"What I meant was, discussing in such detail. I thought you had better things to do than map my face."

I have a feeling I fell for that. I apologised, and he had no idea why. He handed his card to Neera and she passed it on to me. I left it at the table as we finished our drink and walked off. The Brit lady in her red T-shirt and corduroy trousers was still at her beer as we left.

He rang me up home, one day. "Where did you get my number, I asked?" I didn't say that sharply enough. It is the tone that matters on the line, not how you are grimacing or rolling your eyes heavenwards.

He was evasive—his reply was a cross between a snort and a laugh. If he had lied—got it from the phone-book or something like that, I'd have thought poorly of him. He asked me out for lunch and I turned him down. I was happy with myself, my life uncluttered by men. That's how it had been for the last few years—who wants to complicate things?

You run across people if you live in the same city; could be at a clinic, a bar, a *halwai* shop, the Bengali market. I made it a point not to be unpleasant at such run-ins. In fact, I didn't seem to mind him. Then one day, the calling bell rang and I opened the door and there he was.

I laughed. "This happens only in India."

"What happens only in India?"

He had walked in by then. "What happens only in India?" he persisted. (I wouldn't have, if I were him.)

"Well, a man rings the doorbell and calls on a lady."

"You mean a man barging in without a phone call—sans appointment. That's what you meant, didn't you?"

He deserved an honest answer. In any case, I seldom prevaricate. "Yes, that's what I meant."

"I am not going to make the excuse that I was in the vicinity and so thought of dropping by. I just came to see you and know you, know you better."

I am not sure if I felt flattered, but a smile may have made an insidious foray across my lips. I trooped into the kitchen to hide what he had obviously observed. I tried to busy myself with tea cups and things—I didn't want to give him a drink.

"Somehow, I felt I wouldn't be unwelcome," he called out.

"Oh really!" Hmm, didn't say that indignantly enough. When you are not sure whether to deter a fellow or not, your responses become ambiguous. He also mentioned during the evening what I had told him—never hesitate. Things come full circle, sometimes. That's how it began.

Had never been involved with a married man before. What do I mean, *never*? I am making it sound as if I had a string of lovers. Just two, if you please in seven years, since I stepped out, or shall we say flew out, of the parental home. Never wanted to get married. Uggh. The *pheras*, the *suhag raat* and then the post-coital *saveras*—not for me.

I kept him at a distance, more than arm's length, more than a bargepole's length. Something must have told me, keep him out! Just didn't let him touch me. If he sat on the couch, I sat on the chair. Must say, he didn't make any special efforts either. But how long can this kind of a thing go on. Time is the seducer—makes you numb, makes you succumb.

I noticed he seldom, if ever, talked of his daughter. It took me a while to even ferret out her name. "You are fond of her, aren't you?" "Of course," he said—in fact, he seemed riled at the question. I can put my foot in my mouth, sometimes. After that, he started telling me of the toys he bought for her, how she spoke, what she said. "Why didn't you ever talk of her earlier?" I asked. "I thought you wouldn't be keen," he said. I had administered a mild rebuke. "Just because I am not married, you think I am not keen on children?" Much later, it occurred to my cretinous brain that the remark could have been misunderstood.

Earlier on, I must confess I was a bit uneasy on the professional front—he was after all heading a rival travel agency. That could be awkward. But Yash was not interested in the professional aspect—I mean, not with me. We didn't go out much—you don't with a partner who is married. We slid, fairly smoothly, if I may say so, into this relationship, no double entendre intended.

Going back over this travel business, my father had been most unhappy at my choice of a job. (Fathers have the prerogative of being either unhappy with your husband or your job. There's nothing a daughter can do about it.) "You are well read and have literary tastes, Bimla. Why are you getting into this travel business, this Hampi and Khajurao business?"

"So, I can travel."

"You are even stupider than I thought. Others will be travelling. You'll just be booking their tickets and their hotel rooms." He didn't speak to me for a day. But I joined the travel business and never regretted it.

Within two days of resigning from Arora's set-up, I got three offers. I kept them on hold, wanted some free time for myself. I stopped taking Yashpal's calls. That both wife and husband should be dropping their visiting cards at my apartment, was not acceptable. I wanted to be free for a while, from the endearments of one and the insults of the other. I had behaved dreadfully with Devaki, I know; told Neera as much, but you can't afford to be apologetic at such moments. Once you are on the defensive, the other will gobble you up. Still, it was dreadful. I didn't go in for a mouth-rinsing routine, but I couldn't sleep for some hours that night. This too shall pass, I kept telling myself, this too shall pass. Would Devaki be saying the same thing, I reflected.

At last, one day I took his call. He was in a rage. "What the hell do you mean switching off your mobile the moment I call?"

"I think your wife needs you, Yash—must be tough on her these days. Stay by her side."

"You playing Sati Savitri or what? How have you suddenly got interested in her? You haven't even met her? You don't even know the woman."

I switched off the cell. Devaki had never told him about our meeting, I guessed. I could imagine him ranting and cursing, and that gave me great pleasure. Had the evenings to myself and went off shopping.

One evening, I went to a book launch—had heard so much about them. Found some guys from advertising firms there. A lady author (never heard of her before) was waxing hot against Delhi. Corrupt city of bureaucrats she called it—made it sound as if it was Sodom or Gomorrah, (which of the two is worse, incidentally? I haven't a clue—must read the Bible, if for nothing else than to find out more about these twin cities of vice.) She defended Bombay to the hilt, the beating up of the UP Bhaiyas and driving them back to the dust and the silt of the Doab. She "empathised" with the Thackeray types who didn't want people from Benares and Gorakhpur and Basti to enter Malabar Hill or the Napean Sea Road. She didn't want the Bhaiyas even in Dharavi. Smart intellectuals never sympathise; they always empathise. Seeing her age-ravaged face, I was reminded of the Urdu saying: *Khandar bata rahe hain imarat buland thi* (The ruins declare that the building was lofty once). The author must have been beautiful in (what is the phrase?) "time immemorial." I hope I am not sounding pompous when I say that such faces reflect the history of old age and time—the present ravaged, the past beautiful. Badly put, but then I am not an authoress, just an executive in a travel agency. It was interesting just overhearing guys. One bald-headed intellectual, while swilling his gin, was telling others, "The next week is going to be awful. Imagine, no book launch. I don't mind drinking my own whiskey. It is the humiliation I can't stand—drinking your own booze!" I let out a big laugh and the others turned around, gawking at me. Frankly, I wasn't interested in the crowd or the looks of the author or her sociological natter. At book launches, it is the liquor and the hors d'oeuvres that matter. They were great and so was the wine. Who was bothered about the rest?

A month later, I relented, joined a travel firm (higher salary this time) and answered Yashpal's call. You can't cut off someone like that from your life, can you? He didn't show any indignation or anger; talked as if we had never fallen out—must have cost him quite an effort. The next few days, he came home almost every other evening and became very physical. I felt his trawling fingers all over my arm and then over the rest of the body. Unspoken passion can be much more articulate than words. Fortunately, Mom had gone back to my sister, so there was no tension. For a few days, I thought repossession gave Yash a kind of muted elation, an amalgam of cockiness and concealed triumph. But as days went by, and winter and the D-day drew near, he turned a bit nervous.

Winter was busy for both of us—French tourists, Italian tourists. We had to make arrangements for a huge 30-member Italian party going to Halebid and Belur, and another to Ajanta. The Italians were carrying their own guides, which was a blessing. I started reading my Spam mail, for what good reason I don't know. Every day, I won a lottery. Kept shaking my head—what do they want out of me—account number? Bank? Then there was sob mail mostly from Nigeria and Abidjan, Cote d'Ivoire, from young daughters whose parents just popped off leaving millions. Miss Lawrence says, her father "was limited liability in Cocoa and Gold merchant in Sierra Leone. He got into an accident with my mother. My mother died instantly but father died a week later on that 'faithful' afternoon. He left 12 million in the bank in Cote d'Ivoire. He single-handed me the deposit." An Auditor General of a bank wants to send me 15 million in my account. Mayrose Amanda has merely six million to give me. Danguru Arkindale from Burkina Faso has similar requests—or he probably kicked the bucket and his daughter wrote. It took me too much time reading and deleting these messages.

Yash was busier. We normally met late evenings. Sundays were freer. When he trooped in early one Sunday evening, I noticed a crepuscular look on his face. "What is wrong? Have you had a fight?" He shook his head. "Have your cheques bounced?" shook his head again. "Has some employee run away with your money? Then tell me what it is." There was nothing to tell, he said. All was routine, humdrum, yet he seemed to hit the bottle and I had to tell him to go easy on the whiskey. He had to drive back, after all.

The D-day was getting near, I realised. "She should be in hospital any day now, isn't it?" He was intrigued how I got it so right. I didn't want to tell him I had noticed her belly when we met. He didn't even know we had met. A fortnight from now, he told me, but could be earlier. Devaki was feeling very uncomfortable. Could be a week, could be tomorrow, he said.

"Why are you here then, Yash? Shouldn't you be with her?" I said that as gently as I could, and I wasn't putting on an act. He could see that. "You shouldn't be coming now. See me after the whole thing is over."

He thanked me and gave me a warm hug. He was feeling low and when he walked out, his head was bowed.

A week later, through the grapevine I got to hear Devaki had delivered. He'll ring by and by, I thought. He didn't. Even as I was dialling his number I knew I shouldn't be doing it, but curiosity got the better of me.

"Congrats!"

"It's a son! It's a son! Imagine, a son!" He was jubilant. Then, he added a little softly, "Bimla, we are through. Don't call me up again. Ever."

TOUCH

J.P. Das

Madhvi shrank back with a slight shudder as Indranath tried to embrace her, and he was cut to the quick. In the lonely apartment, with no one to spy on them, there was no earthly reason for her strange behaviour.

It had taken Indranath two full years to be able to enjoy intimacy with her, and the whole period had been a time of grim self-control, trial and anxiety. He had known Madhvi for a long time, but had never dreamt of her as a lover. It was a friendship as ordinary, normal, uncomplicated as any. They often met at work and after some time he had fallen into the inexplicable habit of letting her know whenever he went out of town.

"I'm going out for a week," he rang up to tell her one day.

"Isn't a week a bit too long?" she said petulantly.

"Oh, not long enough for anyone to miss me."

"But I'm going to miss you like hell."

The conversation drifted to other things, but her words kept ringing in his mind. He cradled the phone, suddenly drained of energy, cupped his head in his hand and, to his shock, discovered having fallen fatally in love with Madhvi. She occupied his mind in the train, in the town he visited, during and before and after the business deals, in and out of office, every minute of his wakeful life. He tried to phone her but for a long time the line wouldn't oblige. Then, when he succeeded and her voice could be heard on the other end, his heart thudded wildly and he hung up without a word. A long-distance call was a crazy idea anyway.

Seven centuries, which were in fact seven similar days, passed, and his short trip home was a special journey; he felt he was hurtling closer towards the most cherished goal of his life, towards the fountainhead of happiness, joy and peace. He phoned her from the station and she answered politely, even with warmth, but he with his heart all of a patter and a pitter, was strangely tongue-tied.

Afterwards they met, but he was stiff, self-conscious and far from being at ease with her. He knew she had no inkling of what was raging inside him. He could no longer swap jokes; his stomach churned at her proximity, and he sat carefully apart from her, fearing all casual contact of their bodies. Terribly moved, restless, clawed from within, he couldn't put his mind to work. He lost his appetite for everything. He could no longer hold up his monotonous spiel. He tried to keep away from her, but started meeting her more often. He realised he'd go bananas if he didn't do something about it soon and, having made up his mind, he rang her bell one evening. But despite the rehearsals, the words wouldn't roll off his tongue. Tea, trifles and tedious tête-à-tête over, he rose and left. In the street, he mustered his courage and retraced his steps.

"Forgot something?" Madhvi asked.

Now or never, Indranath told himself. "Madhvi," he nearly screamed, "I love you."

She didn't laugh it off, as he had feared, nor throw him out of the house. "Come in, won't you?" she said slowly, staring baby-eyed at him. "Sit down." She flopped down beside him and fell into a reverie. Fluctuating between high hope and black despair, those few moments seemed to him all that was there between life and death. He felt a fever coming on. After a while, she raised her head and met his gaze without a tremor and said, "Look, let's remain friends."

He got the point at once and heaved to his feet. He experienced a strange sensation of lightness despite the numbing pain. *I should have had no illusions,* he sighed, determined to keep away from her. Polite but meaningless social relations with the girl to whom he had dedicated himself body and soul seemed utterly hypocritical.

The next day, she rang him and said, "Come and see me sooner than you can."

Indranath went limp with hope and anxiety. Would she reciprocate his love? Or talk about something else? How would he take the meeting after his loss of face?

Madhvi was her merry old self, welcoming him with the usual warmth. "How about a cup of tea?"

"All right!" he said, adding in his mind, "Oh come, spill it now."

She took her time to serve the tea; then she enquired after his work and his health as if they hadn't met for ages. When she got to the topic of a common friend, he threw up his hands. "What did you want to see me for, Madhvi?"

"Why didn't you give me a tinkle this morning?" she said.

Indranath bit back his words. He knew she'd pounce on any silly answer and turn it into an inane chit-chat.

Madhvi scanned his face teasingly, but he kept his cool. She asked him another question and he still didn't reply.

Finally, putting on a smile of defeat, she said, "I've been mulling it over."

"Well?"

"Haven't decided."

"There's nothing to decide. You either love me or you don't. Surely you know your own mind."

"So easy—knowing your own mind? But tell me, is one-sided love possible?"

"You mean this love of mine which you don't reciprocate?"

"Didn't say a word about not reciprocating, did I? I'm just wondering. Is it possible that you love someone but that someone isn't aware of it at all? Now, what is the meaning of such love?"

Words and more words. The discussion lengthened late into the night, but in the end, he returned empty-handed, without her answer one way or the other. Madhvi wouldn't reveal her feelings.

They continued to meet; the old arguments broke out anew, but he found the distance between them closing. He constantly fought the desire to snuggle up to her, to hold her hand. At his faintest attempt, she tensed. After a while, she let his hand rest on her shoulder and around her waist, but his move to embrace her was always thwarted with stony iciness. Even when she had a fever, she let him feel only her forehead and the nape of her neck.

All this was fine with him, for he was so much in love that he didn't want his physical urge to soil the romance. Lately, they had been candidly discussing sex. And Madhvi was far from being coy. But no amount of academic discussion was getting them into bed.

"Say, you aren't frigid, are you?" Indranath teased her one day.

"Worth checking, isn't it?" she bantered.

He couldn't summon the courage to take her up on her word.

Another time, he clowned, holding out an invitation to her, arms akimbo, and the intensity with which she raced into his arms staggered him.

Not only was she not cold, she was a fiery sensation beyond his wildest dreams. Her frail five-foot-two inches was a voluptuously undulating expanse of dunes, oases, mirages and storms. Her eyes were fire-spewing meteors that seared through the vast atmosphere of his mind and straight into the core of his being. Her lips were volcanic craters, her kiss an explosion, her embrace a swirling band of flame, her breath, hot summer breeze, and her curls tossed around like tongues of fire. Her interior was a blazing ceremonial fire-pit from which he emerged burnished, purified, drained of dross. And she made hungry when she most satisfied. He surrendered himself to this avatar of elemental passion and was the happiest mortal on earth.

Then came the day when she flinched at his touch. They continued to see each other. He made no attempt to touch her. Neither did she. The meetings were meaningless, banal, even hypocritical. The girl who had become a big part of his body and soul sat miles apart from him, and it was so absurd that it made him feel funny, tearful, vapid.

What could have happened to her? he wondered, flummoxed. Was she in love with somebody else? Was she bored with him? Didn't he interest her anymore, even physically? Did she regret her own sexuality?

He ran through the full gamut of possibilities, all of which struck him as equally unlikely. None of these seemed to ring true. He knew Madhvi; she knew her mind. She never jumped into anything but once her mind was made up, regrets had no place. What then could have happened?

Indranath was back at the beginning, with all the agony of having won and lost. He began to see her less and less. He tried to erase the days of courtship and love from his mind. But her memory stole upon him despite all he could do to hold it off. Forgetting was as difficult as it was easy to remember.

Time, he hoped, would heal, but it didn't. He remembered her ever more acutely with each passing day. Memories stabbed at his sides. Peace was gone. Happiness was over. "Madhvi," he often prayed, curled up in his shell, "darling, free me from this terrible curse. Let's be strangers again. I'll start from scratch. I'll declare my love and you'll spurn it. It's better that way. I'll spend the rest of my life clinging to the brittle hope that I might get around you, yet."

(Translated from the Odiya by the author)

VELUTHA BABU

Kamala Das

It was the security guard, the policeman, who told her about Velutha Babu—the light-skinned gentleman. He described him, and she wanted to meet him. Fair, a blood-red kerchief tied around his head, stained, narrow teeth, lips blackened by beedi stains, legs bent like a cowboy's...she felt she would recognise him at first sight. And he would help her fulfill her old desire.

Evading the servant, driver and security guard, she walked the bylanes, took an autorickshaw and finally arrived at ten in the morning, near the Jewish synagogue and the antique shops. The sun's intense glare hurt her eyes. No one recognised her, perhaps because of her Muslim clothes.

She glanced at the rows of shops. Her curious eyes travelled over the *changalavattam*—chained oil lamp—the tower-shaped jewellery boxes, the bearer of the sacred lamp and traditional bronze pots collected from decaying ancestral homes. Utensils of daily use outlive their owners, metal survives mere bone. They reminded her of the bronze lamps that used to glitter in the darkness of her family home. She fondly remembered the village that had closed its doors to her forever. No, I am now a new being. I shall never be allowed into that hamlet of peace, a symbol of my past.

She laboured up the steps to the bookstore. Her poetry books were on display. An anaemic man emerged from the shadows. "We have new arrivals," he said, "books by Latin American writers."

"I have not come to buy books," she said, "I am looking for a man. A young man called Velutha Babu..."

The owner of the shop drew up a stool for her. "There are at least four or five people here called Babu. One Babu, who is fair, sells copper vessels nearby. It is the seventh shop from here. You can tell it by the vessels exhibited outside..."

"My Babu doesn't sell vessels, he is a contract killer."

After a few moments of silence, he asked, "Madam, do you *need* a contract killer?"

She nodded. Her eyes were moist; she was upset.

"You seem to be a decent woman, incapable of cruelty. Who told you about this man?"

"My security guard, who is also a policeman, said Babu would kill anyone for thirty thousand rupees. Spends most of his time in jail. When he comes out, he goes back to his old trade. He doesn't know any other. He's a favourite of politicians, so he has bigwigs arranging for bail and lawyers."

"Now I recognise you—from your voice. Haven't seen you after you converted. Forgive me. Shall I get you a coffee?"

"I never violate my food habits," she said.

"Maybe a Coke, then..."

"No, I'm going back. I'll come another day, before the sun gets too hot. I feel giddy. Would you get me an autorickshaw?" she whispered.

"Of course. Wait right here."

Later, as he helped her into the autorickshaw, he asked, "Who is the enemy? Who is the one who must be killed?"

"The enemy is myself," she said.

(Translated from the Malayalam by Sindhu V. Nair & Antara Dev Sen)

PRECAUTION!

Vijaydan Detha

A jackal and his mate lived in a jungle: their home a neatly nurtured burrow. A pond of clean water was there only four fields away. The jungle abounded in berry-bushes. They selected the best fruit to eat. Every comfort and bliss within easy reach. They expressed extreme love for each other. Each was ready to lay down their life for even the reflection of the other. The she-jackal's professed devotion to her husband was more than what Sita had for Lord Ram. She would not let even a mosquito, fly or bug touch the jackal. Her eulogies made the jackal blush. But her praise encouraged the jackal to boast—his tail cracking like a whip. At its sound, the lion rolled away seven times, till at last the big cat put a straw between its teeth and pleaded to be forgiven. Now the jackal was the king of the jungle. Even a leaf would not move if he wished otherwise. Once in a fury, he hit a sand dune and it got scattered like a toy. His howls made the clouds burst. His spouse felt proud of her mate's prowess.

Once at midnight, she was thirsty and she shook the jackal out of sleep and urged him to escort her to the pond.

The jackal, still feeling sleepy, murmured, "I can't even turn sides to shake off this soothing sleep. You may go alone..."

She disapprovingly said, "How could a female like me go all by herself?"

"Who's there (in this wilderness) to molest you?"

She replied with dignity, "What do you males know of female compulsions? I won't let even the wind and the sun touch me if I could. But I'm helpless."

The jackal, reluctant to wake up, blurted out, "Where's helplessness in it? My reputation is at least there for your safety. As for the sun and wind, I'd tangle them up so inextricably like the bushes that they'd never be the same."

"But first, you escort me. I can't even talk well with a parched throat".

At last, her coaxing persuaded the jackal to go with her. The sky blossomed with the full moon. Berries of all hues shone in the bushes. The whole forest was fast asleep in the lap of the moonlight. The she-jackal looked at the moon. It was gorgeous! Fascinating! Even a horde of jackals would not match its grandeur.

The jackal stood on the bank of the pond. The she-jackal went ahead and drank from the pond to quench her thirst. As she raised her head, she knew of the crookedness of the moon. Hiding underwater, the moon had been kissing her. These males are all so libidinous. Braving the winter, she dived into the pond. How could a devoted wife guard her dignity with all these lascivious males around!

Turning angrily to her husband, she complained, "What are you gazing at? This rascal, the moon is trying hard to kiss me! The moon would have hugged me had you not escorted me."

Her spouse couldn't understand what she was trying to put across to him! Grinding his teeth angrily, he asked, "Who? This pale moon? How dare it? I will batter it to pieces if you so wish!"

Saying this, the jackal gesticulated, striking a blow with his paw like a lion as though the moon was to be done away with instantly. The she-jackal once again raised her head and gazed at the moon. The moon too was eager to stare at her. How gorgeous! How fascinating! She did not want the jackal to take any drastic action and advised him, "Let it be! Or else, the whole world will suffer because of this lascivious moon. Children will be frightened to move around in the dark!"

The jackal brought down his paw with even more ferocity, "Don't stop me, let me reduce this moon to the pulp of a moonlet, if you like!"

She held his hand in her own and said, "Let it go. Why should you take the blame for eternal darkness?"

The jackal was pacified after repeated entreaties from his spouse. Otherwise, the world would have had it.

On their way back to their dwelling, the she-jackal impressed upon the jackal that one's dignity and one's precautions are to be maintained by oneself after all. Let the moon strut as it does. Once inside the burrow, she never peeped out that night.

The jackal entered his dwelling, still grinding his teeth in rage. The she-jackal kept contemplating her beauty and could not sleep for a long while. She could get up only about a couple of hours after sunrise and came out rubbing the sleep from her eyes. The sun was waiting restlessly to admire her beauty. These damned males are all Cupid's cousins! But the sun is dazzling bright. It enlightens the whole world! See, is it not as vicious as the moon? She was not thirsty but she pressed upon the jackal to escort her. The jackal, a bit irritated, retorted, "Foolish woman, what are you afraid of in broad daylight? Go alone, boldly."

The she-jackal argued, "If the great gods like the moon can try to lure others with bad intentions, whom should we trust?"

Her repeated solicitations compelled the jackal to go with her. Whenever she cast slanting glances, she found the sun viewing her closely!

On reaching the edge of the pond, she noticed that the sun had dived into the water. What do these males get by violating the dignity of women? She prepared to drink from the pond but held back. She looked at her Lord and complained, "What I feared has come true! This sun seems to be crazier than the moon. It is full of lust in broad daylight!"

The jackal was at her side in a wink. Infuriated, he asked, "Where? Where?"

She pointed at the reflection of the sun playing on the ripples of water and said, "It's there! The wicked one!"

Now, the jackal's rage was out of bounds. Bringing down his paw like a lion, he said, "If you like, I can dismember this loafer into tiny bits right now."

One again, the she-jackal controlled her ire and counselled, "Leave him alone! The whole world shall have to suffer from our action. It will forever grope in the dark! There will be eternal chaos and distress!"

The jackal underwent great turmoil inside. Enraged, he assured, "No, no, if you like I can swallow this vainglorious sun like a berry! Lick it like a slice of watermelon!"

The she-jackal held his paw and implored, "Forgive him! Be kind! The world would curse you. Why should you take on yourself the blame of the chaos in vain?"

The jackal in his excitement blasted, "In vain? Is it a sin to spare a loafer of this order? Now see what I do..."

"I don't wish to see anything. If I do, the whole world will never be able to see anything! Pacify yourself. One must take precaution and preserve one's own dignity! You just watch this villain while I quench my thirst."

At last, the jackal took her advice. He fixed his gaze on the sun. His looked so scared, the sun, that it just stood there unmoved!

The she-jackal took her time to drink from the pond while she let the sun kiss her. She had never before drunk from the pond with such satiety. Thirst is not within one's control.

Every night, she goaded the jackal to escort her to the pond. The jackal gazed at the movement of the moon! Now, the she-jackal fondly enjoyed the kisses of the sun and the moon as she quenched her thirst. One's own precautions to protect one's dignity is all!

(Translated from the Rajasthani by Madan Mohan Mathur)

THE DEATH OF A MADAM

Arvind Gokhale

The tiny blue villa in that grotesque locality dozed off even as the surroundings bustled with mid-day activities. Behind the closed gate, the keeper slept on a cot in quiet comfort. On the open lawn, a big brown dog stretched. Two or three shaggy dogs slept on the balcony and under the wooden staircase. The big main hall stood in complete darkness with the doors and windows all closed. The suites on both the floors of the house were shut and in the interior, things lay drowsy and cold—mirrors, fans, beds; all of them.

The madam of the house, Erusha Soloman, slept in the room by the hallway, her plump body immersed completely in the big, cosy bed. A big feather cushion lay across her expansive bosom and on it she had brought her left hand to rest, making her breathing completely inaudible. Two large almirahs, a big wardrobe, a safe, and many heavy trunks stood by the large bedstand, and the body of the buxom old woman sprawled on the bed looked like an old museum piece in marble, fabulous yet attractive.

At two in the afternoon, the siren of the mill nearby screamed and Erusha Soloman's sleep was disturbed. She waited somewhat apprehensively for the hall clock to strike two. And soon, the clock obeyed. Still lying on the bed, she opened her eyes and looked up at the white ceiling. The faces of young men which would be visible at night were no longer to be seen on the ceiling. Only a cobweb hung there, uncertainly. After some time, Erusha moved a bit and turned on her side. Contentedly, she looked at the safe and at her reflection in the mirror. Then she closed her eyes and tried to recollect her past.

Suddenly, she reached for her wrist watch under the pillow. "Half-past two," she announced to herself, and then consulted the watch. She had guessed the time accurately. She smiled and then got up. In her younger days too she could guess playing cards arranged upside down—and how the Tommies were astonished! She could guess equally accurately about cigarette brands, labels of bottles of liquor, scents. But that was very long ago, in the distant past—when she was at Cairo or Calcutta and yes, even in this present villa when she shared the room with Gladys. Now she had become the mistress of the house, the madam herself, but her youth was gone and those games were no more. She could only get the measure of time like a clock now.

She picked up her walking stick and leaning against it, walked out of the room. Outside, everything was quiet and dark. She felt like calling out to Shankar. "Boy," she was about to shout but she did not, fearing that her own voice would echo in the house. She walked down the flight of steps. The rooms were closed all in a row. All the girls had left—Gladys, Betty, Nora, Yvonne, Susan, Leela, Akhtar, Ameena, Rosy, Eva, Stella. No, not Stella. She had run away a fortnight back. Leaving the cosy and comfortable life in the villa, she had run madly after a poor and miserable engine driver.

The other girls were not foolish like Stella. They stayed at the villa happily, keeping the madam pleased. All of them earned and enjoyed themselves. Gladys and Betty must have gone home; Nora for her swim as usual and Eva for her dance lessons. Susan and Leela must be eating ice cream cones and striking bargains of cloth. Akhtar must be sitting at the bedside of her ailing sister. Ameena was nuts about becoming an actress. She must be roaming around some film studio. Only Rosy must be home sleeping in her room. She was a quiet, homely child.

Madam tiptoed up to Rosy's room. She had a special liking for this Anglo-Burmese girl with the snub face and smooth, delicate skin. Though not of 'blue' blood, and without a trim figure, she was a quiet bird. She never created any situations like the others often did. Madam peeped through the crack in the closed door. The bed was not made, the cupboard was ajar. Rosy was lying on a mattress, struggling with a Hindi book. Erusha withdrew. She admired Rosy but at the same time she was sorry that her girls were now compelled to pick up this rotten Hindi.

With great effort, she walked up to the hall and rested on the sofa, breathing heavily. Whenever she sat in the darkness at noon, her mind clouded over. What was going to become of this old bagnio of renown? This feeling used to consume her. Thirty or forty years ago, the widow of a colonel in the white regiment had started this house. Then it changed hands and went to the sister of a jockey, and for many years since, Erusha had maintained it under her care and supervision. She had raised it to the high status that it now enjoyed. Nowhere in the whole city was to be found anything comparable to her 'Blue Den'. The name of this blue villa had spread far and wide. Girls from several countries were available at this place. Merchants, sailors, travellers, officers from everywhere adorned the hall of this house flooding it with currency notes. High government officials visited the place for rest and refuge. The English arrogance and European pride were protected and nourished here as much as they were at the Government House, the Fort shops, the Taj Hotel and the lovely swimming pool at Breach Candy. The blue villa remained in seclusion from the dark natives and the ungainly, cheap vamps. Only well-dressed gentlemen who could toss about English words and Indian money were permitted to enter this forbidden fairyland.

But the house was already crumbling. It started with the girls from London and Paris and Aden. Girls from these places did not arrive and that meant reduction in the white clientele. Money became a scarce commodity after the war was over and the white customer became a rarity. The boom just before the British soldiers left proved to be like the last flicker of the dying lanterns. When the sahibs went away, the well-dressed natives, the dark and the ordinary, reluctantly had to be admitted. The vacant lots had to be filled by the native girls. Akhtar, the singing girl, had to be admitted when her voice was cracking and so was Leela who had been kidnapped by soldiers and had ultimately found her way to the house. The white culture of the villa was polluted by such contamination. The callers came, sat like statues and just marched off. They bargained and haggled for money. Occasionally, they stammered in Hindi. They were unwilling to spend on drinks. They did not even know how to sit on the sofa. And the girls? But for Yvonne Young-Husband of Sussex, none of them was of pure English stock. Gladys, Betty, Nora, and Susan were either half English or converts.

These girls dirtied the house and had no training in discipline and habits of cleanliness. The house in which one could once hear enchanting jazz and rhumba resounded with the disturbing noise of Hindi songs. Instead of bacon and ham, one had to be content with cheap Indian dishes. The one and only place of its kind in the city deteriorated from the high standards of entertainment it once boasted of. It pained Erusha Soloman to see this happening under her very nose. Since it was beyond her power to check the rot, she felt like dying. Already she was old, her power and strength were declining. Blood pressure and insomnia were consuming her gradually. She could not bear the sight of the house that was falling into ruin.

All at once, she started perspiring, her heart trying to leap out of her body. Her eyes rolled aimlessly and she thought she would faint. In the darkness of the hall, she felt as if she was being raped by some cheap rickshaw-driver or a massage-boy. Memories of the past and the agony of the reclining present created hallucinations and nightmares that frightened her to death. Her plump body shuddered, and she lay hopelessly crumpled on the sofa.

After some time, Erusha regained consciousness but she broke into tears as she realised that she was entirely and coldly alone. There was no one who would care for her or protect her. This feeling drove her mad. She opened the rear window of the hall and leaned on it. She tried to remember something encouraging and exciting—the big ornament box, the fat bank book, tattooed arms, bubbling wine.

Erusha went on recollecting these things while she stared at the maidservant's hut outside. The memories became dimmer and dimmer, the scene outside excited her. She continued to gaze at the hut. The maidservant sat in the doorway feeding her child. This was more exciting than wine, more valuable than gold, she thought. She looked at that rare sight with deep concentration. She was mad with excitement. Abruptly moving away, she climbed the staircase and stumbled into her room, breathless. In the safe, there was an old handkerchief soaked in blood. She took it and held it next to her heart. This soothed her. But then, all at once, she felt like screaming with all her strength.

It was already dawn, the rooster crowed, birds chirped and the usual routine had begun. Erusha controlled herself. She was awake and happy. She used to get impatient with the dark and the dead noon. The servant opened the windows and the light rushed in. The dogs barked. The girls who had already returned started talking loudly. Erusha hurried out as she heard their sweet voices.

As she descended the staircase, she became serious and dignified like the matron of a girl's hostel. She reprimanded the girls who were laughing. With the door to the street left wide open, they were pottering around shamelessly.

The girls continued to enjoy themselves but put on a show of obedience, went to the kitchen, and started drinking water. Erusha followed them. The frigidaire had been sold and the simple ice box looked like a poor substitute. Erusha suddenly flew into a temper. "How dare you drink cold water at this hour? You came in just now, all of you, didn't you? Well, I don't mind. You catch a cold and the young customers will just avoid you like the plague."

The girls sat around the table and Ameena who joined them, distributed toffee.

"Oh!" Betty shouted, "I have some toffee and chewing gum. That fatty Sikh boy gave it to me yesterday."

"Oh! That bear. He wanted me to go to the movies with him. I would be bored to death in his company, you know."

"Sohrab…Sohrab," Betty cried. "Sohrab has not turned up for so many days. How I wish he had come tonight. I have to pay off the tailor's bill. Certainly, he will pay it…what is the song he sings? Oh yes. 'One Hour of Love…'" Betty started singing.

Standing in the doorway, Erusha looked on in deep concentration, listening to every word with great curiosity. She felt like looking at those beautiful dolls again and again. Betty's bobbed hair, her forehead, her chin, her lips—all were wonderful. Susan had an attractive tapering waist and shapely breasts. Lily had a special charm of her own. All of them were bursting with youth. They had blossomed forth with scents, nail paints, ornaments and the caresses of their lovers. Madam who could not partake of any of these pleasures looked on at their tantalising charm.

As the girls were about to leave the kitchen, Madam collected herself.

"Hurry up, you fools. It's already evening and you haven't put on make-up—any one of you. Where's Gladys?" She was obviously annoyed.

"Oh, Gladys has returned already. She's in the bath," someone said.

"Taking her bath so late, eh? Why does she loaf all over the place all day?" Madam murmured. She suspected that Gladys visited some hotel in the Fort area for business. The girls cast aside the rules of the house. The thought irritated Erusha all the more.

"Shankar, oh Shankar," she shouted and trotted into the hall.

Shankar appeared and started putting the hall in order. Under Madam's gaze, he dusted it, put the curtains in place, placed the sofa in order, and cleaned the ash-trays. There used to be a good Christian waiter on this job before, and now it had fallen into the hands of this South-Indian boy who did this in addition to other work.

When the lamps were on, Erusha's face lit up. She saw that the maids were on duty. She pottered around ordering the girls to make themselves ready. She saw that the water-tubs were ready and the soda water bottles were in place. Everything was okay.

"Seven thirty," she muttered to herself, and it was not necessary to consult her watch. She went around the kitchen, had a bite of cucumber which was cut up and ready for the salad. Some of the ash from the stove settled on her hair. She remembered that she had not made herself presentable at all. In a great hurry, she left the kitchen and leaning on the stick, climbed the steps to her room upstairs. She got busy applying make-up.

The next half hour was spent as if she were in the embrace of the captain of a ship, a man with Saxon blood. Her hair was combed and her lips, brows, and lashes were hidden under a deep coat of paint. Her cheeks and her body were dusted with rose-coloured powder. Then she put on a transparent, sleeveless and neckless dress. The aroma of Parisian scents and Egyptian tobacco spread around. Erusha was very pleased with herself. She did not feel like moving away from the mirror even after her toilet was over. She had made herself up like a newly-wed, ready to meet her lover.

At that very moment, the buzzer at the door exploded into action. Erusha was very much taken aback. She was worried. Was she late? He—her fiancé—had already arrived. But it did not matter. He would wait for her for hours... Then she suddenly lost all her enthusiasm. The cigarette fell from her hands. She would have no visitors anymore. No one was going to wait for her. It was foolish now to try to look young, to dance about and to put on make-up. Once again, she felt very nervous.

Madam reached the hall only to find that the visitor was ready to leave.

"Good evening, Sir," she said to the Baniya in a dhoti. "Do wait a minute. The girls are coming."

Her voice was that of a jeweller proudly showing off his diamonds.

"Send for the girls at once. Oh God, I forget. This was the last of my cigarettes...how I smoke, you know. If you don't mind, I will taste your brand..." Before the girls arrived, she sponged a cigarette from him and had a few puffs.

And then the girls came to in the hall one by one. Gladys, Betty, Nora, Susan, Leela, Ameena, Rosy. They were all beautiful, and enchanting. They started smoking, laughing, telling each other smutty jokes. Madam looked at them with great pride. With what difficulty had she managed to keep this set despite hard times. Her girls were certainly the choicest and the best ever. Madam watched the Baniya trying to judge whom he was going to take.

But the customer continued toying with the match-box in his hand and seemed to be very interested in the pose he had struck, bringing his right leg to rest on his left. He looked at one of the girls, smiled to himself, made faces at the girls. Erusha was restless.

"Come on! Choose any one. They are all beautiful, and clean."

The girls got annoyed. Gladys and Susan left the hall and Susan cursed while leaving. Madam became impatient. If the customers were to hesitate that way, how was she to go on?

How could the heavy expenses be met? Even with the 'come one come all' technique and the low (as ever) rates, this was to be the tragedy then... But the Baniya abruptly got up and walked out.

"No, Sir. You are surely not going to leave un-entertained... Oh, Yvonne, Akhtar, I..." Erusha waited, but the gentleman was gone. The girls returned to their rooms leaving Madam alone in the hall. It was painful. Having to beg for a cigarette from a customer. Once upon a time, she had the owner of a cigarette factory dancing on her little finger. But things had after all come to such a pass. Her freedom, her beauty, were matters of the past. Now it had fallen to her lot to talk of the beauty of other girls to the ordinary man in the street like this one. To pamper these girls and to coax those customers and to be satisfied with the crumbs that survived in this transaction. What a terrible revenge time had taken. Why do I suffer? With what hope? Or is there real pleasure in this way of life? To be a go-between like this, to be a Madam in this bagnio? If this is not so, then the best thing is to leave and go somewhere else.

"I have come..." somebody said from a distance. Erusha was taken aback. It was Stella. She had returned to the cage after a week's honeymoon with her lover. Madam could not believe it for some time. But Stella had returned. The girls who ran away always traced their way back to the house. It was the quality of this house and this trade that the girls would not give up until they were thrown out. The life here was charming and intoxicating. Every girl had a room all to herself. The rooms were well furnished, cosy, and comfortable. They used to be fed four times a day. That, and the lodging cost only eight rupees a day. The girls also shared half of the tips. They could go to the movies, drink, and buy clothes and ornaments for themselves. To give up such a life and run after a vagabond was sheer folly. Even then Madam felt like asking where Stella had been, why she had beat a retreat, how was the house of the man, how did he treat her, did he throw her out himself or did his people not like her... But it was foolish to ask questions. Wasn't it below Madam's dignity? With a serious face, she barked, "You must get ready, you fool... Go quickly and make yourself ready."

A taxi stopped on the street. The buzzer rang and half-a-dozen Punjabi boys rushed in. Madam was happy. They were usual customers. Some were businessmen and others were from movie land. They were quite familiar with the rendezvous. Soon, there was fun and frolic. Erusha bulged happily like a balloon. She had got her fill for the day. The house had got another day's lease of life.

All of them made their choices and disappeared into the rooms. Madam stood up making some calculations. Rosy alone was engrossed in her embroidery. Erusha asked her to stay till she helped herself to dinner.

In the kitchen, Yvonne was having dinner, caring nothing about the business. Erusha was surprised. She was very angry. Yvonne knew it, but she continued to eat, unperturbed.

Tasting the soup, Madam asked, "Yvonne dear, why do you hold yourself back like this? When the men come, you do not come out at all. Are you fed up of this profession, this house?"

Yvonne stopped eating. "I am not fed up with the profession, but certainly I am fed up with this house..."

"Tell me, another..." Madam asked, greatly surprised.

"Yes..." Yvonne said. She put the fork and the knife on the table and continued, "I am going to leave. I've had enough of this country. Can't you see how it is here with girls like me?

Those cheap half-castes, the dirty, nauseating, native visitors... All that bargaining for a few rupees; and no drinks!... I've had enough of all this!"

"Oh, don't talk like that. I appreciate every word of it," Madam said. Her eyes suddenly showed grief and she breathed heavy and fast. Hurriedly, she helped herself to a glass of water.

Yvonne resumed eating. But Madam was unable to do it. She looked at Yvonne in deep concentration. She looked at her blue eyes, her light hair, her chiselled nose and her snow-white skin. Yvonne, the English girl, was the real heir to the house. And she was leaving.

In a low voice, Erusha asked, "What are your plans, anyway? Where do you propose to go?"

"There is nothing certain as yet. None of my relatives are in England. All countries are the same to me now. Hence, I have made all sorts of compromises so far, but now I am fed up. I had enough of this life here. I would prefer Cairo or Shanghai to this."

Yvonne ate and talked. Erusha listened and pondered. She is English, and she is young. Somewhere, she will strike gold. She might settle down happily in some port town. Or she might return to her native country. *But what alternative is left for me? I have no refuge or retreat. I am already an old hag, a roly-poly. I must try to protect this ramshackle house and die under this very roof!* There were tears in her eyes. But slowly she got up, controlling herself, and left the table.

As she turned, a young visitor crossed the lounge after the usher. Erusha halted in her tracks, hypnotised. Greatly astonished, she crumpled into the chair. Her eyes were unsteady, and her bosom was heaving fast. David had returned to the house after twenty-five long years as young as ever! She was stupefied.

David! The sight of David brought back many memories. Their first meeting at a bar. They used to meet often in Calcutta and then here in Bombay. His hairy hands and his two golden teeth. She remembered it all. How he had begged her to run away and get married to him—his crestfallen, disappointed face. The way he made a scene on his last visit. The whole series of incidents flashed before her eyes one after another. But the same dear David had returned today! He has come to cheer me up, to protect me, to take me away with him! Suddenly she got up and practically ran to the hall.

"David...David!" she shouted.

The young man who sat with Rosy was obviously puzzled. "I'm Sam," he stammered.

Suddenly, she came to her senses. Clutching the door-frame for support, she wondered. *How could that be David? He must be twenty-five years older now? He must not be visiting brothels anymore. He should be having a platoon of little grandchildren.* No, there was no doubt about it whatsoever.

She sat before Sam, hypnotised. Then she said, "Not all the folks who visit here tell lies. Tell me, my boy, aren't you a dealer in expensive watches?"

Sam was obviously surprised. He moved away from Rosy.

"Well, how do you know, anyway?"

"Oh. Elementary, my dear Watson. Just a little telepathy and lots of guesswork, I can even guess time, smells, cards..."

"There you have gone wrong, Granny! I do nothing at all. My father used to be a watchmaker."

Her guess was correct then, Erusha was convinced. No doubt whatsoever. This was David's son. Sam laughed but

Madam sat dazed, looking at him in deep concentration. After he left, he must have got married and settled down.

"Where does he stay now?"

"My dear dad? He kicked the bucket you know. Five years back," Sam roared with laughter. Madam's face darkened suddenly. David was dead! For a moment, she could not imagine this!

Sam stopped laughing. "Where are the girls?" he demanded. "I have come to meet them—not my dad. Do you understand?"

Madam found the way back to sanity. She called the girls. Gladys, Betty, Susan, and all the rest followed, each attracting the attention of the young visitor. Madam was quiet; she was immersed in deep thought, some far-off memory. She had thought that David had come at last. Then she had clung to the hope that she could at least meet him, now that his son was here. She was obviously confused to learn that David was dead.

"All these look cute—which one do I take?" Sam asked.

The girls enjoyed this, but Madam had got up in the meantime. "Come up, my boy! I want to speak to you a little in private. Oh girls, please withdraw for a moment."

The girls were astonished, but they cleared off at once.

Madam walked up to Sam and sat by his side. "Oh dear, you mustn't get angry."

Sam tried to move away, pushed her away. But Madam would not budge.

"He was just like you. He looked like you and carried himself like you. Your dad and my fiancé."

Sam lost his temper. "What are you blabbing about?"

"Yes, dear. By God, he loved me. He would do anything in the world for me. Oh, how he loved me! And how he showered presents on me. Once he decorated all the walls of this hall with watches... He was crazy after me. He wanted to get married to me... But I am really the cursed one, the unfortunate one..." Her voice became hoarse and tears rolled down her cheeks.

Sam was confused. Madam was now leaning on his body. He blurted out, "Don't you dare dirty my dad's fair name. Dad would never visit such a house..."

"Oh, such a house! My God! But you are here after all... Anyway, you are meeting me... You are David's shadow. Where are the watches now, won't you tell? The one that made sweet tinging sounds, the one that was fixed in the ball of earth...and David's gun, his camera...all that belonged to him..."

"Oh, leave me alone. Leave me alone."

"No, my dear. My beloved... Don't leave me..." Madam struggled with Sam as he started to go. His touch, his breath—everything was so charming! *How I wish I had married him!... If I had then...*

"Where's your mother? Was she strong and beautiful? Was she faithful to him?"

Sam collected all his strength and pushed her away.

"You bitch! You have gone crazy!" He clenched his fists. "Who do you think I am? I will go get the police to storm this house—this dirty den of yours..."

"Go," Madam shouted. "Go away, David. I won't come with you. I am not going to give up this life to be a maidservant... wife at your house. You...husband for the night. You will never understand young girls...never..."

Erusha lay on the sofa, uncertainly. David had created a big noise in the hall and Erusha had thrown him out. The scenes that had been enacted in the hall twenty-five years ago flashed past.

The girls had already gathered around her. They helped her with some water; they fanned her, and let her get some air. Yvonne patted her.

"What's wrong, Madam?" she asked. "Shall I send for the doctor?"

"Send for David," she said. But her voice trailed off. She gathered what had happened, but could not recollect how she had behaved. Was it madness or just sickness? She was terribly frightened. Suddenly, she broke into tears once again.

"What is it, Madam?" someone asked.

"I am to be cursed for it. Myself... I have spoilt the fair name of this house. I behaved like a damned native. Oh, Yvonne, you were here. The finest jewel of my treasures. But I gave him the cold shoulder. I sent him back. I am damned. I have to wait for another twenty-five years now. Twenty-five long years..."

Erusha started crying. The girls helped her to her room. She stumbled into the room and lay restlessly on her bed. The girls stayed for a while and then withdrew. Long ago, one Irani girl had gone crazy and had to be taken to the hospital. Madam remembered that. She was frightened stiff. She jumped out of bed and rushed towards the door. The door was closed from outside.

Then she realised that she had picked Sam's watch when they were together. She took it out of its hiding place. Holding it to her heart, she felt like crying. But there were no tears in her eyes. She remained unmoved. When David had left for the last time, she had happily run into the dance hall... She got up and played some records on the gramophone. The orchestra was on and that excited her. All the glory of her youth was conjured up before her eyes. English etiquette, white people, costly liqueurs, cigarettes, dances, heaps of currency notes. And she saw the sahibs taking their leave—in planes and steamers, waving their kerchiefs. The record was over, and the whirring noise remained. It never ended in fact. Slowly it was eating into the vitals of the house...the house was crumbling, it was falling to pieces.

But Madam sat there, motionless. The two French girls who charged fifty for a short time were gone and the frigidaire was gone, the queen's big portrait in the hall was gone, and Yvonne was going too. The black rats were destroying her house. There was red betel juice in her clean baths, there were customers in dirty dhotis disgracing the beautiful furniture, there were cheap and ugly girls around in her house... But Madam sat where she was, doing nothing.

The whirring noise of the gramophone stopped. The sounds of vehicles, radios and all the rest had also stopped. All was quiet. In that void, Madam stood up. It was this void which had forced her to follow a man to the brothel instead of going back home from school. It was for the fear of this void that she did not go with David and had danced and tried to forget her agony in the company of the young man.

And today...she craved to see the bloodstained handkerchief in the safe; she wanted to see the maidservant's baby sucking at her breasts. Or should she go in search of Sam? She did nothing of the sort and lay quietly in bed, looking at the cobweb on the ceiling with careless unconcern.

A long time passed. Erusha wanted to sleep. What a bore to sleep all by oneself! She searched for her watch, muttering to herself, "Half-past two..." In the semi-darkness, she looked at the watch. It was just about twelve. She was wrong—perhaps for the first time! She got the fright of her life when she saw the big hands of the watch. Her watch fell from her hands and even as it struck the floor, she took her last breath.

The next moment, she was dead!

(Translated from the Marathi by Bal Gadgil)

DALIA

Gulzar

Her husband was the first to break the news, "I was summoned to the *haveli* at the behest of the Maharaj today—Chhote Maharaj had sent for me—I was quite astonished."

It was her turn to be astonished now. Khuswa was telling her this, his eyes wide open.

"Their servants came to the fields to get me. They tied my hands with a rope. I couldn't think of any fault or mistake I had committed. They took me away and made me stand in front of him. He looked at me with those enormous eyes lined with antimony. I was so scared. Then he ordered those two servants out and instructed them to close the door behind them. That surprised me more." Dalia felt her husband's eyes were also quite large though they had been shrunk to a smaller size by poverty and the sun. Khuswa continued, "Then he asked me in a thunderous voice, 'Is Dalia your wife?'"

Dalia was startled. She said, "Then?"

"He asked me how much I spend on drink every day, and how much went towards household expenses. He said he had come to know that out of my daily earnings of two-and-half rupees, I spent two rupees on drink and gave you eight annas for household expenses. I fell at his feet and said that someone had given him wrong information. I give two rupees for household expenses and spend eight annas on drink. He said he knew it all..."

Dalia understood what had happened. Just the other day, she had met the Maharaj in the desert. She was carrying two pitchers full of water drawn from the well on the other side of the dune when his she-camel started moving closer to her. She could not even look up because there were two full pitchers on her head. It seemed as if someone was speaking to her from the sky.

"Listen, girl, will you give me some water to drink?"

She had stopped. While she was still adjusting the pitcher on her arm, the Maharaj had made the she-camel sit on the sand in a folded heap.

"Will you let me drink some water? My flask has fallen empty on the way."

The enormous eyes lined with antimony had rested on her *choli*. Both her hands were holding the pitchers so she could not even pull her *pallu*.

"What happened? Why are you scared? Aren't you from Jhajure? I am the Maharaj of the palace—the Chhote Maharaj..."

She did not say a word. The Maharaj did not get off the camel but kept staring at her. With trepidation she had uttered, "We are from a lower caste, *Hukum*. It would pollute the dharma."

"Whose dharma? Yours or mine?"

"Yours, *Hukum*." He was silent for a moment, then laughed, and before riding away said, "All right. Don't give me water. I'll drink when I get home."

Khuswa was saying, "The Maharaj told me that Raniji needed a maid in the house, someone who would attend to her bath and Neeti Tai had mentioned my wife's name. He had asked me to send you from tomorrow. You'll get clothes and food grains from the *haveli*."

Dalia shivered. The Maharaj had made all the enquiries in such a short while. Her fair skin had proved to be her enemy time and again. Her mother used to say, "Smear some dust on your face before you step out. Otherwise you will return with a blackened face someday."

And now her husband was saying, "You'll go to work in the *haveli* from tomorrow."

Dalia stood up and stamped her foot. "I'll never go to the *haveli*. Don't you know where the women who go to the *haveli* end up? They go and live in brothels! Their men do not keep them."

Khuswa guffawed and a strong whiff of cheap liquor hit Dalia's senses. "Who is going to pay for you in a brothel? Haven't you ever seen your reflection in the mirror?"

The next day, leaving Dalia with Neeti Tai at the threshold of the *haveli*, Khuswa went off to work in the fields as usual. Neeti took her inside with many words of advice and reassurance. After crossing several doors and entrances, they reached the Maharani's chambers, where she was getting an oil massage. She had taken off her jewellery which lay in a huge heap on a dhurrie. She spoke from behind the door.

"Who is it, Tai?"

"It is Dalia. You had sent for her."

"What for?"

"To assist in your bath."

"Yes, of course. Is she neat and clean?"

Tai gave Dalia a once over and answered, "We'll wash her. She'll be clean then. She is going to be good."

Maharani's laughter tinkled like a silver rattle.

Dalia was reassured to find that her fears about the *haveli* were baseless. Nothing that she was apprehensive about took place there. The family seemed to be nice. However, she was amazed to see the interiors of the *haveli* where rooms opened into more rooms. The *haveli* seemed to have an enormous belly which could easily contain a large number of people. Bade Maharaj spent all his time lying in an opium den in an outer room. There was Chhote Maharaj to look after the estate, but he did not visit the *zenana* too often. However, you could see him in Raniji's room sometimes. Raniji talked a lot during her bath. She would refer to her parental home frequently.

"Bapu had a *stapu* made with glazed tiles for us in the courtyard. The floor used to get spoiled by the lines drawn by chalk sticks, so one day he sent for a mason... Do you know what tiles are? They are coloured bricks made of cement. Bapu had a *stapu* made in the courtyard where we could play hopscotch."

She stopped for a while, then asked, "What games did you play at your parents' home?"

"Where was the time for me to play, *Malkin*?" Dalia answered. "I went to draw water at playtime and worked in the field at mealtimes. My mother used to put an onion and *bajri roti* in my pocket and give me a small piece of rock salt to lick. She instructed me to drink water before and after eating so that I would have a full stomach."

"You have started telling me how poor you were... I was only asking what games you played as a child. All right...will you pour water on me from above now?"

Tai had laughed when Dalia asked her if she could use the water with which Raniji had taken a bath for her own bath. She told Dalia, "Go and bathe with fresh water, you silly girl! There is a well in the house and the wells do not run dry very often!"

The day she had brought a sliver of soap and washed with it, she would thrust her face close to Khuswa's again and again. But his nose, saturated with the stench of liquor was quite beyond smelling the soap's perfume.

One day, when she was giving a bath to Raniji, they heard the Maharaj calling her. Raniji said to Dalia, "Go and ask him what he wants. Tell him I am bathing."

Dalia stepped out and stood before the Maharaj, "Raniji is taking her bath, *Hukum*. She has asked..."

He interrupted her, "Lift your face up. You should look at me when you talk to me." When she looked up, she was stung by those enormous antimony-lined eyes. "Tell Raniji that I am going to the lounge downstairs and ask her to send my refreshments there."

This was the first time she had to stand in the presence of the Maharaj for so long.

He sat eating on the *jhoola* while she stood on one side holding a glass of *lassi* for him. After he finished eating, he said, "Say, Dalia, you did not give me water because it would have spoiled my dharma. How come my dharma is not affected by you serving me food?

"I have served you your own food, *Hukum*. There is nothing of mine in it," she answered.

"I have told you to look up while talking to me," he reminded her.

She tried hard but could not lift her eyes. She did not realise how heavy one's eyelids could be. She lifted them up but they dropped back like a limp cat.

"Look up again," he demanded.

"How can I look at you like that, *Hukum*?" she said, diffidently.

He took the glass of *lassi* from her hand and placing its rim under her chin, lifted her face up so that she could look at him.

"Like this," he said. "Look at me and talk to me, like this. In what way do you look at that drunkard? At Khuswa?"

"But he is my husband, *Hukum*," she said, defensively.

Neeti Tai came to her rescue just then. God knows how long he would have made her stand there if Tai had not come. Neeti Tai said, "Come Dalia, let me give you your food. Please let her go, *Hukum*. It is getting late."

"Hm..." the Maharaj snorted and asked, "do you give her enough food?"

"*Malkin* has told me to give her three *roti*s and a lump of jaggery..."

Dalia summoned the courage to ask, "Could I please take the *roti*s home? May I eat them at home?"

"With Khuswa?"

She nodded, "Yes."

"Tai, pack her food and give it to her. And don't count the *roti*s...give her a whole basketful," the Maharaj ordered.

Dalia was pleased to see Khuswa eating the butter she had brought from the *haveli*. Tai had put such a large blob of butter between the *roti*s she had brought home.

"Didn't Raniji object?" Khuswa asked.

"Well, not everything takes place in front of Raniji," she said, playfully giving one more twist to Khuswa's moustache with her butter-smeared fingers.

You could see the clouds come swirling by every day, but they just dissolved and evaporated in the sky over the desert. However, a certain current of moisture-laden breeze had pervaded the atmosphere. The earth was getting softer and Khuswa was much in demand as a farmhand. For the first time in years, he had seen the little granary in his house fill up with foodgrains.

Dalia was rubbing oil in Raniji's hair when the Maharaj entered the room without clearing his throat. He sat down before Raniji.

"Your *Mamaji's* daughter is getting married," he said.

"Sheetla?" Raniji asked.

"Yes, it is Sheetla's wedding and they have asked you to come early. In fact, they want you to come right now."

"You'll come too, won't you?" she asked.

"What would I do going so early? I'll be there for the wedding. You must go. You can stay with your parents for a few days. Ma Saheb misses you a lot," he answered.

"And who is going to look after you for so long?"

"She is here," he answered, looking at Dalia, "she can take care of me. Would you, Dalia? She can stay here with Tai."

Dalia broke into a cold sweat at the Maharaj's jocularity. Raniji said, "But for her husband, I would have taken her with me."

"What husband?" the Maharaj said. "He is no husband. He is a bottle of liquor that rolls here and there."

Arrangements for Raniji's departure were completed in two days. A caravan left for her parents' place. Dewanji escorted her.

Dalia stayed away from the *haveli* for several days after Raniji's departure. She stayed back deliberately even after Tai sent for her.

By now, Khuswa was receiving higher wages from the *haveli* and his drinking had increased ever since his stock of grain had started remaining full. Quite often, Dalia had to fetch him, from the *theka* at night, in an inebriated state.

On one occasion, he picked up a fight with the village *purohit* after drinking and in a rage, he spat at the door of the temple. That created a furore in the village. He was beaten up by the men from the police station and put in the lockup. Dalia visited the police station again and again. Every time, she would tremble to see the state in which her husband was kept there. However, her appeals were ignored completely and ultimately, she ended up going back to the *haveli*.

She became stiff sitting on the threshold of the *haveli*, all day. After sunset, Neeti Tai came and took her inside. She made Dalia have a wash first and then served her something nice to eat. As she asked her to change into fresh clothes, Dalia was flabbergasted. It took her no time to understand Neeti Tai's intent and purpose. She could read it all in her eyes.

Neeti Tai said in a soft whisper, "Come, change your clothes. This time, Khuswa is going to be kept in the lockup for several days. And who knows what happens afterwards!"

Her voice was tremulous as she went on, "This is how I too came to Bade Maharaj and stayed back in the *haveli*. I was left with nothing with which I could go back. The Maharaj did not leave me worthy of anything! Come, get up and change your *choli*!"

Dalia looked around with terrified eyes. Imprisoned in the belly of the *haveli*, she could hear someone bellowing close by.

(Translated from the Hindi by Masooma Ali)

THE SHIP OF BUTTERFLIES

Thomas Joseph

A ship which had begun its voyage years ago swam many latitudes and longitudes and one day reached the island of butterflies that lay in the middle of the ocean.

Everywhere, butterflies emerging from the breaking cocoon of life hovered over the shimmering waters, dancing. As the loud talk and gay songs of the sailors wafted towards the island, the butterflies, like guests just arriving, rose and flew in the direction of the ship. All those places the butterflies reached, straying from their fast-burning, intense lives, were the secret domains of the shapes of man, mixed with dream and blood, all changed beyond recognition. Amongst them the ship too lay huddled, immersed in its own destiny, cold and frozen under thick shrouds of mist.

Here is uncovered a vast world in which the deep rumble of the breakers prevails and stray human forms climb towards the summit of the rocks. In the centre of all this, the ship lay still in a pool of deep quiet, like a gigantic butterfly with many wings and petals. The captain, who now and then came out upon the deck, clad in his ceremonial attire on which silver stars and the ribbons of his rank were sewn, stood there in sombre majesty, casting his fearless glance upon the distant seas. Lighting his pipe, he stood there smoking, motionless, for a long time. The butterflies had become still upon the body of the ship, folding their wings, unknown and unseen. Intently gazing at the captain's face sunk in thought, they now joined his endless voyage as the guardians of a prescient life possessing visions of coming sorrowful events. Wrinkles and the fatigue of lost sleep filled the captain's face with signs of indescribable hints of coming events.

Through the telescope, he cast a far-reaching glance, mastered by only him only, beyond the oceans, mountains and valleys, faraway, to his native land, far beyond the reach of human sight. His wife, Susanna, was sitting in the garden in front of his house, sewing butterflies upon a silk handkerchief.

For many years the captain had, through the startling thunder of his orders and shouts, led his sailors and steered the ship through dangerous and fearsome sea currents to unchartered continents. He would stand fast even when all the weapons and tools of war had collapsed under the onslaught of a sea-battle and everything lay in ruins around him. It would be at the last moment when everything had crumbled and was about to sink into the ashen waters of death that the surface of the waters would bloom with spring-bursts of calm. And the ship would heave forward covered in foam and spray. It would be at a time when they despaired that it would take months or even years to sight land again that the ship would float into a harbour where light, falling in shafts, appeared like swords strewn about. The waterfront resounds with the happy yells and loud exchanges flowing out of the ship. And the captain stands on the deck, in the firelight of resurrection, his coat fluttering in the wind, making him look like a huge bird.

At all the harbours the ship anchored, the broad streets and wine-shops and restaurants that lined them, received the captain and his sailors as their guests. He returned to the ship drunk, after buying fine gifts from the shopping malls. As he lay alone in the darkness of his cabin, his eyes were filled with the sights of suburbs haunted by gangs of desperadoes wearing daggers and revolvers under their waistbands, and the shocking familiarity of the faces of certain lonely people who had passed into the realm of death. His own figure, wandering under a scorching mid-day sun in strange towns, looking for what he could not say, also entered his reflections. And at last, the ship, tossed about by the hot ocean currents and miraculously escaping from tempests, had reached the island of butterflies. It lay, at anchor, calmly resting and expectantly gazing upon the moment when the next voyage would begin. The days of violent seas and fearful waves now become sounds floating from far away and soft whispers from nowhere, all boiling together under the hot sun.

Although the sound of Susanna's prayers or of her calling out his name gently had risen out of the moving waters outside and caressed him, his awareness of its being unreal plunged the captain into great melancholy. At the same time, he was not able to escape those invisible calls. From beyond the ocean currents and the distant mountains and valleys, a Sunday morning enters. The captain and Susanna are climbing the steps of a tranquil yet tense church. Circling their beautiful bodies, butterflies flit and dance under the golden yellow sunlight.

Suddenly, when Susanna falls back in a swoon, the captain's hands hold her. When they return home from church, a telegram awaits, asking him to get back to the ship immediately.

As he lies now in the cabin of the darkening ship, all events obtain a flow of added meaning. He thought he saw Susanna, standing motionless and silent, staring into the limitless ocean, among the many hands that rise and wave farewell as the ship swims out to the ocean on an evening when the waves are high, and a cold wind beats violently. Memories that shone from the telescope glitter and die over the mirages of the ocean.

Even as he thus rested upon a bed of butterflies in the ship moored so far away, he could see the figure of Susanna, fatigued by despair, lying among the broken plates and flower-pots of his home. Her face was covered with wrinkles, her clothes dirty and smelly and her feet caked with mud. The captain dreamt that he reached her in the wink of an eye, held her hand and lifted her out of the soot and smoke and, together, they flew up into the vast universe. He dreamt that in one moment he had arrived at his distant country's borders, protected by barbed wires, and stood gazing into a magical land, but alien, filled with people, vehicles and concrete apartments. He dreamt that his clothes and his bones were filled with the roar of the ocean and with the spilled blood of the creatures that live in it. He returned, unable to see a beautiful house on a riverside, the radiance of Susanna flitting through its rooms, sometimes seen and sometimes not, and the flower-pots of his garden. He woke with a start, thinking that his ship was plunging headlong into the angry waters of a strait. As he tossed about on the bed, he heard, like the sound of raindrops falling upon water, Susanna's prayers for voyagers being washed in from distant seas. Then he sank down into the bottom of sleep, and the depths of its oceanic stirrings.

The butterflies that rose up from the words of Susanna's prayers and from the silken kerchiefs she embroidered, usually vanished for some time, somewhere, after presenting to the earth rare shows of magical beauty. They vanished, swimming into the springs of the sun and the moon's soft light. Those butterflies that disappeared into the inner reverberations of a secret life are, perhaps, being transferred by beautiful fingers unseen, onto cloaks and coats. Sitting in the garden of her house, Susanna immersed herself in this duty which was of another world.

The captain, as he stood upon the deck, attentive to the tremendous changes taking place in the ocean, could not find a way to escape from the stranglehold, like that of an octopus, of the loneliness of his life and the silent cries of Susanna. During these days and nights of conflict, he would sometimes walk into the midst of sailors and loudly upbraid them or shout with horrible laughter, joining them in their lives filled with strenuous labour and hard-edged jokes. Then, singing a sorrowful song in a deep and sombre voice, he took the ship across the anxiety-filled hot currents of future, and, passing shores where water lilies swam upon the waves, onto coasts of white bears and penguins, and dropped anchor.

The captain tried to be content by taking out the gifts he had bought for Susanna over the years and stored away in chests and drawers, and touching them all over; inhaling deeply the smell of garments and undergarments Susanna would never wear. He lit his pipe, and, smoking, set flying for Susanna, beyond the infinite horizon of the eyes, kissing lips and a proud smile. Knowing these secrets of the captain, butterfly-wings fluttered. The soliloquies and sighs of the captain blew into their wings along with the wind, and the butterflies rose into the air in large numbers. Filling their wings with extraordinary winds of beauty, they landed upon the butt of revolvers and on boxes full of cartridges. One or two of them went, like adventurers, down the barrel of a gun as if it were a deep well. Their wings gathered the odour of gunpowder and smoke and they became engulfed in the invisible presence of death.

One afternoon, the captain set out for the island of butterflies. He was received into a door filled with darkness which looked like the cavernous depths of a bar. For the captain, one more night of the butterflies had arrived. From the midst of darkness and mysterious dialogue, a cup full of blood was delivered into his hands. He sat there immobile, experiencing unfamiliar glances and languages, as the glasses were being filled and emptied. In the dim light, upon the lips and hands of people, were visible the images of butterflies. On every wine cup, a butterfly sat still. When the captain left the bar all of a sudden, the butterflies opened their wings, flew up from the legs of tables and chairs and followed him.

The captain came to a street lined with many shops. All the things of the earth were sold there. Puzzling and shocking the shopkeepers, he purchased women's dresses and children's garments in large numbers and hung them in bundles from his shoulders. He also showed extraordinary interest in buying from the fruit stalls all the sweet varieties of fruits available. He bought, paying heavy prices, portraits of beautiful women and many other paintings. Carrying them all on his back, his revolver stuck under his belt, he kept wandering around the houses and the stalls of the marketplace. Inexplicably, hearing the happy voices of women and children after a very long time, he only felt immensely sad. In his drunken stupor, he saw the merchants who visited Susanna in their house for mysterious reasons and thieves who made off with money and ornaments. He fell to the earth upon his face. Dust covered the captain with its ancient scales. The fruits of the earth filled his eyes and mouth. He kept kissing the soggy dust again and again.

At midnight, the captain woke up on the bed of butterflies. He looked out and saw floating upon the surface of the ocean a faded shadow. As it slowly approached the ship, he saw that it was the body of a woman, her hands crossed upon her chest, her body covered with a white shroud and white veil upon her head. As he feared, it was the body of Susanna. He felt that her face, and the pupils of her eyes which were filled with tenderness, were rising and floating towards him, trembling in shock. He also saw himself crouching with his head between his knees, near Susanna's body in a vast cemetery, amongst monuments and broken-down crosses.

In the ship, he became engrossed in the strategies for a battle against himself. He wore his armour, his ribbons and medals and got ready. He took out a bloodstained sword upon whose hilt the figure of a butterfly was carved.

When he reached the shore with the unsheathed sword raised in his hand, he found that the whiteness of dawn had spread in the east. The captain's figure, climbing the rocks, was bathed in the light of the sun. He seemed to flutter in the wind. Then he began to execute the warlike footwork of a soldier. His sword rose and flashed in the air. The sharp point of the sword was reflected in the pupils of his eyes. Sometimes, he turned the point of the sword against his own body. All over his body, like a bloody memory, eyes and cells of life opened. The butterflies flew high above the rocky summit, keenly watching the fate of this unique human guest. The fish and the great sharks that flung themselves above the sea's surface gazed at the captain's battle against himself and sank back into the sea.

The murmur of flying wings rose like the sound of a whirlwind in the island of the butterflies. Flying up out of the earth's life-blocks and grass, the butterflies swam into the realm of the soul's outcries where blood-drops glisten. The captain, fighting his way up, reached the high summit of the rock just below the clouds. His sword looked like a waterfall as he sank it into his own body. A spring of blood rose from the wound. His feet faltered upon the rocks and he fell far down into the open hands of water. Where he fell, an immortal memory of blood spread through the water.

The captain's body floating upon the bloodstained water, bathed in peace. The butterflies had increased in number and their swarms flew over to the captain's body and rested upon it.

In the course of time, upon the shore of a continent hidden and unmarked in the maps, the captain's body was washed up. Plants and butterfly wings began to sprout from the body that lay enwrapped in the grass and the earth.

(Translated from the Malayalam by A.J. Thomas & Paul Zacharia)

KURUKSHETRA

Suresh Joshi

At two in the night, I enter the house. In the darkness, an impression of city lights continues to hurt my eyes. I walk to the lamp in the corner and raise the wick. Breeze shoots into the chimney and the flame leaps. The house rears like a ship in a storm and I grip the clothesline to keep from falling.

The mass of darkness inhaled in city lanes sinks lower into my body. It settles to my feet and I stumble again. Quickly, I find the edge of the bed. In the front room, the old man snores softly near the window, flat on his back, a think cloth webbing feet and face, awaiting the bier, one would think. Clumsy mass of wooden logs—his unshapely life of sixty-five years—how comfortably he stretches across the pile!

Mother and my brother's wife lie on the floor, breathing in the dank kitchen odour. Brother is on night shift; my wife and I have the middle room. Demons of the night dishevel my sister-in-law's clothes. Mother's toothless mouth is poised open, a hesitant snuff-box.

My wife by my side. Wife, wife. Girl too fragile for the weight of the world. Supine, defenceless, the young bride's

Monday story, the Bible under her pillow. So will she appear at death's hour, and I shall shut her eyes and her mouth, and I do not know why I should have such a thought today.

The cold entering with me has settled into the warm corners of the house. I lower the wick and lie down. I watch my wife's gaping face. That blandness! May I laugh please, please may I laugh? Without a notion in the world to launch herself into this! Momentous! Would you hold me? Smashed into a thousand fragments, scattered across a thousand paths, I, wanderer, would she hold me, collect my pieces into her inadequate womb, give me shape and deliver me back into the world? Such innocence, such faith in a young wife's Monday book.

A tiny tongue of flame continues to flicker in the corner. I lie now and shut my eyes. The mice start their invasion. The day's voices hover, echoing frailly. Fragments of thought gyrate illogically, planets out of orbit, swinging and crashing. All these adhere to me, fasten on to me, and in my sleep continue their attentions. I always turn a deaf ear to the conversation of the moment. On purpose, I allow my mind to wander, and later, argue vehemently to make up for inattention. These days, I notice, I become desperate over trifles, fiercely take up arms to justify even so simple an act as drinking water.

No surprising then that Chandrakanta, daughter of Manubhai the teacher, received from me today—a slap. I compose songs. Cause enough, it would seem, for Chandra to lose her head. O Spring and Summer, O Radhe Shyam, a few such words strung together and there we are! An ounce of my soul, true enough, takes shelter behind such words. And she sings passably. Then, as is my habit, I draw her out a bit, hold her thirteen-year-old chin and declare with theatrical charm, "Chandra, if you will always sing so sweetly, I shall lay a heap of songs at your feet, a heap of blossoms will I shake down for you!" She gapes. But look at her friends—without a care in the world they hop about, they spin, they twirl; Chandra squats like a cretin. Then suddenly she is in my lap, searching my eyes for a sign. I am revolted. Like a shock I am up, down tumble Chandrakanta and her play-acting, still clinging on to my feet. I bend low to help her, but the clammy greed of those hands infuriates me. I slap her across the face and amble away.

A dim flame reaches me through the tired flesh of my eyelids. It clings to my eyes like Chandra's humid hands. I turn off the lamp.

Dark, dark. A cigarette in hand—I need that—need to watch the steady glow of burning ash. I stretch, and my wife's arm is crushed. It conjures up a vision—Ketki Mehta! The foul, plush restaurant, with her pouring tea into my cup. The flesh of her arm—bare. The down on it, the soft fullness of it above the elbow. The slightest exertion and blood rushes into her milky skin. I watch the stream of tea rushing into the cup, and her arm, gauze-white in the milky flood of tubelights, steam from the cup mingling with the odour of her silk dress. I would like to say something, but she softly withdraws her arm. I draw a blank.

A woman, to me, has no unity of being. Some little quarter of her body tells me all about her; and that quarter is accessible to me in an instant. It's a knack I have, to detect how one plays gently with her foot; another, without reason, curves her neck and looks over her shoulder; a third pats her hair back into place. And some allow their lips to flicker like lights. The essential woman is laid bare. From then on, no other part of her will interest me.

Now I am aroused. My slumbering wife can't recognise my touch. She prattles on like a lost child; she turns and sinks again into stupor. All her friends' detailed instructions, advice fetched from their own conjugal experiences—wasted. See, now she wanders in the dream pastures of her childhood.

The bare outline of her form is visible in this darkness. Darkness activates my mind. I see—Rita! The bold grace of her ponytail. And Rekha—a flickering tongue. Flicker mouth, flicker tongue, half and go on. Her words hardly register. I listen only to the voice; not sweet but binding, creator of atmosphere; bitter in its tang like a mature peach. So Rekha's voice. And Minal? Her brows contracting at any excuse. And Shilu—the pointless, unreasonable movements of her body, an unwilling tree pushed by winds, breezes. In darkness, I gather fragments. In the dense womb of darkness, I conceive the image of a new woman. Into the outlines of the woman sleeping by my side, I arrange these fragments.

The sleep that will not come burns my eyes. My blood throbs rhythmically and, as though in sympathy, I hear echoing heartbeats in my wife's body. Her leg veers unsteadily as I turn her to me. With a jerk it falls on me. Losing no time, I draw upon the fragments—Shilu's mindless swaying, Minal's brows, Rekha's voice... Sleep percolates downward through the heaviness of that leg. I lie still and helpless under its weight. My old father sits up, clears his throat. He opens the door to leave the room. Air wafts in and the streetlights enter furtively. I summon up courage to remove the leg.

Masses of air captive in the house rush headlong as the door shuts, crash against the wall and collapse. An odour of sweat and hair oil rises to my nostrils. I gasp. Prone in bed and single-handed I seem engaged in mortal combat. The impact of battle shakes my body and my wife wakes: "What? Who, who?"

"It's me." Softly.

Up she jumps.

"What's wrong?" I ask.

"The milk's been put away. Wait, I'll get it."

"Don't want any. Let it be."

She is about to reply and I jerk her nearer to me. Darkness veils my annoyance. She interprets passion, slithers towards me and latches on like a child. I choke in the warmth, I want to explode—out, out—into the streets, but I am arrested. Immobilising arms! Arms that swing playfully from trees, draw water, patch floors with dung, those very arms!

The old man next door comes through a marathon cough, spits out phlegm like a storm, mutters, 'O, God, Great God...' Then it is silent again.

There it is—the darkness, the silence. And two pulsating bodies, under a sheet of darkness. The world is hatched in just such a womb. The foetus sucks upon darkness. Will I never have it in me, this pitch of black I wander the world in search of? This child beside me would gather my quintessence into her being and give me a new body. And for that, there is no dearth of darkness in the mother's womb. It links birth to birth. But I shall let her have such fragments of flint, such pieces—too various to integrate—that they will course through her veins like missiles and pierce their walls. My body flies at her in fury. The house's smothered breath, its anguished, fractured inhabitants—all these cling to my mind as my body clings to hers.

Mother rises for a drink of water. Her feet scrape on the floor and my wife's arms freeze across my back. Unbearable heat fumes between us stream like lava through my body. I creep in by inches. Sleep floods across my walls and I collapse.

And now another picture appears: On a vast battlefield, I lie prostrate among a heap of bodies. I am spread over an area larger than that occupied by a body intact. I see an arm here, another flung far, a severed head rolled some yards away as though by its own volition. Upon this field my wife arrives, torch in hand, looking for me among the bodies. She gathers my limbs. Crimson adorns the parting of her hair, vermilion tints both her palms. She collects my parts, with her own hand lights my pyre, and sits upon it. Flames spin and twine around us, scorching our flesh. My eyes open.

The sun is out and some of its fragmented rays slant and scatter into my eyes. My eyes burn. I rise, pass into the kitchen. Mother reheats tea for me. It is hot ash; I sit and swallow, watching the light pick up, grain by grain, the ash in the courtyard. And all at once the poem arrives:

The nineteenth Dawn rises over Kurukshetra. Light rings and crinkles like smashed bangle. It scatters from the caverns of the East like vermilion from a Sati's palm...

Now I stumble across my brother's voice reciting his tables. In this rising day, I take my poem for an unsteady walk in the street. She will not open her eyes to this day's dazzle. To this sightless poem I will give refuge, awaiting again the silent dark desolation of night. In darkness, the poem awakens. This is the sum of my courage, leading me to the end of one more day.

(Translated from the Gujarati by Gieve Patel)

THE SEMINAR

Mamta Kalia

She was amazed at the invitation. She did not respond, thinking that if the offer was dispatched by mistake, there will be no next letter through which the conveners usually write, "Please do come, the seminar will be incomplete without your active and thought-provoking participation." When such a letter was usually received, Pakhi had to decide to go or not to go.

Delhi was boiling under 48° Celsius. The mercury was still rising. The seminar was to be held in Shimla. Writing the word 'Shimla' on the envelope imparted a relief. The room was occupied by a decent cooler and fan—both were lifeless because of the load shedding of four hours—daily schedule. It was impossible to relax, or read or write.

As it was, Pakhi's life was quite hard. There was no space for blessings like holidays, sightseeing, tête-à-têtes and peace. She had received letters from three or four magazines whose editors insisted that she should send them her contribution. She had written to all of them on the basis of this single short story, "I'll be sending the story posthaste". Pakhi always hoped that given better weather, electricity supply and home front, she would be able to keep her promise. This invitation from Shimla could relieve her from all that trauma, albeit for a few days. She sent her consent.

After her acceptance, Pakhi was overcome by a sense of regret. She felt she was becoming too cunning, like a cat. She knew she would not meet like-minded writers and thinkers in the seminar. Instead, there would be people whose thinking would be quite the antithesis. Then why should she be going? Immediately, a skunk-like head of compromise rose from within her and announced, "You have agreed to go because it is needed to get close to your enemy to know it fully well. If you do not know your opponent, how will you fight?" The agreement pacified Pakhi. She felt she could participate in the seminar without losing her identity.

Pakhi and the other delegates of the seminar were put up in a hillside house. The rooms had heavy curtains on three sides of the wall, and the fourth wall was left bare for a panel view of the Shivalik range. The pine and cedar trees looked too good and green, as if they were paper-made. The room was air-conditioned. You could sense the botanical grandeur of the forests up to the foothills of the Shivalik range. Pakhi's eyes were unaccustomed to so much of greenery, what with years of staying in crowded colonies of her town. She looked at the landscape for a long while to convince herself.

After a shower, Pakhi gave a good shake to her head to get out of her domestic mindset. She took great care to dress up and went to the dining hall. It dawned upon her that this place was agog with such fine fiction fabricators who had been crafting the short story genre for a long time, though their fiction remained where it was. For these craftsmen, literature outside their own parameters, was no more than a dustbin.

There were twenty participants who had come from far-flung destinations. They dazzled like the Queen's necklace in which Pakhi's presence was like a black-bead string. She was here as per design or stupidity. Also present were a poet and a literary critic who were at the height of their honour, hence they were above sanction. Their works found favour with the publishers, and were in every textbook.

There were four other women writers besides Pakhi. Two were young and pushing hard to look mature, and the other two who were older, were trying to look younger. Pakhi was familiar with the older two because they too belonged to Delhi University. They were at the centre of the capital's literati. There would never be a book launch, conference or seminar without them. During discussions, if they fell out, they pounced upon their victim. Their arguments were aggressive, though without logic. They used pedantic terminology that made every seminar seem sombre and selective. There was this Surekhaji, who was into writing some very individual sort of stories. Her fiction reflected her personal life, her love, and lost loves, her frustration and her fetishes. The readers would know from her fiction when Surekhaji was to go abroad, when she was getting out of one love affair to get into another, when she was going to build a house and when she was to buy a pup of a rare pedigree. In the beginning, Surekhaji used to write lyrics, etc., but she was soon influenced by some foreign magazines to become real mod.

Not only did she cut and dye her hair, she also did the same with her writing.

She had a small band of admirers who looked upon her as an A-one artist and intellectual. It added to her fan mail in whichever magazine she was published. Surekhaji regarded herself as a top-ranking writer because of her fanfare.

The other woman, Veena Jaitly, was an art critic with an eminent daily. Veena was tall, slender and pretty. Her age oscillated from 25 to 45. She wrote in Hindi, but spoke English. Her short stories were midway between fantasy and symbolism. Her lips appeared purple as a result of chain smoking, but her tapering fingers showed the ashenness of nicotine. She had to lug quite a few things when she lifted her seat. Veena carried a big tote, but liked to hold a cigarette and matchbox in her hand. The other hand often held her glass of gin and bitters. She would drag another chair near hers, and put all her things thereon. She closed her eyes while listening to an argument, and when no one expected, she'd open her eyes and say, "Now that was a point." Then she spoke in great detail about the timeless truths that had no relevance to the point of the seminar.

The initial two sessions made it clear that writers were quite confused in their ideas. Some had not yet come out of Sartre's existentialism, while some interpreted the short story as though it belonged to the Red Riding Hood days. They would quote a few European critics, highlight Premchand's shortcomings, elaborate Prasad's creative parameters, and explain how the short story can survive and revive human values by avoiding platitude, media mediocrity and political commitments.

The reading session was in the evening. Four authors were to read their short stories to a select audience. Veena Jaitly and Pakhi were in this session. The other two participants had already made a name in English by translating their Hindi stories themselves. It was rumoured that they were paid handsomely in dollars for their overseas contributions.

Chandrashekhar was dressed in a yellow kurta and blue jeans. He announced, "I've been at the beer bar since the morning to be able to cope and present my story in a credible manner." He read out his story which had neither characters nor action. He was recounting his views on a heap of garbage in a playground. He received an applause from the audience.

The chairperson said, "A good work of art surpasses theme and thought, character and action. In order to break the rut, the short story should get out of its framework and code."

Veena was to read her short story now. She moved to the dais with all her paraphernalia. She lit her cigarette, drew the ashtray closer and began on an attractive note. Pakhi was finding her fabulous, but her story was beyond grasp. Veena's story fabricated a symbol around an eagle's droppings.

At the end of the story, there was thunderous applause. Veenaji's art was likened to that of Camus's and Kafka's. Veena walked back to her seat and kept smoking. It seemed she was listening to someone else's compliments for some other author.

When it was Pakhi's turn to read, at the outset she apologised by saying, " I am sorry to say my short story speaks of real-bodied people; they have a milieu, there is some action and it does not break free of any framework..."

Young critics and offbeat listeners winced a little, and wore a ginger expression during her reading. Pakhi knew she was here with the wrong armour. She was hardly surprised when there was no follow-up on her short story.

Going for long walks on the road, going down the hills, etching names on rocks and clicking cameras too were part of the seminar on the final day.

They started out in a huge group, but soon split into smaller units. Veena joined Pakhi. There was a small bazaar ahead that had everything a small hill-town market should have: two or three liquor shops, one photographer, a few stores of woollen wear and a few sundry shops like a tea stall, kerosene oil stall and a grain merchant's shop.

Chandrashekhar and Vivek paused at the liquor shop. Veena approached them, "A quarter for me too, okay?"

Veena spotted a nearby shop. It displayed wicker baskets, brooms, jute cord and handmade fans. Veena was drawn to the broom. "Oh! How beautiful", she said.

She lifted the broom. Certainly, it was a very artistically woven broom where all the wicks were gathered up in an arch. The front portion was thickset and stunted. The broom was tied by a thin cord. Veena untied it and held it round her thin waist. "How do I look now?"

"Fabulous", said Vivek and clicked his camera.

Chandrashekhar sighed, "Oh! I'm going to swoon." By then, two other women writers had joined them. Veena showed them the broom. They went gaga over its craftsmanship. Veena said, "I shall use it as my central wall-piece. I will give a black velvet background and you'll see the charisma."

Surekhaji said, "One of my bedroom walls appears glum. I shall put it over there."

The third intellectual held her hand over her heart, "Oh please, let me have two. How can do with one?"

All of them tried to persuade Pakhi to opt for one. But Pakhi declined point blank. "I cannot switch over from the short story to a broomstick."

"Oh Pakhiji, this is not a broomstick. This is a masterpiece awaiting a Picasso." Surekhaji felt quite sorry for Pakhi.

"Perhaps, but I'm not interested", Pakhi gave a brash retort.

All the post-modern writers came back to the guest house, holding their art objects close to their hearts.

There was still some time for dinner. After the second peg of gin, Veena started upon her pet subject. Her voice was sensitive and she was standing by the window facing the hills. She recounted how her parents had brought her up by putting her in a hostel and keeping their pets Tixy and Pixy close by. Even today, when she recalls her childhood, she can only see fog and inferno. The man she loved died in a car accident. Her present paying guest accommodation was in a colony where there were at least five murders a day. She writes in order to identify better all those hazards.

Pakhi was overwhelmed to hear Veena's soliloquy. Her own life was terribly tame, mundane and eventless. In fact, her writing was to get over the monotony, melancholy and boredom of her existence.

Veena's confession was sincere; it might have been true too, but all this did not reflect in her writing. In fact, her short stories were so disguised in symbols, they read like fantasies.

Surekhaji pressed her temples, "Oh, my past! Oh, no! Who has put me to the end of the road! Oh, oh!" Surekhaji rose to slip into the balcony.

Veena and Pakhi tiptoed there to find Surekhaji resting her head against the wall.

"Please Surekhaji, get over it and join us inside," Pakhi requested.

"Leave me alone, I'm very tense," Surekhaji gasped.

Veena signalled Pakhi to move away. "Tonight, Surekhaji will create some masterpiece. This is creative tension."

Anita Jain was a new young writer. She was looking at things as if she were Alice in Wonderland. She asked Pakhi,"Do you undergo such bouts of creative tension, Pakhiji?"

"Never", said Pakhi. "I write about ideas. Tension seems pretentious to me."

Chandrashekhar intervened, "Literature that's written without creative tension is mediocre, mundane and propaganda."

Veena added, "Yes, ideas and ideologies do limit a work of art."

"I don't think so", said Pakhi. "If you don't have an ideology, what can you give society besides your sick psychology and complexes?"

Chandrashekhar was finding Pakhi's presence an eyesore. He said, "You think the society is a godown of the Indian Food Corporation that has to be jam-packed with your jaded ideas and faded ideologies? Writing, after all, is a personal and subtle art."

Anita was getting amazed at the exchange. This was the first seminar for her creative breakthrough. Chandrashekhar and Vivek were interested in giving her a makeover, whereas she was full of awe for every author.

Pakhi said, "If you consider writing to be so personal and subtle, why do you get it published? Better to leave it in your diary."

"Sure, I don't care to get it published and read. I write for myself, not for the society."

"So do I, so do I," came several assents.

The seminar secretary walked in with the most literary critic of the Hindi world.

"Ah! The air is full of fire and firewood," he commented.

Surekhaji smiled, *"Raat ka waqt hai, mahaul banaye rakhiye."* Her tension and depression had long disappeared and now she was full of giggles.

Veena pressed the bell. Mansingh, the waiter came in.

"Remove these soda bottles and glasses," Veena said.

A bat had made its entry into the room. The shadow of its forelimbs flitted on the walls ominously.

The bat kept fluttering and flying towards the ceiling, only to descend like a copter.

The room was replete with sounds of 'ouch' and 'ugh'. Surekhaji was covering her eyes and gasping, "Oh God! How ominous!"

Veena said, "*Chhi, chhi.*"

Just then, came the secretary's command, "Mansingh, check it out."

Mansingh was quite short in height, but kept slouching his head as if to avoid the bat's contact.

Very soon, the bat completed another round and ultimately, it collapsed in a corner.

Mansingh picked up one of the brooms and hit the bat with all his might.

"The bastard is dead," saying so, Mansingh picked up the dead mammal and went to throw it outside the balcony.

"Oh no! Oh no!" Surekhaji, Veena and Vivek advanced forth, but had no guts to touch the broom that had accomplished this heroic act.

When Mansingh came back to the room, they all screamed, "Aiy Mansingh, you have ruined a decoration piece of ours, how mean of you."

Mansingh replied smugly, "*Arrey*, this was a mere broomstick. If you don't kill a lizard or a bat, you think you can kill a leopard or what?" he dropped all the brooms from the tabletop. "A broom's place is in the balcony. Why have you put it on a table as if it were a god?"

Veena felt deeply hurt, "I won't have a meal today."

"Nor will I," said Surekhaji, "I am very upset."

The senior literary critic rested his hands upon two junior authors, asking them to stand up for dinner. He said good-naturedly, "Now come on, don't make a fuss."

Pakhi declared loudly, "I'm famished. I must have a hearty dinner now."

The arty authors were trudging lifelessly towards the dining hall. Their faces expressed that they were undergoing much tension.

(*Translated from the Hindi by the author*)

THE ENIGMA

Amin Kamil

He spoke rather exasperatedly, "This is a matter beyond your understanding—too technical for you—surely not as simple as it might appear." He picked up his packet of cigarettes from his desk. I was rendered speechless.

He lit a cigarette and leaning back, spewed out of his mouth a cloud of smoke which thinned away slowly, filling up the room. Purged of its acridity, the smoke now became air, mingled with the air.

Breaking my train of thought, he said, "Listen, the body is not important. What matters is the head. What have I to do with the skin and the flesh? In which direction did the head lie? This is what concerns me. This, in fact, is the crux of the issue." His tone was emphatic. I wondered, what indeed was the worth of a man without his head or brains? All vanities reside in the skull. Pulling myself together, I asked just for the sake of asking, "Don't you know, Sir, in which direction the head lay?"

"There is nothing that is not known to us," he said, clenching his teeth. "They are big oafs if they think they can bungle the issue and beat us out. We are not novices but sheep keds, not like those folks who have just finished college and after paying bribes, manoeuvred their way to a *thanedar's* position. For the past thirty years, we have been drawing sustenance from the police department. So no hanky-panky with us."

How true! One can't defeat a sheep ked. He who is preyed upon by two sheep keds has his fate sealed and should prepare to make his exit from the world. A sheep ked is, after all, a sheep ked. Once it gets stuck to a limb, you just cannot remove it from there, do what you will. This is exactly what had happened with the corpse sucked off by the two sheep keds.

Whatever little I knew of the matter was based on hearsay. The details I didn't know. Of course, I wished to get to the heart of the matter to satisfy my curiosity. I must admit that I have no flair for mediation, and am little interested in sorting out disputes between contending parties. Even otherwise, for me, mediating in the face of the two sheep keds would be out of the question. Only diamond cuts diamond. However, to get a clear picture, I said, "The information must have reached you late. Else, how could the *thanedar* of Khanpur have outpaced you?"

I could see that this flattered him, for the muscles of his neck relaxed a bit and a smile flashed across his lips. His eyes shone with a devilish glint. Knitting his brow, he said, "The devil take constable Amma who messed the whole thing up. I wonder if you know him?" he asked.

"Yes, I do," I said, although I didn't know who the devil he was.

"The bloke didn't hold up the man," he said. "He didn't even send word for me. Otherwise, I should have been able to know what was what. But I made sure that my records were put straight."

"Sir, what man was it?" I said to get more information on the matter.

"There is no knowing that, thanks to the accursed constable Amma," he said in a surly tone. "These ragamuffins can't make their livelihood even from begging. Which is why they enlist as constables. Brainless lot! They hardly perceive the delicacy of a situation. The numbskull came to tell me, after the man had vanished, that it was a rider who had said that he had come across a dead body under a Chinar at Poshmarg. Now, what do you do with such an oaf? You ass of a man, why did you let the man go away? Who was he? Where did he belong? What if he himself had slain the person? Well, anything is possible. Do you agree? A *thanedar* must consider various aspects of a situation, mustn't he?"

"What you say is perfectly sound, more so as it comes from a *thanedar* like you. Now, what is the difficulty about the case?"

"What is the difficulty, you ask?"

He opened his eyes like an owl, took off his cap with his left hand and put it down. Then raising his gaze, he said, "There is no bloody difficulty about the matter. We have gone through such situations. Our papers are perfect. They can hold water, you see. I will make him see his worthlessness as a professional. My papers will speak."

Saying this, he burst into a guffaw. I felt tempted to laugh with him but restrained myself, not knowing why he was laughing.

He picked up something like a little ball of sugar from a plate on the desk and threw it into his mouth. "Try this, it is such a sweet thing," he pointed to the plate, making me a generous offer.

I took a ball and put it into my mouth. It was indeed very sweet. *The stuff has sweetened his mood. So I can draw him out,* I said to myself.

"The *thanedar* of Khanpur will not sit still. He must have thought out a strategy."

"Who cares? He will only knock out his own brains. When had he a head for strategies?" He stretched up his arms in order to relax. Then he put on his cap, and went through the act of yawning. "The mischief he wanted to do has been done. What else can he do now? We are watching out."

"What kind of mischief has he done?" I asked, naively.

"Well, I will tell you," he said, giving a jerk to his head which suggested that he would let the cat out of the bag.

"As soon as I heard that a dead body had been spotted under a Chinar at Poshmarg, I proceeded there, taking my men with me. It took us some time to arrive there. Our *thana*, mind you, is not like the *thana* of Khanpur, which is worse than a shanty. Ours has a vast jurisdiction. As we arrived, I found that he was there already with his scraggy constables. The body lay there under the chinar. I sensed his mischief. No duping me. I wouldn't let the apprentice outsmart the master." He helped himself to another sugary ball and munched on it.

I wanted to know why two *thanedar*s had to rush to the spot for a single dead body. It was the funeral of the *thanedar* in whose jurisdiction the body lay. So I asked him, somewhat in astonishment, "Sir, in whose jurisdiction did the corpse lie?"

"It lay in the jurisdiction of neither but on the demarcation line between the two jurisdictions. So we had to be there. The other party had to be there too. It would be unwise on our part to question their presence there. We will never say a thing which is illogical."

Craning his neck, he looked out of the window. Down below, two constables were roughing up someone. The spectacle was within my sight too.

"Even then, only one of you should have instituted the inquiry," I said, straightforwardly.

"Whatever do you mean?" he asked with a snarl. "The right to investigation belongs to him for whose jurisdiction the victim was headed for."

"But, Sir, didn't you say the body was on the demarcation line?" I said.

"Yes, I did. But the point is, in which direction did the head lie? That is the issue to be sorted out."

I was at a loss. He had made a remark earlier too about the head, but I hadn't given it much importance.

"Sir, what has the head to do with the matter?" I asked.

"There is a vital connection between the two," he said, emphasising each word. "I have already told you that such technical matters won't sink into your head. If a body is found on the demarcation line between two police stations, the matter is investigated by the station in whose jurisdiction the head is found to lie."

I was flummoxed. "Well, Sir, in which direction did the head lie? This point had come up earlier too, but I didn't realise then how important it was."

"That is precisely where the whole villainy lies," he said, shaking his head. "The scavenger of corpses from Khanpur had already appeared on the scene at Poshmarg. A devil of a man! But I am quick to see through stratagems. He had turned the head of the body towards his own jurisdiction so as to give himself the right to investigation. But, being an old-timer, I didn't let him have his way."

The whole thing was clear to me now. Only one thing remained unsolved.

So I asked, "What action did you take?"

"I would be the last man to let him have the body. I had his lousy men charged with batons. This generated a row. But I don't care. The papers are there to speak. So the matter is pending now."

I fancied the dead man being revived, rising up and walking in the direction of his home. But, another thought crossed my mind. I said, "But the corpse...lying there it will rot. How long...?"

He didn't let me finish. "Let it rot. The moot point is that of the head. In which direction did it lie? Until this matter is resolved, the case shall remain pending."

I couldn't utter another word.

(Translated from the Kashmiri by Mohamad Amin)

GIRLWATCH

Lakshmi Kannan

By the time she walked around Ortega Park for the second time, the gentle drizzle became a purposeful rain. Savitri covered Malaika's head with the end of her saree and hurried into the first shelter near the water fountain. The place was already crowded with the compulsive Californian morning walkers huddled within. She recognised some of them as the regulars from Sunnyvale and around. Four people stood at the fringe of the crowd, waiting for the first clear moment to step out. Savitri recalled how just ten minutes back, they were performing *tai chi* gracefully, led by their nimble Chinese instructor in an open section of the park.

Savitri wiped Malaika's face and shook her head as the child begged her to let her walk in the rain. She wiped her watch, removed it from her wrist and carefully put it away in her small wallet. No, it certainly wasn't waterproof. At 5 USD, it was the most inexpensive watch on sale—'dirt-cheap' as they called it—so there was no question of it being waterproof. Far more expensive watches at home had stopped working because of water seepage. A good amount was spent repairing them. But her watch could never be repaired, said her son Vijay Bhaskar. In case it stops working, it just has to be thrown away, that's all. It was a disposable watch. "Here, Mom," Vijay had said, giving her the watch. "I got it for you. Can't guarantee for how long it'll work though. It may keep going for the next four or six months or it could stop after a week from now. You never know. Depends on your luck," he laughed. "Ah, I did check if it's a lady's watch. They claimed it was unisex, so you can use it," he smiled.

That was a good two years ago, but the watch had showed no signs of stopping. Ever. It had gone on ticking resolutely until Vijay Bhaskar and his wife Asha grew tired of marvelling at its tenacity. They grew tired of joking about it too and consigned it to the background as one of those things that could be expected to function on its own steam.

"Come, my pet," said Savitri to Malaika. "It's stopped raining. Let's hurry or we'll get late."

There were lots of others who walked along as they came out of Ortega Park. Americans, Chinese, Indians of various origins—Gujaratis, Punjabis, South Indians, a few Bengalis. Savitri and Malaika crossed the school ground. Home was just two streets away. Savitri held Malaika by the hand and crossed the street. A steady drizzle continued. *Why did I forget the umbrella*, Savitri thought. But it was so bright in the morning with the sky a clear, innocent blue. That's California for you in November. Unpredictable.

On reaching home, Savitri took out the watch from her wallet and placed it in the right end corner of the kitchen counter, its reserved place. She gave Malaika a bath, dressed her, opened the shelves in the kitchen and asked her.

"What cereal do you want today? Wheat Checks, Cheerios, Lucky Charms...?"

"Cheerios!" Malaika said. She settled her at the dining table, poured milk into her bowl of cereal and said, "Come on, hurry. You must get ready. Mummy and Daddy are taking you out in a while."

Malaika scooped up her cereal and smiled at her grandmother.

"Want some fresh strawberries with the cereal, precious?" Savitri asked.

The child nodded happily. Savitri put the fruits in, stood for a minute enjoying the sight of luscious strawberries vanishing into her small mouth. She shook herself and returned to preparing a picnic lunch for them. Briskly, the *paranthas* were getting done on the hot griddle when Asha, her daughter-in-law came in, floating in the aroma of her shampoo, her skin glowing with health.

"Will lunch be ready, Mummy, for us to take along?" she asked.

"Of course. Come and have breakfast, both of you. Where's Vijay?"

"Having a shower. Anything I can do to help, Mummy?" Asha asked, standing at the doorway.

"Nothing really. You get ready."

"All right. I'll go dry my hair. Sure you don't want to come with us, Mummy?"

"Actually, I've tons of things to do. I'll come with you another day," Savitri said, garnishing the potato-onion masala to go with the *paranthas*. Lemon rice was ready. She packed the *paranthas* in a casserole, packed the rest of the stuff, kept bottles of water, juices, Goldfish, Graham Crackers and Nilla cookies for Malaika, fruits and then napkins, paper plates, spoons and so on into the boot of the car. She hurried in from the garage and glanced at her watch. Ten already!

"Vijay, Asha", she called and laid out their breakfast. She served them *upma* with coconut-coriander chutney.

"It's yummy!" Vijay said, taking large helpings of the *upma*.

Savitri collected a few of Malaika's toys for the rear seat, gave her the favourite velvety monkey and panda bear in hand and strapped her to her seat.

"Why don't you come along, Mummy?" Vijay asked as he eased himself into the driver's seat. Savitri smiled and waved them goodbye. With one touch of the remote, the garage door came rolling down and she was plunged in darkness.

She switched on the light. It flooded the huge pile of laundry in a large rattan basket. And showed the huge utensils on the left, holding soaked rice and black gram, waiting to be ground for *idli* on that motorised stone-grinder. With other things strewn around or stashed away, the garage looked comfortably shabby, like the common room back home in her father's house in Tumkur. Three daughters and their mother shared it. Savitri hurried into the kitchen, dashed across to the washroom, had a bath, lit the lamp in the shrine and made herself a cup of coffee to go with her breakfast. Sunnyvale had decided to be sunny again. Bright light poured in through the window and the sky wore its clear, innocent blue as if nothing had happened. *Mustn't waste this bit of sunlight, must get the laundry done quickly,* she said to herself, gulping down her coffee.

Back in the garage, the clothes swished in soap water, the machine droned on as she sat waiting, sitting on a low stool near the grinding machine.

Thak! Thak! Thak!

Sounds of damp clothes flung on a sloping, rough stone-topped platform in the backyard with a tap at the side for running water. That was how they washed clothes way back in

Tumkur. *Thak! Thak!* The clothes got a beating on that pitted stone platform. Then they were hand-rinsed in water, squeezed and put out to dry. Savitri, her elder sister Mangalam, and younger sister Radha, took turns washing the clothes of the entire household, taking particular care to brush and clean their brother Madhav's shirts, shorts and undergarments. These had to be dried in the sunniest part of the washing line.

Savitri's elder sister Mangalam was the first girl-child of the family. '*Mangalam*' meant the completion of an event. She was named Mangalam in the fond hope that it would be the end of girl-children for the family. But Savitri followed Mangalam, and then there was Radha. Madhav came next after three girls, ushering in much celebration and exchange of sweets. By now, all the three girls realised that they were born experimentally, as a means towards that eternal quest for a son. Girls number one, two, three were just passages to make way for that one boy-child, Madhav.

Madhav didn't have to wash clothes. The girls washed his clothes, they assisted in cooking, cleaned the house, ran errands for the family, sewed clothes and the household ran like a well-greased machine. Mangalam and Savitri were good at studies, but were pulled out of school so that the money could be saved for Madhav's school fee. Year after year, he failed to qualify. Hesitantly, Mangalam asked if she may resume her studies now. She was told to take responsibility of the house like a proper eldest daughter and look after Madhav. She took him to school and brought him back every single day. As for Radha, she never saw the face of a school but spent time languishing at home, reading her sisters' old schoolbooks.

"Madhav needs extra nourishment. His health isn't too robust, which is why he is unable to study," the parents said, plying him with thickened milk, butter, lentils, vegetables, creamy yoghurt and fruits. The buttermilk for the three girls got further diluted with water; they did not get any vegetables and for them, fruits were to look at. Yet, Madhav continued to fall ill frequently. At the first whimper, he would be rushed to the doctor, medicines would be procured, and more water added to the buttermilk for the girls. The doctor's advice for sports, exercise and diet control to combat his increasing obesity went unheeded. They changed his doctor and resumed giving thickened milk, creamy yoghurt, butter, rich *kheer* and sweets as before. New clothes were made for him as he was fast outgrowing his shirts and shorts.

Mangalam and Savitri registered themselves for their studies through a correspondence course as it cost the family next to nothing. Mangalam did exceedingly well and studied hard well into the night. A week before her exams, she came down with a raging fever.

"Don't give her anything to eat," declared her father. "You must always starve a fever. Just put a damp cloth over her forehead and she will be all right in a few days."

Her mother made her a thin rice gruel. The fever couldn't stand so much starvation. It left Mangalam within two days.

"See?" the father exulted. "I told you that a doctor is quite unnecessary for such fevers. Good. Mangalam, now you can go to the ration shop for this month's supply, and Radha, go with your sister and help her carry the stuff," he commanded. Savitri had her exams the following day. She stayed at home studying and helped her mother prepare snacks in the evening.

Images swirled in her consciousness. There was a marriage that left no imprint in her memory. Her husband was years older than her. He died soon after Vijay Bhaskar was born.

Savitri spent an entire lifetime bringing up Vijay and educating him. It was rewarding, for he had done very well for himself and effortlessly made it to the US.

Suddenly, Savitri became aware that all the noises were coming only from within her head, and that the garage had indeed fallen silent. It was so quiet in there. The washing machine had stopped. The laundry was done. She glanced quickly at the steel utensils with things waiting to be ground for *idli*. She took the pile of clothes in two buckets to the backyard and put them out to dry. On the way back to the kitchen, she noticed that there was another pile of clothes, clean and dry, on the sofa in the living room. She rushed to the kitchen, checked the *kabuli chana* that had been soaked overnight, put them into the pressure cooker with some baking soda and set it on the gas stove. *Asha loves* chana *with* puris, *not* chapatis. *Must make them all a nice dinner after they return from their tiring trip,* she thought.

Oh dear, she glanced at the watch on the counter. It was 10:45. But it felt like she had spent twenty years in the garage. *Must rush with the* idli-*grinding,* she said to herself and set the stone-grinder in motion. First rice, then black gram. The grinder swung into action rhythmically as Savitri stepped into the kitchen and briskly prepared the garnishing for *kabuli chana*. She also made Vijay's favourite green bell pepper *sambar*. The pressure cooker whistled furiously. Savitri looked at her watch. *I'll let it cook on low fire for another fifteen minutes till the* chana *is soft and tender*, she thought, lowering the flame.

Back in the garage, she scooped up the black gram paste over the rice paste, sprinkled salt and mixed them evenly with a long wooden spoon till her arm ached. Fatigue washed over her body. She sat in the stillness for a minute, doing nothing.

Dinner items done, she sat down to a simple lunch. Had no appetite whatsoever. The yoghurt was so unnaturally thick. She mixed it with water till it looked like the buttermilk of Tumkur, and washed down her rice with it. She put some of the newly-made *sambhar* and *kabuli chana* on her plate to taste. They were fine enough. The dough for *puris* was also ready. Oh God, she had forgotten that pile of dried clothes on the sofa in the living room. Hurriedly, she folded them up neatly. They were a mix of clothes. *I'll separate them later*, she thought. *Let me put them on my bed for the time being.* She carried them over to her room and stacked them in two tidy rows on one side of her bed.

Must pour out a glass of orange juice and put it out of the fridge for Malaika. They'll be back any moment. Malaika will rest a bit. She poured Minute Maid into her favourite doggie-face mug, covered it with a small lid and picked up her watch. It read 2:30. *There's time for a small nap. I'm dropping dead with exhaustion.*

Savitri went to her room and stretched herself on the free side of her bed, placing her watch beside the row of folded clothes. It felt blissful to close her eyes. *After Malaika rests, I'll ask her about the day's trip. Then, read her a story and see everything through her lustrous eyes. Tomorrow, I'll take her to Ortega Park, make her sit on the swing or watch her come down the slide with a shriek of delight, her dress billowing in the wind, her sleeves flapping like a butterfly.* Malaika, the new-age girl growing up in California. A lovely butterfly with the sun on her wings.

The caterpillar Savitri shuffled about awkwardly toward the ration shop in Tumkur, forever hungry, looking for green leaves and fruits to chew. It searched on its six true legs, three on each side to help it wobble along. The legs in the middle made it slow. There were no leaves in sight, still it kept moving, not sure if it can starve its way to staying alive till the next week. But it stayed alive somehow, so out came the chrysalis from the larva, raising its head confidently as it shook itself free of the integument to become Asha in Sunnyvale, a hard-working professional who brought home plenty of green leaves and fruits. And from the chrysalis, there is now the beautiful butterfly Malaika, catching the sun on her billowing skirt as she went forward and backward on the swing. The larva, the pupa, and then the butterfly. Malaika smiled at her grandmother. For Savitri, it felt like drinking in a clear, sparkling spring water. She ran her fingers through the soft, young hair of her grandchild. The bed felt soft and downy too, after the day's work.

They called a doctor known to a close friend, or else who would home-visit anyone in the US? He made for the bed straightaway and took in the sleeping figure of Savitri and pushed away the neat stack of washed clothes kept in two rows beside the sleeping Savitri.

"For God's sake, allow her to breathe. What's this? Take them away," he ordered with impatience. Asha moved in, embarrassed, and took one pile of clothes in her hands.

"Mummy must've..." she began to explain, her voice agitated.

"No, no. She needs to breathe freely...take them away," the doctor cut in, stethoscope around his ears. He placed the end piece on Savitri's chest while he felt her pulse at the same time. He looked in silence at the calm figure on the bed and folded his hands in front. He shook his head, and then turned to Vijay—

"I'm sorry. I'm really very sorry. Your Mom..."

"But, Doctor, she was fine when we left her," Vijay protested, his throat going dry. Asha moved in to collect the next pile of clothes. The doctor pushed it towards her, and then saw the faded brown wrist watch beside Savitri.

"What's this old watch doing here? It stopped at three. It's nearing six now!" he said, giving it to Vijay.

"Three? Then that's the time my mother must've died," Vijay said, his eyes filling up.

"What! How can you say for sure?" the doctor retorted. *Strange. How incomprehensible he is,* said his eyes.

"Because, Doctor, this watch stopped working at last. At long last," Vijay replied, burying his face in his hands.

"Vijay Bhaskar, what are you saying? I don't understand. Get a grip over yourself. I know this is hard on you. It's very shocking indeed to come home and see your mother gone. I'm really very sorry," he said, placing his arm around Vijay's shoulder. It shook, racked by his sobs.

(Translated from the Tamil by the author;
Acknowledgement: Ç̣onfluence, *Sussex, U.K.)*

HANDS

Shiv K. Kumar

I walk through the lounge which resounds with the chatter of the coffee-drinkers, their faces fuzzy in the cigarette fumes. But it's different in the rear courtyard—hardly any smoke or noise. As I look about, I feel relieved to find my favourite corner seat unoccupied. Is it because the table is still messy, with several used cups and saucers lying on it? But I shouldn't mind if the waiter (whom I see cleaning up tables at the far end) doesn't show up here for a while. If I come to this coffee-house, it's to stay away from home as long as possible. Only the other day, my neighbour barged into my room to say—"Now that you're single," (I don't know how people can sniff out a divorce, even though am not yet out of it) "why don't you let me get you something to eat or drink?" I surely felt like snapping at him—why don't you eat my flesh and drink my blood? Will you leave me alone, you bumptious intruder? But I just smiled back and mumbled—"No, thanks."

So you see, I come here to be alone with myself—and yet feel the presence of others somewhere around, but not too close. Like a bird-watcher, I like to view people from a distance, gesticulating with their hands, because I believe that hands can articulate more effectively than words. Aren't hands almost living organisms with a distinct identity of their own? Well, you may call me the hands-man, if you like. Show me your hand and I could tell you everything about yourself. But I am not like one of those street palmists.

So I always feel secure at this coffee-house, at peace with myself. I get rattled only when someone recognises me and walks over to talk. I'm particularly scared of my fellow-writers because they are so snooty and malicious. Only last week, Nirupam, that journalist-turned-poet, spotted me. Then, with his chapped hands bearing down heavily on my shoulders, he said—"What's coming up next, feller? A new novel or a play?"

"No," I replied, "I've been commissioned by the Department of Telecommunications to proofread the New Delhi Telephone Directory! Now, isn't that exciting?" He grinned and walked away, somewhat befuddled. *Good riddance*, I said to myself.

But let me first secure my corner seat. You see, how I get embroiled in my vagrant thoughts. So, leaving my scrapbook open at the table, with my Reynolds black ball-point uncapped across it (as a sort of my 'Reserved!' sign), I hurry to the service counter in the lounge to get myself a cold coffee. But the concoction tastes rather insipid on this cold, dreary afternoon. Or, is it the hangover of my deep annoyance with my lawyer, Ram Kapur—that floundering, stolid fool? How I wish I could shake him off even at this late stage, but now he knows too much about my personal life. He'd surely blackmail me if I give him the boot. But, oh God! How he kept me on the edge of my nerves all of yesterday morning in the court! Why didn't he try to stir up some emotion in the judge—some poignant remark about the mental cruelty I've suffered at the hands of my wife—the focal thing in my case? Above all, he could have done something with his hands, some touching gesticulation. But there he stood with his hands locked behind his back, arguing as though at gunpoint. And all the time, I watched the judge caressing the round paper-weight in front of him as if it were a young woman's breast. Here was, surely, someone quite susceptible to an emotional overture. A rare opportunity lost! Or is it my imagination gone haywire? What have hands to do with a lawsuit?

"May we join you, please?"

The words splash into my stream of thought. It's a middle-aged woman, with a man in his early fifties. They look tense; the woman's hands, I notice, are somewhat shaking.

"Welcome," I reply, and beckon them to the other side of the table. Although I'd have liked to say, *No, why don't you unload yourself somewhere else?* But by now, the coffee-house is almost overflowing.

I pick up my Reynolds and feign to scribble something in my scrapbook. But, in fact, I am watching the couple from the corner of my eye. The woman's right hand now moves toward her partner's left arm and stays there for a few moments. As the pressure deepens, her face glows.

"How long can we carry on like this? Sneaking into corners?"

The woman's voice is a poignant whisper, but it carries a spirited urgency about it. Then her hand begins to move up and down the man's left arm, her fingers rippling as if across a piano's keyboard—light, tender and fluid. At this point, I lapse into a direct stare at the couple. They look flustered as if they have been caught in some immoral act. Instantly, they rise and vanish into the lounge, leaving their coffees unfinished. So the bird-watcher, I realise, has scared the pigeons away. But those two pairs of hands—the woman's so sensitive and impassioned, and the man's so angular and unresponsive. No, I tell myself, they'd never be able to sort it out.

So it's the same pain everywhere and I am not the only one. But while I know how to empathise with my friend's sorrows, nobody seems to give me anything in return. And all that I need is a kind word, a gentle press of a hand... It's such little things that make for love and compassion.

I must get myself another coffee if I have to hold on to my fortress even though the beverage doesn't excite me at all this afternoon. Maybe, if I feel the taste of cow-dung on my palate, it's because some invisible hand is at work against my peace of mind—even here. I can't believe how I got into marrying that scorpion with multiple stings. Living with her for ten long years—oh God! And then picking a lawyer who is stupid like a sparrow. Let's try out just mental cruelty, he says, when it's been stark physical cruelty too all the time—her hands and nails flying at my throat. Why didn't he spit it all out in the face of Rita's lawyer, and also let the judge see that she has hands like a vulture's talons?

Why did I give in to my mother to get into this arranged marriage? She's now gone, and I am left alone to fight it out in the courts which treat humans like pawns in a game of chess. I don't know how long I'll have to endure all this. At least Rita has her brother to fight her battle, whereas I have none. All my friends seem to enjoy seeing me bleed in the gladiatorial arena. Except perhaps Jagdish. But here also, I'm not too sure. So, I guess, I must learn the art of self-communion. All right, then let me talk to myself: be patient, my dear. It'll soon be over. You're going to win this case. You'll come through, finally. And, look, if God has put you through this fire, it's because all this suffering will be grist to your mill. Hasn't this agony already sharpened your sensibilities, endowed you with a double vision to see things in their true perspective? And, incidentally, why don't you practise the time-theory that you have been preaching to others? Jugal Kishore, for instance—how you cured him of depression over his suspension from service. Didn't you advise him to install in his house a statue of Kal Dev, the deity of time, with his right hand raised in benediction? Just a few months, or a few weeks, and one's pain is gone. So why don't you worship this God yourself, write hymns in his praise since he is the only redeemer? All other gods are mere brass and tinsel.

"Hi! How are you?"

A male voice impinges upon my thoughts. I look up to see Kohli and his daughter, Geeta. Oh, gracious heavens, how I wish I could duck under the table, or jump over the compound wall to escape these pests. How did they sniff me out here? It must have been Geeta, a fellow divorcee, who shadows me everywhere. If only Kohli knew how I hate all sorts of formal greetings—"How are you?" and all that. For one thing, such a greeting may provoke me into thinking about my relationship with phenomenal reality. And, in any case, if I choose to respond truthfully, I'd like to say, "Right now, I'm burning in hell since my divorce has run into sands."

"Why don't you come home sometime and see Geeta's dance on the video?"

Why not have her live-dance, dear Kohli, I say to myself. And can she dance at all, with those large, leathery hands, too brittle to lend themselves to the lotus posture, for instance? No plastic surgery could ever give her hands any nimbleness. But I know that if you want me to 'come home', it's to get me hooked to your daughter. One divorcee waiting to catch the other on the rebound. Isn't it as simple as that? Maybe all divorcees should club themselves into a new caste, with its own norms and rituals. But I am not for you, dear Geeta. Find somebody else—and you should have no problems whatsoever since your Dad holds in his hands sacks of gold he has smuggled out of Dubai.

"I'll certainly come over one of these days. It's just that presently I'm deeply embroiled..."

"Oh, yes, how's the case going?"

"Not too well. But I can wait. I have learnt to take life stoically, you know... But I am sorry I was just about to leave—a pressing engagement with my publisher at Volga's, and he's known for his vicious punctuality."

And then, without waiting for any reply, I walk away.

I go down the street past the Jammu & Kashmir Bank, beyond Bhasin's Garage which buys and sells cars and scooters. I hang about the Madras Hotel Bus Terminal for a while, not knowing what to do. Then, suddenly, my eye catches a pavement fruit-vendor with his basket poised, almost precariously, on a wooden tripod. What intrigues me is the dexterous movement of his hands as he slices off, with his scimitar-shaped knife, little pieces of each fruit—papaya, banana, guava, apple or orange—and mixes them all on a plantain leaf. Then, with his right thumb and first finger, he takes a pinch of salt and pepper to spread over the entire stuff, shakes it thoroughly and hands it over to each customer. To me, he seems to be a priest moving gracefully through some ritual. I too feel like tasting this colourful, invigorating fruit-blend, saying to myself: isn't it better than that insipid, inert concoction? But I also know that a coffee addict's priorities never follow any rationale.

As I start eating this fruity-mixture, I hear boisterous applause behind my back—*bravo!* Turning around, I notice a pair of young street-performers—an eleven-year old boy, his ribs showing through a ragged shirt, and his four-year-old sister. The boy has lifted her up in the air on the palms of his hands; then she does a somersault and lands, like a diver, on the cobbled curb, straight up on her feet. She beams as the commuters, queued in a long line for their bus, give her a hand. But when these performers walk down the entire length of the queue with their hands stretched out for a coin or two, everyone looks away. But the little ones don't look disappointed; they seem to take life too as a sort of game. So does it matter if one scores or not? I walk over to the little girl and hand in a tenner which might have been their entire day's picking. Her face sparkles out of gratitude. But when she kneels to touch my feet, I wave her off gently, looking awfully embarrassed. As I start walking back to the coffee-house, hoping that the Kohlis would have left by now, I wonder if these performers come from the labourers' colony beyond the Jamuna embankment, or from the hutments sprawling under the flyover bridge, linking the Shadipur Bus Depot with the Karampura Terminal. And what do they eat to shore up so much sap in their bodies? My only regret is that I couldn't have a close look at their hands. But the girl's, surely, looked tender and agile. She would have not only done the lotus posture better than Geeta, but also the ballet—with the elegance of a gazelle.

I must get back to the coffee-house soon enough lest I miss Jagdish. I'm sure he'll show up this evening. When I telephoned him last evening after the court hearing, he did sound concerned. He is one person with whom I can communicate even though there's little in common between us. While he is a civil servant used to formalities, I wear my heart on my sleeve, and look about for crumbs of sympathy from anyone, anywhere. It's strange I have never asked him if he has read any of my books. But does it matter? In any case, one writes to communicate with one's own self only.

But let me first see if my corner seat is still available. No, some leviathan Sikh has grabbed it. But there are two seats unoccupied at the next table. Suits me fine; I can take one for myself and hold the other for Jagdish. So, leaving my scrapbook on one and my hanky on the other, I dash off to get myself another coffee, even though I'm going to let it sit in front of me, untouched.

Back to my seat, I begin to analyse my feelings for Jagdish. First, I like the way he sits at the table with his strong, male hands interlocked. It always reminds me of the ad put out by the Life Insurance Company of India—a pair of cupped palms protecting a tiny candle-flame. Well, in his presence, I too feel like that flame myself, although I don't remember him doing anything special for me. But since friendship is not a give-and-take transaction, I don't care. This evening, I intend sharing with him my theory of friendship, the great theoretician that I am. I'll tell him that on Judgement Day (which, as a Hindu, I don't believe in, but never mind), God will ask each soul only one question. Did you have, during your life on the earth, any true friend, someone who was willing to put his right hand into fire for your sake? But, mind you, you are not permitted to mention your wife, any of your children or relatives. If you can claim one such friend, I'll let you have a place in heaven. Otherwise, the other place, you know.

Well, I guess I may not put up Jagdish as such a friend... but we have stayed together since our school days, and he listens to my tale of woe now and then. I'm sure he'd comfort me this evening, saying I'd get my divorce soon, that lawsuits are like ever-changing phases of the moon. If my last hearing was frustrating, the next one may turn out well. Then the celebration, I'd respond, not just the cold coffee, but Johnnie Walker or champagne. His right hand may even caress my arm to soothe my tangled nerves—and this will work for me as both physical and psychic therapy.

"Hello, old boy! I'm sorry for being late."

(So there he is. I knew he wouldn't let me down).

"Come and sit there," I say, pointing to the seat with my hanky on it. "I've saved it for you."

As he sits there, with his hands interlocked in front of him, he breaks into words.

"You know, I had a nasty time in office today. Everything went upside down. You see, my boss asked me to prepare a note urgently, a case of promotion. But don't you think he should have given me some time to look into this man's background, his service-record and all that? After all, I am not a computer... But, presumably, he was under some pressure. Then, in the midst of it all, the phone kept ringing. You see, I couldn't even have my lunch in peace. Terrible! So I decided to have a breath of fresh air after leaving office. Parked my car near Empire Stores and watched the crowds for a while... And look, who says dental floss is not available in Delhi? Well, I found some in the shop next to Bharat Leather Emporium, and unwaxed too!"

And so he runs on, his right hand now rising up as though for some special gesticulation. I try to lend him an attentive ear. But what was this talk about dental floss, waxed or unwaxed? I've never had any dental problems; in fact, my teeth are as strong as a tusker's. But, maybe, this is only a prelude to what he will say next—a consoling word to pull me out of the blues. But suddenly he rises, saying, "Oh God, I'd nearly forgotten to pick up my wife's saree from Rainbow Dry Cleaners. Do you know what time they close?"

"No idea, Jagdish."

"See you later," he mumbles, and rises to leave.

"Bye," I respond, with a lump in my throat. And then I say to myself, *et tu, Jagdish*.

I already feel the evening descending, layer by layer. I know it'll soon be closing time. But I intend to stay on as long as possible. I wouldn't feel humiliated if the waiter comes over to say, "It's time, Sir."

Then, surprisingly, I see my right hand caressing my left arm, just as I hear myself saying, "Look, my dear, don't let anything get you down. You'll come through, finally. Remember, there is Father Time to heal all scars."

BONDED CHILD

Kuvempu

"Subba! Subba! Eh Subba!"

A dark night in the rainy season. The darkness was dense. The whole world appeared to have been erased by darkness. There was a continuous torrential downpour. Heavy winds lashed sometimes; sometimes they would stumble and blow.

The hills in the Malnad forest seemed to have disappeared. When the wind blew swiftly, the whole forest appeared to be roaring. Raindrops fell on the trees, the arecanut and the plantain groves, and on the tiles of the houses, making *chutpat, turtur* and *pat-pat* noises. As a result of the movement of the wind and the rain, thousands of frogs came out from all directions, garbling, causing a headache. Along with them, some of the night-moving insects cried harshly from the hollows of the trees. The palm fronds caused a constant murmur and increased the noise all around. Sometimes to unravel the mystery of the night, as if the day had peeped in, lightning flashed in the sky like the tongue of a snake and disappeared. The universe was replete with the sound of music, of darkness, of the rain and water. All around the houses, the canals were flowing, roaring like lions. Thunder rolled on the horizon. Who would not fall asleep if they lay down at home in that rain, in that continuous noise, that cold? All were asleep at home. Suddenly, a thunderbolt struck as if the universe had collapsed and splintered like a dome of glass. Gowda woke up.

"Subba! Subba! Eh Subba!" he shouted.

Subba did not wake up. He had fallen asleep like a bent bow in the corner of an open verandah, covering himself with the torn blanket donated by somebody. A young boy like him was tired after working in the fields the whole day along with the adults. He lay like a log in the lap of the Goddess of Sleep—the mother of orphans. Gowda grew wild. He shouted several times. He could not hear his own voice amidst the rain and thunder. Yet, he shouted. He got up from bed and came down to the verandah to pick up a stick.

Gowda was the head of the family, a very affluent one. He was also the head of the entire village, but very hard hearted. He was over sixty. He had married thrice. He had lent money to four or five families at a high interest and destroyed them. Everyone was very afraid of him, like being afraid of a tiger. Gowda mistook it for respect shown to him. He could not sleep without consuming brandy. But he was not less orthodox. He used to smear his body with holy ash and worship Lord Shiva every day. While pouring brandy into the mug, he did not want that noise to be heard by outsiders. So, he recited loudly, "Hari Narayana, Hari Narayana..." This Hari Narayana chant was heard more during the rainy season.

Subba was a ten-year-old boy. His father, Ranga, was a tenant of Gowda's. Subba's mother had expired within two years of his birth. Ranga tried his best to marry another girl. The marriage was fixed, but the bride's party demanded three hundred rupees as bride price. Poor Ranga asked his master Gowda for a loan. Gowda drew his attention to the already pending loan of three hundred rupees with him and rejected his request outright. As such, Ranga's marriage was stalled. Within a few days, Ranga died of the plague. Gowda, in return for his loan, made Subba his bonded child and made him carry a huge load like a donkey. The boy was forced to do hard labour. Whether Subba was capable of it or not, he had to carry out the assigned work. Gowda used to beat him with a stick now and then in order to make him work. Subba became emaciated day by day. Even when he fell sick and lay down, Gowda would rain down blows on his back and push him to follow the routine. The boy, even while shivering due to fever and cold, attended to his work. Sometimes, other grown-up servants, out of sheer pity for Subba, asked him to go to sleep and did his work themselves. But, on sensing Gowda's arrival, they would wake up Subba. Even in his feverish state, Subba would return to work. Thus, the poor orphan came closer to the grave every day.

When Gowda called Subba, he was asleep. But the sick do not sleep without dreams. He dreamt of pleasures that he could not enjoy. The desires that were not fulfilled in reality were fulfilled in his dreams. Subba dreamt of enjoying life in a stately mansion with his parents. In his dream world, he wore different types of expensive clothes. There was no need for him to do any work. There were many servants to attend to him and he even had friends to play with. He could eat varieties of sweets. When Gowda beat him mercilessly with his stick, he woke up, shouting. He threw aside the blanket with which he had covered himself and entreated, "Oh, generous master."

Gowda chided him, "You rascal, even if I shout, you pretend to be asleep."

Subba stood up, shedding tears, screaming with pain. He could not understand anything but pain.

Gowda shouted, "Go, go over there and look for the fishing net in the fields," and lifted his stick again.

"Yes, going..." cried Subba.

During the rainy season, when the fish are found in large numbers, the farmers catch them with fishing nets. More than seven or eight baskets of fish can be caught each day. That day, Gowda had found out that four or five baskets of fish would be available. At night time, he was anxious that the fish would be washed away in the flood of water. That was why he had woken up the young boy by beating him.

Subba, carrying a big basket, left with a lantern in hand. Gowda went back to a sound sleep.

It was still pouring, the storm raged with thunder and lightning. The darkness was deep. The path was full of wet soil and it flew about wherever Subba trod. He lifted the lantern high lest Gowda beat him for letting the wet soil fall on it. There were still five or six furlongs left for him to reach the net. There was no other living being around except for wild nature. On his way, while jumping from one part of the field to the other, he slipped in the mire and the lantern broke. The light went out. It was as if Subba had drowned in darkness. He sat sobbing at one end of the field, upset about breaking the lantern. He continued to weep, lest he get severe punishment if he returned home without collecting the fish. He sat fearfully in the darkness, and then, walked a few steps in the midst of the storm and heavy downpour. In that merciless and horrible situation, he floated like a straw.

It became very cold. He covered himself with a blanket. At last, he reached the place where the net was located. He put down the basket. The net was filled with fish and they were making a *chol-chol* noise. Some of them were leaping to the other side of the net. Subba lifted up the net and took out a funnel. Suddenly, a snake that had entered the net to swallow the fish sprang up and bit him. By that time, the storm and the rain had subsided to some extent. Subba screamed and collapsed as the poison entered his body. Water was gushing around him. The wind blew over the crops. The sky was shining with lightning. Without any consideration for his routine, the wheel of the universe kept revolving.

At dawn, Gowda was upset as Subba had not returned. He looked for him, assuming he might have hidden somewhere in the house instead of going to find the net. He could not be found anywhere and Gowda shouted in anger. He thought that Subba might have gone to sleep in somebody else's house. At last, he himself went in search of Subba, along with a labourer. On the way, he found a broken lantern in a corner of the field. It upset him all the more. "I shall break his bones if I meet him," he roared.

He walked towards the net. On finding it lying upside down, he lamented, "Alas, what a rascal! He's spoilt my chances of getting the fish."

He stepped closer. There was Subba lying in the mire, in the midst of the field. Gowda was shocked. He shouted at him, but there was no response. Subba neither got up nor moved. Gowda asked his companion to lift him up. He was lifted up. Only the dead body stood there, mute.

Gowda felt very sad.

"Three hundred rupees gone," he said with a sigh!

(Translated from the Kannada by M.S. Raghunath)

GUL

Prabhakar Machwe

Dewdrops in the morn
Said, "A rose is born
Upon a thorn!"

"I don't believe a word of what you say."

"But, it's a true story."

"Such things don't happen." I persisted with my doubts.

My friend had escorted me to the house of the ailing Jivanbhai. Reclining on a white cushion, in a homespun *dhoti-kurta*, Jivanbhai's face brightened upon seeing us.

But before we proceed with the narration, an insight into Jivanbhai—a quiet sort of a guy. A Gandhian social worker. Went to jail in 1930 and then again in 1942, but refused the freedom fighters' pension. Worked mostly in the rural countryside for the uplift of the tribals, Bhils in Madhya Pradesh, apart from contributing his services to the Harijan Sewa Sangh. Content with leading a life of solitude and maintained a low profile. Earned only for his needs, which were few and far between. A man of simple habits.

We listen intently as he narrates the story of Aatish Syed Khan.

"I met Aatish Khan, a tall hefty Pathan, in the late thirties. I was the young son of the jailor at Bhairavagarh Jail. He was serving a six-year imprisonment under suspicion of an alleged involvement in a dacoity, though there wasn't sufficient evidence against him. As he had turned a government informer, he had gotten away with a shorter sentence. He was a well-behaved prisoner. He was in charge of the garden in the jail compound.

I was a well-behaved kid, and I would tell him tales of valour of national leaders, which he listened to with rapt attention. We shared an easy-going and fun-loving relationship.

One day, Aatish Khan said, "You know my name is Aatish. Aatish means fire. When I am released, I will join the revolutionaries, make bombs and hurl them at the Britishers."

"Why? Aren't you afraid? Haven't you any family?" I asked.

He pulled out a faded photo from his pocket, and showed it to me. It was the photo of the Pathan and his burqa-clad wife, with a smiling, seemingly camera-shy girl between them.

Pointing to the girl, he said, "This is Gul, the flower of my heart. She must have grown up by now. She was ten when I was arrested. I don't know whether my uncle married her off or not.

"We get our daughters married off when they are young, you know. I was married when I was not even fifteen. My wife bore many children, but alas! Only Gul survived by Allah's grace," his voice quivered.

I returned the photo to him.

Aatish Khan had an abundance of tales to retell. He would tell me stories about plants and trees, birds and beasts, and reptiles and termites invading his garden. He had tended to every plant with parental care, as if every flowering plant reminded him of his daughter, Gul.

He got a three-month reprieve on account of good conduct. There were tears in his eyes on his release. He thanked my father for being sympathetic towards him, and presented me with a specially made rose bouquet. He fondly used to call me 'the young master'.

His parting words to me were, "You will become a jailor one day, won't you?"

"No, I won't!" I had protested. "I hate it. I'll never become a slave of the government."

"What will you do then?"

"I don't really know."

"What will you do now that you are out of here?" I asked.

"I hope to have a big farm, a big orchard and a flower-belt. My Gul will sell the flowers."

"Can one make a living out of selling flowers?"

"I don't really know, young master."

"But you're a Pathan. You'll terrorise poor people with a gun, and extract heavy interest for the money you lend."

"No, my young master. Lending money against interest is *haram,* unholy according to our religion. I will never sell my soul. I will never trade my religion for money."

"Then you should change your name! For Aatish means fire, and thus it means you will deal in firearms."

"What does your name mean, Jivan?"

"Jivan is water. Water is life, and fire and water are opposite elements."

"We can't co-exist then, little master. Anyway, we shall do what Allah ordains us to do."

Aatish Khan was given a fond farewell by the inmates. Everyone had a good word about him. The criminal in him, if there had been one at all, had been tamed.

But does the nature of fire ever change? If it does not get any wind, hay or dry wood to feed it, the fire dies away, unused. Does the fire in man, the animal within, also atrophy? Can it change its original form? Does it get easily transformed?

A Pathan does not always remain a Pathan. Khan Abdul Gaffar Khan became a *Khudai Khimatgar,* a servant of God.

I had never imagined that there would be another opportunity to meet Aatish Khan again, but I ran into him during the 1942 movement.

I was underground, helping my socialist associates. We needed money, food, information. I had become a police target. To avoid arrest, I had disguised myself as a Sikh. One day, two men kidnapped me for a ransom. I was taken to an undisclosed destination, like a prisoner. I was doubtful about the religion of one of my kidnappers. His voice was distinctly familiar, but I could not place him.

It took a lot of time to reach the underground hideout. The blindfold was removed from my eyes. I demanded that my turban and false beard be removed too. Most of the men were standing in the obscure, darker area in order to avoid being identified.

One of them admonished me, "So, you're not a Sikh! You're a cheat, a smuggler. Where is the pile of gold?"

Instinct compelled me to hum the Urdu couplet that Aatish Khan used to sing to me:

Dewdrops in the morn
Said, "A rose is born
Upon a thorn!"

This had a magical effect on the man with the stern baritone. He spoke in a softer tone, "Are you Jivanbhai, my old little master?"

"Aren't you Aatish Khan?" I enquired.

The suddenness of the chance meeting stunned us both. So did the strangeness of the circumstances.

Then Aatish Khan commanded the man covering me, "Leave him alone, Sher Singh. He is an old friend."

Aatish held me firmly in his arms and hugged me, showering blessings.

"Are you thirsty?" he asked. "Bring some cold water for our friend."

We both made ourselves comfortable on a quilt-covered cot in a corner.

"Why were you impersonating a Sikh?" Aatish Khan asked. "And what were you doing in that wealthy house?"

In all humility, I explained, "Now, we have nothing left, but a fight to the finish. Gandhiji has given the call, *Quit India—Do or Die*! Thus, we are in hiding, helping our comrades plan a big subterfuge. Some of them are languishing in jail. Their families need to be looked after. We collect money, clothes, medicines, food items—anything that is voluntarily donated. But, what are you doing in this dilapidated cell?"

Aatish Khan let out a threatening laughter. "You want money, we create money. We print counterfeit currency here. But no one knows about it."

After treating me like a royal, Aatish said he wanted me to reach my hideout safely. He stuffed my pockets with counterfeit notes. I tried to stop him. "Friend, I won't take any money from you. Not this kind of money, anyway. If I'm caught, they are bound to extract a confession from me." I said.

"Please don't misunderstand me, little master. We are also patriots. We want to help those who are sacrificing their lives, and taking risks to bring us freedom. This is our humble tribute."

I tried to intimidate him, "Suppose I inform the police about you and your gang?"

"No, little master, I know you won't. A Pathan always speaks the truth. But you must carry some money," he said, handing me a large envelope and a cotton bag. "Put the money under the vegetables in the bag. It will give the impression that you have been to the market. We will secure you close to your hideout. After dusk, one of my trusted men will take you back."

Before parting, I asked him about his daughter, Gul.

He stared blankly at a wall and said, "My wife died. Gul was married off to a rich tannery merchant in Calcutta. I don't know what is going to happen to them. I believe the Japanese are coming to Bengal via Burma. I wish I could see her at least once before this bloody war ends."

He gave me the Calcutta address. I thought to myself that if I were in Calcutta, I would receive the hospitality that Gul's father had bestowed upon me.

I never went to Calcutta.

In 1950, I happened to go to Madhya Pradesh, in one of the districts near Ujjain, in connection with some nationalist celebrations. We needed marigold flowers and rose garlands to deck up the venue. Enquiries revealed that one Mr. S.A. Seth could fulfill our requirements. The man had a roaring business and was contemplating opening a perfume factory. I presumed that he was a local moneylender. I approached him for a donation for the Kasturba Ashram that was being planned to rehabilitate destitute widows and Harijan women.

Syed Aatish Seth operated from a two-storeyed house equipped with modern amenities. Except for his beard, which had greyed, there was no sign of the erstwhile criminal, or the ferocious outlaw. The fire seemed to have been only in his name. He had remarried, and had a happy family that had assimilated well in the Hindu neighbourhood. People had all praises for the man. The Hindus would partake in the milk and *seviyan* pudding on Eid. Mr. Seth would generously supply the flowers for the Hindu festivals.

He immediately recognised his old acquaintance, and escorted me to his private chambers. Tea and snacks followed. I was introduced to his new family. We talked, laughed and joked about the good old days. The family understood and left us alone.

I asked him casually, "What brought about the change of heart? The change from manufacturing guns to growing flowers. From guns to Gul is an interesting switch, isn't it?"

He didn't answer for a long time, and stared blankly at the facing wall. I realised my mistake, by mentioning Gul, I had touched a delicate cord.

As his family rejoined us, he deftly changed the subject and began to narrate an incident.

"In my previous wicked life, I once kidnapped a little girl and demanded ransom from her parents. She was as delicate as a flower, and was named thus. Her name was Kusum. By the time her parents came with the ransom, she had died in my arms.

"The parents had laid a trap by intimating the police. All my co-conspirators were arrested, but I managed to escape. The dead girl's eyed still haunt me. The episode changed the course of my life—Allah alone can give life, and he alone can take it. Man has no right to take lives…"

He talked like a saint, a philosopher. He gave me the rose garlands and marigold flowers free of cost. He counted the floral bends in the garland and said matter-of-factly, "The years of my life are limited like the beads of this string."

Whispering, I asked again, "Where is Gul?"

"Allah alone knows. She went away to East Pakistan after the partition. I have had no communication with her ever since. I hope she is safe."

Presuming that the tale of this strange friendship between Aatish Khan and Jivanbhai was over, I asked Jivanbhai, "Did you ever see him again?"

"No, though I did get to know that he had left Ujjain and gone to Pakistan after the 1965 Indo-Pak conflict. The state took over his estate. On making enquiries I learnt that he had been an important name in Yahya Khan's regime, and was subsequently killed."

"What about his family?" I asked.

"No one knows what happened to them."

"And what about Gul? Did you meet her?" I asked.

"After the creation of Bangladesh," he said. "I went there in 1972 as a part of a delegation. While passing by a college building, I saw this graffiti on the walls from Mao's *Red Book* —"Political power grows out of the barrel of the gun," not by ballots, but by bullets, and I suddenly thought of Gul."

I sat pondering. What could have happened to Gul? Was she still alive? Could she have gone to Pakistan, to her father, or maybe she was in India along with other refugees. Maybe after the decline of her fortunes, she was selling flowers in the bylanes of Calcutta? Would she ever know that her father had grown flowers and used to sing:

Dew drops in the morn
Said, "A rose is born
Upon a thorn!"

Perhaps Gul never returned from Bangladesh, and was a rebel leader and a suspect in the eyes of the new regime. Perhaps she had written the slogan on the wall. The delicate rosebud in a veil—that was the cause of Noorjahan's famous discovery of 'the Attar of roses'—might have been forced by the cruel logic of circumstances to tote a gun.

From a gun to flowers, and from flowers back to the gun... is that the destiny of man?

What crime, what punishment?

Drops of blood and blushing petals are both red—what ascent, what descent?'

After Jivanbhai had narrated the story, he was suddenly wordless. He let out a deep sigh. We hurriedly wiped away tears from our eyes, and left the room. The picture of Gandhi meditating hung on the wall. Someone had tucked a flower there. It was fading. All flowers fade away. All guns go silent, after the smoke and thunder. Water quenches fire. Jivan goes on. Aatish is lost in some wilderness...

(Translated from the Hindi by Suresh Kohli)

A LESBIAN COW

Indu Menon

A shaft of light that moved like smoke fell into the bathroom through the ventilator glass. While bathing, at times, Mehrunnisa turned back like a small child. In those moments, raising her interest, the shaft of light touched her navel like an umbilical cord. Otherwise, it would submerge inside the orange bucket like a bright submarine tail. If not, then on the broken tiles of the roof, it shone as a small shimmering ring.

Sometimes, Mehrunnisa tried to catch it with her hands. Or else, she would turn it towards her wet hair. If not, she would keep watching the crores of tiny particles dancing inside the shaft of light. Many a time, this delayed Mehrunnisa's bath.

But that day, Mehrunnisa was in a rush to finish her bath. She didn't think of the sunlight that day. But while lifting the last mug of water from the bucket, she realised that the sunlight's transparent fingers hadn't reached down to touch the water. Panicking, she turned towards the ventilator. *"Ayyo!"* She screamed and took the clothes kept for washing and held them close to her. Two eyes were watching her calmly. Slowly, half of the face withdrew and moved away.

Mehrunnisa was shivering after coming out from the bathroom, dressed up. It was her—the lesbian cow!

Mehrunnisa was washing her clothes when Mehmood Khan came to visit her rented house on his moped. Mehmood Khan was astonished at the changes in his daughter over the past three years. He realised that his daughter had become a mature woman and he understood that time had erased all traces of childhood from her.

At the same time, Mehrunnisa's elder sister, Eid, was becoming more and more naughty and childish, which was odd for her age.

Even after ten years of marriage, Eid did not show any signs of getting pregnant. Since the Ravuthar family followed matrilineal succession, Eid Kamal's husband also stayed with her in Mehmood Khan's wife's home. Even though people gossiped that Raftas Junish did not divorce her because he lived at her place, the fact was that their love made them inseparable like a fever and a fever's temperature. Still, Khan regarded his daughter not getting pregnant as a curse on his family.

But the news of his younger daughter Mehrunnisa, who had eloped with her lover, getting pregnant thawed all his anger.

When she turned around after squeezing the water from the clothes and put them over her shoulder, Mehrunnisa noticed him. She was startled. At first sight, she thought it was the lesbian cow which was trying to intrude for the last five-six days. It showed extra courage after knowing that Shrihari Venkatesh was away.

Mehrunnisa was surprised. At six feet, like a man carved out of stone, it was her father who was standing near the moped. She pulled down her saree. After three years, Atta was smiling at her like a dream seen during a siesta. Mehrunnisa also smiled back. Mehrunnisa laughed with her brown eyes, her beautiful brown eyelashes dancing, her mouth wide open.

Mehrunnisa invited her Atta in. While he was entering the rented house, she noticed Atta stepping on the three-day-old *lakshamankkolam* drawn by Shrihari Venkatesh. After three years, she complained like a child, "Atta, move."

The sour taste of lemon in the *suleimani* made Atta cringe and frown. She started crying when Atta reminded her that whatever heights a Ravuttar girl reaches, if she doesn't know how to make good *suleimani*, she is of no use.

"Is he a painter?"

Relishing Mehrunnisa's tears, Mahmood Khan looked at the *kolam*.

"No."

"What is his name?"

"Shrihari Venkatesh Pai."

"When will he return?"

"By evening."

Mehmood Khan shook his head gravely.

"Any photo of his?"

"No."

"What about your wedding album?"

Mehrunnisa twisted her fingers nervously. "We are not married."

Mehmood Khan kept shaking his head as if he had heard nothing unusual.

"Have you changed your religion?"

"No."

Mehrunnisa noticed Mehmood Khan's face suddenly turning red like a smouldering ember.

"You should have changed your religion. It is more dignified than what you have done now."

He put down the *suleimani* cup on the sill. "I did not know that you are living in such pathetic conditions."

While drinking his tea, Shrihari decided to ask Mehrunnisa a question. Because Shrihari believed in signs. The signs he had witnessed while entering the house indicated the presence of three people.

"Who were the visitors?"

"Atta."

"Atta!" Shrihari felt ashamed. He knew that Mehrunnisa's Atta was a rich jewel merchant. He assumed that after seeing his daughter's present rented residence, he might have snubbed her.

Shrihari did not enquire after Atta's well-being. They always avoided all traces of conversations typical of men and women, as if decided by an invisible law.

Before Shrihari could ask her anything, Mehrunnisa started talking about her dream.

Shrihari scratched his head, surprised. It was for the first time since they had started living together that Mehrunnisa was sharing her dream with him.

"It was not a dream like you think."

"Then what Mehru, a daydream?" He poured tea in a saucer and gave it to her.

"No. I think it started the day before yesterday. I felt an unusual restlessness. I vomited. Finally, vomiting became just a gesture last morning as if nothing else could come out of my body apart from a light yellowish watery fluid. I went to wash my face near the well. And at that time, the cow hugged me from behind. I fainted. That dream came to me when I was unconscious."

"Mehrunnisa," Shrihari called out to her. He couldn't control his happiness. He kissed her on her forehead and on her eyelids.

Mehrunnisa lay down on the bed like a biological clock. Her eyes shone like a digital watch.

The villagers were unhappy when Mehrunnisa and Shrihari Venkatesh started 'cohabitation.' People debated about the rights and wrongs of two people from two different religions living together in the same house without getting married. Mehrunnisa and Shrihari had written a letter saying that they were going to live together when they shifted from the hospital to the rented house.

It was at the complaints reprisal committee of the Ayurveda Hospital that the sixteen-year-old Mehrunnisa first met Shrihari Venkatesh. More than being a social welfare officer, he was a handsome young man with a bluish face. His face with blue and green veins was shining because of excessive oil.

Mehrunnisa's small teeth and bright smile sparked Shrihari's interest. At the time, he was approximately thirty-six years old.

It was a complicated problem. The accused nurse looked at him like a ferocious cow. She couldn't tolerate him looking at Mehrunnisa.

Mehrunnisa had come to the hospital to get treated for paralysis. Even the most sophisticated medical processes could not faze her. But when the accused nurse started treating her, Mehrunnisa understood that the nurse was deriving pleasure out of massaging her instead of doing it properly. In the complaint given by Mehrunnisa, Shrihari read:

"Sir, that woman smells like a cow. Same shape. Rough feet like a cow's hooves. She keeps staring at me always. Do you know how much I hated that creature for doing that?" When she heard the word 'hate,' her face hardened. Shrihari was observing the accused.

Her eyes were like ancient battleships. Like a voyage of gun smoke and roaring canons, tears flowed from her eyes. They stuck to her cheek like a bullet, a sea wave, a melted glass shard.

"She kicked me hard on my chest with iron soles," Mehrunnisa placed her hand over her bosom.

"From the beginning, I felt something unusual. She kissed my daughter while she slept. How could she behave like this with my sick daughter?" Nihad Begum testified.

"My body became looser than clay. After every foot-massage, like human flesh getting fried in oil, I was cooked into a state of drugged sleep. At that time, all the nurses took turns to clean me. But all of them showed the compassion and respect which should be given to a sick patient. Apart from this dirty cow."

"I loved your body, Mehru," the nurse told her while looking at her face with desperate love, "like a cow loving another cow."

Even Shrihari was perplexed by her shameless revelation.

Her name was Nandini Gomata, and she hailed from the Gomata family. She was punished with a three-month suspension and lifetime prohibition from Mehrunnisa's ward.

"After that, she used to visit my room in stealth. Once, when I woke up from sleep, she kissed me with obstinate determination."

"Shrihari," Mehrunnisa opened her eyes, "that dirty cow proposed love to me when I came back to consciousness."

Shrihari frowned and sat up straight.

Shrihari woke up when stars of fire and shining moonlight appeared in the sky. He usually slept without closing the window. He was not afraid of that. But he felt the presence of the cow's ears and battleship eyes in the darkness. A fruit wrapped in a paper fell before him. Somebody ran behind the wall and vanished into the darkness. Cows from the dairy farm started crying. Written on that paper was the line, *"Return Mehrunnisa."*

The next day, when Mehmood Khan, Nihad Begum, Eid Kamal and Raftas Junish entered their home, Shrihari Venkatesh forgot to offer them a seat out of shame.

Khan openly asked him to marry Mehrunnisa. Khan repeated his offers of a generous dowry, traditional Pathani jewellery and other material wealth. But Shrihari replied in a different way. He retorted frankly that as long as he is a feminist, he cannot accept the institution of marriage.

"Women should enjoy maximum freedom. Mehrunnisa deserves it."

Khan started swaying his leg restlessly and hid the long line of sweat that flowed down on his cheek, with his hand. "Every human organ has a clock," Shrihari remembered his father who taught him this. He touched Mehmood Khan's legs. "Baappa, please forgive me. The problem is of my principles. Don't take it as an act of rebellion."

Meanwhile, Nihad Begum was anxiously asking about the lesbian cow. In fact, after reaching the rented house, Mehrunnisa had never thought about her. The nearby dairy farm situated on a five-acre land and the huge cows which came to eat the white flowers inside the gate did not remind her of Nandini Gomata. But recently the lesbian cow had came inside with the other cows and peeped with craving eyes into the bathroom while Mehrunnisa was taking a bath.

"Come, let's get married," she said.

Nihad Begum was scared. She had heard of men following women in the heightened craze of romance and of lonely male lovers rolling on the ground where the shadows of the women they loved fell. But she couldn't understand why one woman was chasing another woman in the name of love and desire.

"On certain nights, she would be observing our rented home from her room on the top floor of the dairy farm. While closing the window, I could see that her skin was tough like a cow's and her face compressed like dry leather on gloves."

"Daughter, maybe she is a sorceress..."

Mehrunnisa and Eid were scared.

"But don't worry, Mehrunnisa. Your Atta and I had stayed for five months in a village which had many like them. At that time, people used to call them Panans. Villagers considered them beasts since they ate beef. In that village, the cow was worshipped like a sacred animal. Panans took care of the cows. If one of the cows died, these caretakers would drag the corpse to their huts in celebration. They would grill and eat it. I have seen with my own eyes those villagers whipping people who resisted eating it."

Mehrunnisa felt paralysed.

"I think these Panans get the divine essence of the dead cow. Therefore, they become sorcerers and magicians. They have special powers using which they vanish into thin air. They can then take any form. But they will be naked. Most of them run around in the form of a cow."

Mehrunnisa felt as if her head would explode. Loud noises thundered inside her ear...the mooing of a cow.

"Sorcerers chase the women they love in the form of a cow. They avenge themselves by kicking the stomachs of pregnant women."

Mehrunnisa tried very hard to believe that all these stories are embroiled in superstition, and that the stories of belief and disbelief of the sorcerers were a myth. She became scared of the lesbian cow which shook the gate violently once Shrihari left home. Does its forehead have two lumps? Lumps hiding the sharp horns within the sheath of the skin?

That evening, while coming back from the market after buying milk, Shrihari was chased by the cow's noisy footsteps. The lesbian cow! Shrihari observed her cautiously. She wore clothes that reminded him of the leathery sheen of the skin of a cow. The *dupatta*'s end shook in the wind like a cow's ears. High-heeled iron-soled shoes on the feet, her eyes were battleships. Her skin was mild pink and shone like freshly-curdled, soft butter.

"Return Mehrunnisa to me. You should leave her. Since it is a non-contractual marriage, it will be easier to leave. She is not even your wife."

"*Chee*," Shrihari Venkatesh fumed. "Stop disturbing Mehru. I will call the police."

"Look, Shrihari. There is no use getting angry. Listen to me. I have more rights on her than you. I have touched her bosom twice as many times as you have. I remember every single grain of her body waking up to the touch of my fingers," she said with desire.

"Get lost!" Shrihari Venkatesh shouted. He pushed that woman.

The change on her face was sudden. From the warmth of lust, her face became distorted with anger. From her veins, blood rushed to her face. She smelt of gunpowder.

"You!" She screamed and hit Shrihari's chest with her head. Kicked him hard with her tall legs with ringed hooves. She pressed down her leg with force on his face. "I will kill you," she shouted, a mad cry.

While lying like dead meat on the corridor of the beef stall of the market, stinking of cow dung and urine, Shrihari Venkatesh decided to marry Mehrunnisa. Meanwhile, the lesbian cow stormed off. Her plaited, thin hair resembled a cow's tail.

Shrihari Venkatesh married Mehrunnisa according to both Hindu and Muslim traditions. That day, the lesbian cow destroyed the walls of the dairy farm. From the broken gate, more than two thousand cows entered the village in a mad rampage. Rumours spread that the cows were let out because they were infected by the mad-cow disease. Villagers ran around scared. Children did not go to school. The village became silent like a post-war terrain. Some young guys started roaming around, with nailed sticks, lamenting the disaster that was brought upon their village. They attacked, killed and assaulted the cows with stones and tins.

That afternoon, as if out of revenge, Shrihari married Mehrunnisa legally. On the way, while returning from the registrar's office, they saw piled up bodies of dead cows.

Shrihari expected a Hindu-Muslim riot. Like a riot-inflicted place, the roads were deserted. Half-dead, head-smashed, mutilated cows were crawling on the roads, crying.

Shrihari and Mehrunnisa saw a crowd on the western part of the dairy farm. Shrihari stopped the car and went there, anxiously. The lesbian cow was lying on the road. She was naked. Blood flowed from her chest onto the dark tar and it was boiling without drying up.

The place smelled of cow's milk.

"People killed her with stones and nailed sticks since she was attacked by a mad cow's horns."

Shrihari Venkatesh felt a sense of relief. "Oh, it died," he said with the same ease as if he was talking of a cow.

"Who are you talking about?" Mehrunnisa enquired.

"Nothing, people killed a mad cow. That's all..."

Shrihari closed the car's door.

The next morning, Shrihari stopped Mehrunnisa from reading the newspaper which carried the news, 'People Killed Dairy Farm Owner Thinking She Was A Witch.'

"Go, get a cup of coffee." Then he leaned back on the armchair with all the arrogance and pride of a husband.

(Translated from the Malayalam by Premjish)

THE PRICE OF FLOWERS

Prabhat Kumar Mukhopadhyay

Vegetarian restaurants are to be found in various parts of London. One day, I tired myself out walking around the National Gallery, looking at pictures. It was nearly one o'clock and I was feeling extremely hungry. So I slowly made my way to a restaurant of this kind which was not far from there, in St. Martin's Lane. London restaurants in lunch hours were not so crowded in those days. I found not more than three or four hungry people scattered around the restaurant. I chose a table, seated myself and opened the newspaper.

A waitress came up and waited politely for my order. I raised my eyes from the paper, glanced at the menu and told her what I required. "Thank you, Sir," she said and went briskly and noiselessly away.

At that moment, my attention was drawn to a table not far from mine. A young English girl was sitting there. She had been watching me with interest but turned her eyes away as soon as I looked at her. There was nothing new in her surprise, for in white countries, people are often charmed by the beauty of our coloured complexion and we receive more attention than we deserve.

The girl was thirteen or fourteen years old. Her clothes betrayed her poverty. Her hair hung like a heavy stream flowing down her back. Her eyes were large. They had a sad expression. I watched her when she was not looking at me so that she would not notice. My lunch was served as she was finishing hers. The waitress brought her the bill. Bills are paid at the desk as one goes out. The desk is near the door.

The girl stood up. My eyes followed her. As she paid her bill, she asked the cashier in a low voice, "Please, Miss, can you tell me if that gentleman is an Indian?"

"I think so," the cashier answered.

"Does he come here all the time?"

"Perhaps not. I do not recall having seen him before."

"Thank you," the girl said, looked at me once more with a startled air and stepped out.

It surprised me. Why? What was the matter? Her interest in me aroused my interest in her. When I had finished my lunch, I asked the waitress, "Do you know the girl who was sitting over there?"

"No, Sir, I hardly know her to speak of. I notice she has lunch here on Saturdays."

"Doesn't she come on any other day?"

"I never see her on other days."

"Have you any idea who she is?"

"Perhaps she works in a nearby shop."

"How do you know?"

"Saturday is pay day. That is when she comes. On other days, she may not be able to afford lunch. Perhaps she does not earn very much."

I was moved by what she said.

The curiosity I felt about the girl persisted. Why had she enquired about me? Was some mystery the cause of her interest? Her poverty-stricken, sad and anxious figure took possession of my thoughts. Who was the child? Was there any possibility of my being of any help to her? On Sunday, all London shops are closed. So I set out to look for her after breakfast on Monday morning. I looked into the shops on the streets near St Martin's Lane, especially the shops on the Strand, but did not see her anywhere. The pockets of my overcoat were bulging with dozens of picture postcards, pencils, studs, ties and other things I did not need, for in each shop, I had to buy something. But I found no trace of the girl.

The week passed. Saturday came again. I presented myself at the vegetarian restaurant once more. As I entered, I saw her sitting at the same table as before. She was eating. I walked up and took the chair opposite hers, saying, "Good afternoon!"

"Good afternoon, Sir," she responded, hesitantly.

By making one brief remark after another I was able, slowly, to start a conversation. At last, she asked, "Are you an Indian?"

"Yes."

"Excuse me, are you a vegetarian?"

"Why do you ask that?"

"I have heard that most Indians are vegetarians."

"How is it that you know anything about India?"

"My elder brother is in India. He is a soldier."

"I am not much of a vegetarian," I answered her question, "but I enjoy a vegetarian meal now and then."

The girl seemed disappointed.

I learned that her only guardian was this elder brother. She lived in Lambeth with her widowed mother, who was old.

"Do you hear from your brother?"

"We have not had a letter from him in a long time. My mother is very worried. People tell her that India is full of tigers and snakes, and fevers. She is afraid something has happened to him. Is it true, Sir, that India is full of tigers and snakes, and fevers?"

"No," I smiled. "How could people live there if it were so?"

The girl sighed softly. "Mother says she would like to ask an Indian about these things. If she can find an Indian..." the girl looked at me with entreating eyes.

I understood how she felt. She wanted me to see her mother, but she did not have the courage to ask me to accompany her home. A keen desire to meet this poor, anxious mother took hold of me. I had not had the opportunity to visit an impoverished English home. I wished to see how the poor lived in this country, to know what they thought.

"Will you introduce me to your mother sometime? Would you like me to accompany you home? I can go some day."

The girl's eyes brimmed with gratitude. "Thank you ever so much!" she said. "It is so kind of you! Can you come now?"

"With pleasure."

"It will not interfere with anything else you have to do?"

"No, no, not at all. This afternoon is entirely my own."

The girl was delighted. We finished our lunch and got up together.

As we walked, I asked her, "May I know your name?"

"My name is Alice Margaret Clifford."

"Oh! Are you Alice of *Alice in Wonderland*?" I joked.

"What is that?" she was alarmed.

I was nonplussed. I had imagined every English girl must have read the incomparable book.

"That is the name of a very nice book," I explained. "Haven't you read it?"

"No. I have not."

"If your mother permits me," I said, "I shall make a present of it to you."

We chatted pleasantly until we passed St. Martin's Church and reached Charing Cross Station. Double-decker buses were dashing up and down the Strand, rushing from both directions. There were innumerable cabs. We stopped in front of the telegraph office. "Let's wait for the Westminster bus here," I said.

"Would you mind walking?" she asked.

"Not at all," I answered, "if it is not difficult for you."

"No, I walk home every day."

This gave me the opportunity of asking her where she worked. To ask bluntly is not polite in England, but there are many ways of circumventing the rules. For instance, it is not offensive to ask a fellow traveller in a train, "Are you going far?" but to ask him, "Where are you going?" is considered very rude. The fellow passenger may, if he wishes, answer, "I am going to such-and-such place," or, if he does not wish to disclose his destination, he may say, "Not very far." The question is thus answered, while at the same time a certain reserve is maintained. So, I asked the girl, "Do you come this way often?"

"Yes," she answered, "I work as a typist at the Civil Service Stores. Every afternoon, I come home this way. Today is Saturday, so I am off early."

"Let us walk along the Embankment. It will be less crowded than the Strand," I said and, taking her by the arm, guided her carefully across the street.

The street known as the Embankment runs along the North shore of the Thames. "Do you usually go this way?" I asked as we made our way along it.

"No, it is less crowded, it is true, but the people are dirtier. I go home by the Strand and Whitehall."

This poor unsophisticated girl had defeated me. I admitted it. This was not the first time the English sense of beauty had disarmed me. We approached Westminster Bridge.

"Shall I call you Miss Clifford or Alice?"

"I am not a grown-up yet. You may call me what you like. I am usually called Maggie," she laughed.

"Are you very anxious to grow up?"

"Yes."

"Tell me why."

"When I grow up, I shall be paid more for my work. My mother is old."

"Is the work you do to your liking?"

"No. The work is very mechanical. I want work that will make me use my head, brain work. Like the work of a secretary."

Guards were pacing up and down outside the Houses of Parliament. We left them on the right, crossed the bridge and arrived in Lambeth. It is a poor neighbourhood. "If I ever become a secretary," Maggie said, "I shall take mother away from here."

"Why are you called by your second name instead of your first?" I asked as we pushed through the crowd of ill-dressed work-people.

"My mother's first name is also Alice, so my father called me by my second, making it my nickname."

"Did your father call you Maggie or Magsy?"

"When he was very affectionate, he called me Magsy. How did you know?"

"Yes, yes," I answered, mysteriously, "we are Indians, you know. We know about the future and all kinds of magic."

"That is what I have heard," she said.

"Indeed?" I was surprised. "What have you heard?"

"I have heard that there are many people in India who have occult powers. They are called yogis. But you are not a yogi."

"How do you know that I am not a yogi, Maggie?"

"Yogis do not eat meat."

"Is that why you asked me in the beginning whether I am a vegetarian or not?"

She smiled without answering.

We had reached a narrow doorway. Maggie took a thin latchkey out of her pocket and opened the door. She entered and said, "Please come in."

When I was inside, Maggie closed the door. She went to the foot of the stairs and, raising her voice a little, called, "Mother, where are you?"

"I am in the kitchen, child," the answer came from below. "Come down."

It is necessary to explain here that London streets are above ground. Kitchens are often below street level.

Maggie looked at me, questioningly, "Do you mind?"

"Not in the least. Come on." I said.

Together, we descended the stairs to the kitchen.

"Mother," Maggie said from the doorway, "an Indian gentleman has come to see you."

"Where is he?" the old woman asked, eagerly. With a smile, I stepped into the kitchen, trailing behind Maggie. She introduced us. "This is Mr. Gupta, Mother," she said, "Mr. Gupta, my mother."

"How do you do?" I said and held out my hand.

"Excuse me. My hands—" she said, holding them out for me to see. They were covered with flour. "Today is Saturday," she explained, "I am making cakes. People will come to buy them this evening. They will be sold on the streets tonight. This is the way we make our living—lots of trouble!"

Saturday night is a time for festivity in poor neighbourhoods. All sorts of things are sold from countless lighted pushcarts. The streets are more crowded than on any other day. Saturday is the day the poor are able to spend a little for they receive their weekly wages.

Ingredients for cake-making—flour, sugar, fat, raisins, eggs and so forth—were set out in readiness upon the dresser. Several freshly baked cakes in tins were also there.

"Sitting in such a poor kitchen will not be very pleasant for you, will it?" Mrs. Clifford said, "I have almost finished my work. Maggie, take him to the sitting room. I'll come in a minute."

"No, no," I protested, "I can sit here well enough. The cakes you make are nice ones, I must say!"

Mrs. Clifford thanked me with a smile.

"Mother makes good toffee also. Will you try some?" Maggie opened a cupboard and took out a tin. I ate several pieces and praised them.

"What kind of a country is India, Sir?" Mrs. Clifford asked as she resumed her cooking.

"A beautiful country."

"Safe to live in?"

"Certainly. But not cold like this country. It is somewhat hot."

"Aren't there too many snakes and tigers? Don't they kill people?"

"Don't believe that," I laughed. "Snakes and tigers keep to the jungles. They get killed themselves if they come too close to place where people live."

"And fevers?"

"In some places in India, there is more fever than in others. It is neither the same everywhere nor the same all year around."

"My son is in Punjab. He is a soldier. What kind of a place is Punjab?"

"Punjab is a fine place. There is little fever there. It is very healthy."

"I am glad to hear that," Mrs. Clifford said.

Her baking was finished. "Maggie," she said, "take Mr. Gupta upstairs. I'll wash my hands and bring him tea."

Maggie showed the way to their sitting room and I followed. The furniture was cheap and there was not much of it. The carpet was old, torn in places. But everything was extremely clean. Maggie drew the curtains back and opened the windows. There was a glass bookcase. I stood in front of it.

A few minutes later, Mrs. Clifford came in carrying the tea tray. All traces of the kitchen had vanished from her person. As we drank tea, I talked about India. Mrs. Clifford showed me a photograph of her son. It had been taken before he left. His name was Francis or Frank. Maggie brought out a book of pictures he had sent her for her birthday. There were many pictures of Simla and the surrounding mountain country. On the inside page was written, "To Maggie on her birthday from her loving brother Frank."

"Maggie," Mrs. Clifford said, "Show Mr. Gupta the ring."

"Has your brother sent you a ring?" I asked her. "Let me see what kind of a ring it is."

"It is a magic ring," Maggie explained. "A yogi gave it to Frank."

She brought it and asked, "Can you see the past and future in it?"

I had heard a lot about crystal gazing. A crystal was set in the ring. I took it up and examined it.

"When Frank sent the ring," Mrs. Clifford said, "he wrote that if you concentrate on a distant person as you gaze into it, you will be able to see him and what he is doing. This what the yogi told Frank. Maggie and I have concentrated upon it again and again because we have not had any news from Frank in a long time. But we have not been able to see anything. Why don't you try? You are a Hindu. You may be able to do it!"

I realised that superstition is not confined to India. I did not have the heart to tell the mother and daughter that the ring was nothing more than brass with a piece of ordinary glass stuck on it. They believed their Frank had sent them a new and miraculous thing from a distant land, a dream India. How could I shatter their faith?

Urged by Mrs. Clifford and Maggie, I took the ring in my hand and stared at it intensely for a long time. "I cannot see anything," I exclaimed at last, giving up.

Mother and daughter were disappointed. To change the subject, I said, "Here is a violin. It is yours, isn't it, Maggie?"

"Yes," Mrs. Clifford answered, "Maggie plays quite well. Maggie, please play something for us."

"Oh, Mother!" Maggie looked at her, protesting.

"Maggie," I pleaded, "please play something! I am very fond of the violin. I have a sister at home about your age. She used to play for me."

"The way I play is not at all worth listening to," Maggie said.

My entreaties at last persuaded her to play. "I do not know many pieces," she said. "What would you like to hear?"

"Shall I choose something? All right, then, give me your music. Let me see what you have."

Maggie brought out an old music-case bound in black leather. I opened it. Most of the pieces were light airs like,

'Goodbye Dolly Grey,' 'Honeysuckle and the Bee,' etc. There were a few really good though old-fashioned ones, things like 'Robin Adair,' 'Annie Laurie,' 'The Last Rose of Summer,' etc. There were several Scottish songs. So, I selected 'The Blue Bells of Scotland' and handed Maggie the music. Maggie played, and I hummed the tune to myself.

When the song was over, I praised her playing lavishly as I thanked her. "Maggie has never had the opportunity to study," Mrs. Clifford said. "She has learned what she knows by herself. If our circumstances ever improve, I shall arrange for her to have lessons."

"Maggie, play something else," I said.

Maggie had overcome her shyness. "What shall I play?" she asked.

I went through her pieces. Not a single composition fashionable at the time in cultivated circles was there. I realised that no echo of them had yet reached the poorer neighbourhoods.

There was a minor classic among her pieces which I at last found: the 'Flower Song' from Gounod's opera, *Faust*. I picked it up and said, "Please play this."

Maggie played it. When she finished, I was silent with astonishment. My astonishment was occasioned by a sudden insight into the extent to which culture had penetrated even the lower levels of society in the West. Maggie played the difficult score beautifully, yet she was only a girl of the people. It occurred to me that if the daughter of a distinguished Calcutta barrister or well-known civilian were able to play this well at her age, a furore would be created in social circles.

"Did you learn that also by yourself?" I asked Maggie as I thanked her.

"No," she said, "I couldn't do that by myself. The daughter of the minister of our church helped me. Have you heard the opera?"

"I have not heard the opera," I replied, "but I have seen *Faust* staged at the Lyceum in English translation. Goethe's *Faust*."

"At the Lyceum? Where Irving acts?"

"Yes. Have you ever seen him?"

Maggie answered, ruefully, "No, I have never been to a West End Theatre. I have never seen Irving. I have not seen more than his photograph in the shop windows."

"Irving is acting in *The Merchant of Venice* now. If Mrs. Clifford and you are free to accompany me some evening, I shall be delighted to take you."

Mrs. Clifford consented, gratefully. "Which would you prefer," I asked, "the evening performance or the matinee?"

A word about the London theatre must be said here. Unlike Calcutta, where the performance of a play is the subject of much comment, plays here are staged every night with the exception of Sundays. In addition, there are afternoon shows called matinees in some theatres on Wednesdays or Saturdays or on both days. A play causes little stir. Once it starts, it is staged every day and runs as long as there is an adequate audience. Some plays run for two months, some six. A popular musical comedy often has an uninterrupted run of two or three years.

"I am not very well," Mrs. Clifford said, "the matinee is best. We can go some Saturday after Maggie's office closes."

"Fine!" I said, "I'll go on Monday and buy tickets for the first Saturday available. I'll let you know the date."

"But Mr. Gupta!" Maggie said, "Don't buy expensive seats. We shall be very sorry if you do."

"No," I assured her. "Why should I buy expensive seats? I am not an Indian Raja! I'll take seats in the Upper Circle. One thing. Have you read *The Merchant of Venice*?"

"Not the play itself. The story was in our textbook at school, Lamb's *Tales*. I read that."

"All right. I'll send you a copy of the play. Read it carefully beforehand and you will be able to understand the acting."

It was growing late. I took my leave.

I presented myself at the box-office of the Lyceum Theatre at ten o'clock on Monday morning and asked, "May I have three tickets in the Upper Circle for the Saturday matinee?"

"No, Sir," the ticket-seller said, "not for the next two Saturdays. The house is sold-out."

"The third Saturday?"

"I can give them to you." He took out a plan of the theatre marked with the date and showed it to me. I saw that many seats in the Upper Circle for that day too were already sold. The numbers of the seats sold were struck through with a blue pencil. I took the plan, examined it, chose three seats in a row and gave their numbers to the ticket-seller. I took the three numbered tickets, paid twelve shillings and came away.

Three months passed. I visited Maggie and her mother several times at their home and took Maggie to see the zoo once. She rode the elephant, Indian Raja, like all the other boys and girls. How delighted she was!

But no news had come from her brother. Urged by Mrs. Clifford, I went to India House one day and made enquiries. I was told the regiment to which Frank belonged was fighting on the Northwest Frontier. Mrs. Clifford became extremely worried when she heard it.

One day, I received a postcard from Maggie. She wrote:

"Dear Mr. Gupta,

My mother is very ill. I have not been able to go to work for a week. We shall be extremely grateful if you take the trouble to come see us.

Maggie"

I had told the family with whom I lived about Maggie and her mother. At breakfast, I spoke of the letter.

My hostess said, "When you go, take some money with you. The girl has not been able to go to work for a week. She has not received any pay. It is probable that they are hard up."

After breakfast, I took some money and set out for Lambeth. I knocked at the door. Maggie opened it.

She was looking very tired. Her eyes were ringed. "Oh, thank you, Mr. Gupta!" she exclaimed when she saw me. "It is so kind of you."

"How is your mother, Maggie?" I asked.

"She is sleeping now. Her condition is very serious. The doctor says it is aggravated by her anxiety for Frank. There is no news from him yet. She may not live."

I tried to console Maggie, wiping her tears with my handkerchief. Maggie controlled herself with much effort and said, "I have a request to make of you, Mr. Gupta."

"What is it, Maggie?" I asked.

"Come to the sitting room and I'll tell you," she answered.

We tiptoed carefully to the sitting room lest the sound of our footsteps disturbed the sick woman. I turned when I reached the centre of the room and remained standing there.

"What is it, Maggie?" I repeated my question.

Maggie gazed at my face with beseeching eyes. I waited. Then, she covered her face with her hands and wept silently.

I was in a fix. What could I say to console this child? Her brother was fighting on the Frontier. Only God knew whether he was alive or dead. Her mother was the only person she had on earth. If she lost her, what would happen? Where in London could this girl, on the threshold of adolescence, go?

I pulled her hands away from her face. "Maggie, tell me what you wish me to do. If there is anything I can do to help you, I shall not hesitate."

"Mr. Gupta," the girl said, "I do not know what you will think of the request I am going to make. Please forgive me if it is very, very wrong."

"What is it? What do you wish to ask?"

"All day yesterday, Mother kept saying that if Mr. Gupta would come and gaze into the crystal, he might learn something about Frank. Mr. Gupta is a Hindu, she said. If only he would come, she said. That is why I wrote to you."

"If you want me to try once more, go and bring me the ring, Maggie. Of course, I'll do it."

"But if you don't see anything again this time?"

I understood what Maggie meant. I was silent.

"Mr. Gupta, I have read in books that Hindus are extremely truth-loving. If you could bring yourself to tell mother only once, after looking into the crystal, that Frank is all right, that he is alive—will it be too much of a lie? Will it be very, very wrong?" As she spoke, tears streamed from her eyes.

I thought it over. I am not very virtuous. I have done my sinful things. So, I decided to do this. It would be the least of my offences. "Please, Maggie, don't cry. Where is the ring? Let me take a good look at it this time. If I do not see anything, I shall do as you suggest. God will forgive me if it is wrong."

Maggie brought me the ring. I took it and said, "See if your mother is awake."

Fifteen minutes passed before Maggie came back. "Mother is awake," she said. "I have told her you are here."

"May I see her now?"

"Please come."

I approached the mother's bedside. The ring was in my hand. Wishing her a good morning I said, "Mrs. Clifford, your son is alive. He is well."

The old woman raised her head a little off the pillow. "Did you see that in the crystal?" she asked.

"Yes, Mrs. Clifford," I answered without any hesitation, "I have seen it."

Her head dropped back. Tears of happiness welled up in her eyes. She whispered faintly, "God bless you! God bless you!"

Mrs. Clifford recovered.

It was almost time for me to return to my country. I wished to go to Lambeth to say goodbye to Maggie and her mother. But the family was in mourning. Frank had been killed in the fighting on the Frontier. A month earlier, Maggie had sent me a card with a black border. I checked the date and found out that Frank had died some days before I told his mother he was alive and well. I felt ashamed to face Mrs. Clifford. So I wrote a letter to them, announcing my departure and bidding them goodbye.

The morning of my last day in London dawned. I was to leave before night. As I was breakfasting with the family, there was a knock on the door. A minute or two later, the maid came in and announced, "Please Mr. Gupta, Miss Clifford has come to see you."

My breakfast was unfinished. Maggie had come to say goodbye. I took permission from my hostess and left the table. Maggie was standing in the hall. She was wearing black.

I took her to the adjoining library and made her sit down.

"Are you leaving today?" she asked.

"Yes, Maggie, today is the day of my departure."

"How long will it take you to reach your country?"

"A little more than two weeks."

"In what part of the country do you live?"

"I have entered the Punjab Civil Service. I shall not know exactly where I am posted until I arrive there."

"Is the Frontier very far from there?"

"No, not very."

"Frank is buried at Fort Monroe near Dera-Ghazi-Khan." The girl's eyes filled with tears as she spoke.

"When I go to that part of the country I shall visit your brother's grave and write to you."

"It won't be troublesome for you? Or inconvenient?" Maggie asked.

"Why should it be? Dera-Ghazi-Khan is not very far from where I shall be. It will certainly be possible for me to go there, someday. I'll write and tell you about it."

Maggie's face filled with gratitude. As she thanked me, her voice choked. She took a shilling out of her pocket and put it down on the table in front of me, saying, "Please buy flowers with this shilling when you go and lay them on my brother's grave."

Overwhelmed by emotion, I lowered my eyes. The girl had earned the shilling with so much toil! I felt like returning it to her, explaining that in our country, flowers grow in great profusion and do not have to be purchased.

But, I reconsidered. Why should I deprive her of the joy this sacrifice would give her? All that this shilling could have given her, she was foregoing for the love of her brother. The joy of doing it was beyond all price. The grief in her heart would be eased a little. What good would it do to deprive her of it? I picked up the shilling.

"Maggie," I said, "I shall use this shilling to buy flowers and put them on your brother's grave."

Maggie stood up. "How can I thank you?" she said. "Now, it is time for me to go to work. Goodbye. Remember to write."

I got up and took her hand in mine. "Goodbye, Maggie. God bless you," I said and pressed her hand to my lips. Maggie left. I wiped a tear or two from my eyes and went upstairs to pack my bags.

(Translated from the Bengali by Lila Ray)

MA

Pritish Nandy

"This is where we played as children, with the tassels of the sun," she smiled quietly as she led me into the courtyard of the old house, into the eye of memory, where the shadows and the sunlight wove a strange tapestry of the past.

"My father died when I was very young and my eldest brother, who was the doctor I told you about, brought me up. You didn't see him either because he died when you were very small. Or was it before you were even born?"

I looked at her. The tired sunlight was in her eyes. The bronze of her skin had lost its shine; the quiet of autumn grew around us tenderly, with a strange vengeance. We were alone in the ruins of that old house. The sun lit up the corners, the nooks and crannies of the past. I was thirty-three. She, seventy.

Father had died three years ago. But it seemed like only yesterday. The small hospital room. The smell from the open drain outside, and we—all waiting for him to die. The saline drips. The oxygen. He, without his false teeth, looking old and almost ready to go away, the sixty-watt bulb lighting up the tender violence of the scene. We all knew it was over and yet none of us would accept. Except perhaps Ashis; after all, he was the eldest and in many ways the wisest of us three brothers. Even as I pleaded with an imperfect God to spare his life, I knew it was useless. I knew there was no God.

"You see that old guava tree there; that is where you buried your doll once. An old rag doll one of your cousins had made for you. I don't quite remember who. We would come here in summer, when your school would close. The journey was long in those days; it would take almost a full day, but the train would stop right here, outside the house. For they all knew us. Daktarbabu's house was an important landmark in those days."

The crows were winging homewards. In the distance, I heard the whistle of a local train. Dusk creaked in gently. Cattle bells tinkled. There was a smell of lostness in the air.

I remember the faltering carriage in which they took my father away. A brown horse limped through the traffic, pulling the carriage into the strange muted colours of memory. Ashis and I sat together. Manish was miles away.

Ma went through all the rituals, unbelieving. I didn't know how to react. The black box atop the carriage kept bobbing up and down. The fierce afternoon sun was upon us.

"At night, we would all sit here and chat. The stars would come up one by one. Someone would light the lantern inside. After dinner, you would come to me and lie down, and I would then tell you the stories my grandmother told me. Slowly, the night would grow in your eyes."

It was the same priest, dressed in the same fierce white. Four grave-diggers shovelled away in the sunlight as he kept mumbling strange verses from the scriptures. Aunts, friends, a few stragglers—they all stood in silence, and after the coffin was lowered into the ground, threw in a fistful of earth. How could I dismiss a man I had loved and known with such a simple gesture? Is that a way to say goodbye? I wondered.

Ma was dressed in white.

"Once we came for a marriage in the family. The entire house was packed with relatives and we all slept on the floor. You can hardly believe it, seeing this ruined courtyard today, but we were almost a hundred people. The family was very big, you see. We were seven brothers and three sisters and all of us were very close to each other. Well, almost all. Mejda and Probodh stayed a bit aloof."

With father going away, it left only us three. Two aunts, one blind and ailing. Only us three brothers and Ma. All her brothers had gone away, except Probodh, and he was distant anyway. Even the sisters had died. Nothing remained of the family except memories and a few scattered children, far, far from each other. I remembered a sense of helplessness. Who was there to share my hurts and my triumphs, now that he was gone? He was, after all, the only one who knew me, understood me, and not just as a son.

Ma must have felt even more lonely. He was all the world to her.

"You see that tree in the distance. It is an old neem tree. We were told as children that an ancient witch lived there. She had long, silver hair and a voice like a cracked copper vessel. So, at night we never went that way even though we were curious to know what a voice like a cracked copper vessel sounded like. My mother, whom you never saw, was a very religious and superstitious person. After my father, Suleiman—or Solomon, as he chose to call himself after conversion—died, she began to believe in everything. God, witches, devils, *rakshasas*, ghosts, spirits, anything you told her about. Religion played no role in her beliefs. She had faith in everything, everyone."

That is the way father was. He trusted everything, everyone. Even me. Sometimes he found me strange. Which was not surprising, considering that I did the same myself, at times. But he had faith in me. Even when things went wrong, which they often did. Even when I lost faith in myself.

The four grave-diggers worked away. Dust unto dust we shall return...the nasal intonation almost put me to sleep. The heat, the long vigil through the nights, the tension of watching a man die–it had all accumulated. I was beaten.

"Don't go away, son. No, it is not for me that I speak. It is for your own good, for the good of your children. Nothing matters for nothing stays. Like this courtyard. Like memories..."

The light was faint. In the wistful magic of dusk, we looked backwards, each into our own worlds. There was the sound of cattle bells and the hush of dusk.

I stood lonely in my dreams. She was there, wandering in her past.

KHODU BABA'S TOMB

Joginder Paul

Khodu Baba and the evening entered the *jhopadpatti* one after the other. Shadow by shadow, the evening slid ahead on its own. On seeing Khodu Baba, a well-fed dog barked, as if to say, come, follow me. He went ahead of him and passing through narrow paths drawn amidst small huts and shacks, stood in front of the door of an extraordinary hut. To say something to himself, or perhaps to call someone from within the *jhuggi*, Baba shouted out, "Hak-k!" Offended by this, the dog started barking, "Wahun, wahun! It is my job to call or not to call Choudhuri, Baba!—Wahun!"

"Yes, yes, I hear you, Bandhu," pulling up his salwar, Rakha Choudhuri emerged from the hut. As he came towards them, he paused to tighten the string of his *salwar*, which was loosening at the waist, "Who have you dragged here?" His voice seemed to leak from his nose and acquired a tingle. "You establish a relationship with any Nathu-Khera! How many people can I accommodate? Tell me!"

Bandhu withdrew a little in fear and growled as he raised his head towards Khodu Baba, "Wahun wahun, tell me."

But Baba stood silent, staring at Rakha Choudhuri.

"Why do you stare at me this way, Baba?" Rakha said, twirling his moustache and feeling a little disturbed. "I am none other than my own self."

"No, Khodu," Khodu Baba opened his mouth from within his dense beard. "How would Khodu know who Khodu is?"

Choudhuri was beginning to feel angry, "Baba, my name is not Khodu." Khodu's anger was hardly over when he suddenly let out another "Hak—!" And he picked up a stone and threw it towards his feet.

"Arre...re!" Choudhuri sprang back and on seeing a crushed scorpion, stood still. *"Baap...re!"* He thought he was just a beggar, but now he appeared to him a saviour. "You want a *jhuggi* to stay? Sure, I'll give you one. I charge others fifty over five hundreds for a single *jhuggi*, but it'll do if you give me fifty over two."

"Oh no! I am guilty of murder, Khodu." Although Baba was reassured that Choudhuri was saved, he felt bad that the scorpion lay crushed.

"My name..." Choudhuri wished to tell Baba that his name was not Khodu, but he restrained himself. "Why should you feel bad about killing a scorpion, Baba? It is better to kill the one who stings."

"Scorpions too say the same, it is better to sting those who kill."

God knows what got into Bandhu that he began to roll at Baba's feet.

"*Arre*...run away, you son of a bitch!" Rakha Choudhuri raised his arm and moved towards him, "Go, do your own *chowkidari*."

But Khodu Baba bent down and patted the dog's back lovingly, and before raising his head, he took a fistful of dust from the ground below and put it on his head.

Somewhat surprised, Rakha Choudhuri kept looking at him, and then he folded his hands across his chest in reverence, thinking that Baba must be a miracle man. "Baba, how long will you stand on your two feet with all the burdens of the world? But never mind," he began tightening his *salwar* chord again, "come inside, take my money and hand it back to me," he laughed out. "Actually, Choudhuri can give away his life for free, but he won't give the *jhuggi* for free—come Baba, come inside." With folded hands, Choudhuri turned towards the door and like Bandhu, with his tail wagging, he walked ahead with Khodu Baba trailing after him. Behind them, Bandhu stood on his hind legs, trying to fold the other two across his chest just like his master. Failing in his efforts, he released from his throat a one-word bark which sounded like a "Hak—k!"

Inside the *jhuggi*, Rakha Choudhuri wished to serve Baba the liquor he had brewed with his own hands. Baba, he imagined, must be a fakir of a high order. Must be a resident of at least the fourth or the fifth heaven. As his gaze would rise further, he would reach the seventh heaven and ask me, "Hak...! Come on, ask for something—tell me what you wish for." He started wishing for something, keeping Khodu Baba in mind—what more was there to ask from Baba! Ramcharan's wife does not come around even after relishing all those *jalebi*s from me. I'll triumph only when she comes to me! But as soon as he placed the glass in front of Khodu Baba, Baba raised the slogan of 'Hak' and smashed the glass on the floor. And while he did so, he hurt his hand. He cleaned the blood on his palm with his beard and as he was getting up, Choudhuri fell at his feet, cursing Ramcharan's wife in his heart—if only she'd come around straight and direct, there'd be no need to get into such trouble.

Having fallen at Baba's feet, Choudhuri began to collect the scattered pieces of the broken glass.

"Those who cannot forgive, Khodu," Khodu Baba settled himself again comfortably, "they too deserve the same punishment as those they need to forgive."

Choudhuri was relieved and in his happiness, he brought out the bag full of sweet *jalebi*s from the cupboard—the *jalebis* he'd kept aside for Ramcharan's wife.

"Have some *jalebis*, Baba!" She herself does not do any good deeds. Let me earn some blessings for her.

Khodu Baba waived the *jalebi*s away, "No, Khodu, those who eat sweets become victims of *khwab-e-khaflat*."

"*Khwab-e-khaflat*! Wah!" Fascinated by his language, Choudhuri kissed his fingers as though he were kissing Khodu Baba's words, "If it is possible, Khodu, then, in the name of Allah, maybe you can give me a plain dry roti to eat."

Choudhuri had kept two—three rotis for the dog, Bandhu. He told himself, Bandhu will surely manage a roti for himself from elsewhere. He brought him the rotis, wrapped in a piece of cloth, and after keeping them before Baba, he got up to bring him a glass of water.

"Just one," Baba took one roti in his hands, "Am I taking your Bandhu's share?"

"You know it all, Baba, just wait a little and I'll make some fresh rotis for you in a minute."

"No, make fresh ones for Bandhu, Khodu," Khodu Baba offered his thanks to God and took the first bite.

"Put a little bit of salt on the roti, Baba."

"Yes, Khodu, do give me some salt so that I will never forget your kindness, for fear of being untrue to your salt!"

As Baba laughed for the first time, Choudhuri felt that his hut had suddenly brightened up.

"No, Baba, don't say such things." Choudhuri kept the little box of salt in front of Baba and seemed to love his own modesty. Baba took a sip of water and looked at him attentively. Choudhuri turned and looked back, confused.

"Who are you looking at, Khodu?"

"Why, the one you are looking at, Baba. But I am here."

"Hardly...you are hardly..." Khodu Baba began to sprinkle salt on his roti, if only to look casual.

"Only Baba can comprehend Baba," Choudhuri told himself. And then, he asked Baba, "Baba, can you tell me something? Why do you call me Khodu?"

"Because I am also Khodu," Baba swallowed a mouthful of roti and answered. "Except for my name, what do I possess, that I can offer to another? I give what I have, to everyone—that is, my very own self."

Choudhuri felt like stopping Baba from eating so that he could kiss his fingers first. "Baba, there are a lot of empty *jhuggis* here. You put your finger on anyone of them and that'll be yours. One of them has a very high roof. It's very airy."

"No, I want the absolutely highest roof, that of the sky, Khodu," Baba finished his roti and wiped his hands on his beard, "I don't want any *jhuggi-vuggi*. If you can give me a little bit of open space, I'll settle down."

Choudhuri decided he'd give Baba that raised platform a little distance away, from where the graveyard commenced. And from within his good intentions, crept a cunning smile, almost involuntarily. It would be easier for him to grab some land from the graveyard this way.

"Hak...!" In a short while, tired as he was, Baba's eyes started to grow heavy with sleep. He was about to lie down there itself.

"Wait, Baba, let me spread out a sheet first."

"No, whether for a moment or forever, death should be felt on the raw ground, Hak...!"

Khodu Baba started to snore as soon as he lay down and Choudhuri pulled out his earnings of the day from his pocket and got down to counting it. He wanted to sleep then—"Hak"—God knows what he tried to say to himself as he, like Baba, produced this sound.

God alone knows what stories Rakha Choudhuri created and spread amongst the people of that *jhopadpatti* that crowds of believers gathered the very next evening at Khodu Baba's *chabootra*. Baba half reclined on the platform, resting his back on a pillow of bricks...he appeared to be a corpse who had to come out into the open, unable to cope with the suffocation of his tomb. The overawed people sitting around him were like shadows for him. Suddenly, he called out, "Hak...!" Most people raised their heads towards the sky as though Baba's voice had descended from somewhere there.

Many of them had placed their offerings by his side. He spotted a dry *roti* peeping out of a newspaper-wrapping, amongst these. He bent forward, picked up the *roti* and put it into his mouth. By the time a man ran and got a jug of water for him, the whole *roti* was in Baba's belly.

"Hak...!" Baba's mouth was still full of water. When he opened his mouth, from behind the wild bushes, a natural spring burst forth growing into a fast stream. When Baba's beard and moustache were drenched, the eyes of the devotees popped out. Baba turned his back towards the graveyard and bent over the other offerings. He picked up a turban and gave it to a bare-headed man, here, take it Khodu—and the sheet; he passed it on to a naked man—take it, Khodu—the bottle filled with honey was given to a pale-faced woman and shoes—he called out to an old man with cracked feet—"Come, Khodu, take this."

Badhwa Chamar stood up when he saw this, "But I spent my whole day on this shoe for your sake, Baba, and made it of a magical size for anybody's foot to fit into it."

The old man quickly wore the shoes lest Baba changed his mind on listening to Badhwa. He trembled with happiness. "Baba, my babua always said, don't worry, Bapu! When you die, I'll send you away in shoes." The old man seemed to be dancing in a frenzy.

Although the sky was absolutely clear, two-three drops of water fell on their cheeks. And they were very comforting. After calling out to the old man, Baba called out to Choudhuri, "Take this." He gave a fistful of dust from his *chabootra* to Rakha Choudhuri, who poured it on his head the same way Baba had earlier done.

Baba then spotted a bag of *laddoo*s. He was perhaps wondering what he could do with it when he thought he heard a voice behind him. "*Arre, haan.*" He turned around. "Here, take these *laddoo*s and share it amongst yourselves." He dropped the bag to his left.

"But, there's no one on this side, Baba," Choudhuri looked at that side and said.

"You are blind in your head, Khodu. Rub the dust properly on your head and then look. There—that old woman, the two young men and three children sitting there—who are they?"

"Where?"

"Rub some more. Those who rise from their graves cannot be seen with the eyes but with the head."

Perhaps all of them could see with their heads now…those six corpses sitting on the edge of the graveyard. Some were frightened, but with Khodu Baba around, why fear? So they kept sitting there, even though they were scared.

Baba told them, "You too are living only as much as you can in your speculation. Tell me, is that right or wrong?"

"Absolutely correct, Baba, absolutely right."

"Dear Khodus, corpses come alive if they are loved."

"Yes, Baba," the pale-faced woman, who had been given the jar of pure honey, said. "Haji Hakim had told me, lick honey, dear lady, and you'll start living."

Some young men from this side summoned the courage to go and sit over there, near the graveyard. "*Shabash!* Always live like this—mixing well with each other. And share everything and then eat."

When it was nearly dark, Choudhuri wanted to send a man to get a lantern and light it.

"No," Baba stopped him, "except a human being, have you seen any living creature igniting a light, Khodu?"

Baba looked at the sky, "Look up, there are so many lights. Now you should all go." He addressed everyone and said, "Hak…! Hak…!"

To surrender to himself, he closed his eyes even before he lay down.

Rakha Choudhuri followed everybody else towards his hut. He saw the band-master walking hand-in-hand with his wife. He began to think, 'No wonder, *sala*, when he plays his band, the sound reaches the skies!—Ramcharan's wife is not an item to be eaten—even if she were, she was just not getting into my grip. Shall I eat Ramcharan?' He told himself, 'Throw her out of your heart—but then I can throw her out only when she first steps into my heart—*saali!*' Then the face of Bebe Bashiran's widowed daughter loomed before his eyes—so simple and so humble. 'Why don't I ask Bebe for her hand? She'll set an example for me to pray and fast. I shall become a better person. So what if she's forty? After all, I too have fifty years behind me,' he thought very seriously. But on one condition—even if it's just pretence—if the widow has to win my heart, she too will have to say no to me like Ramcharan's wife. "Hak!..." He cried out spontaneously.

The next day, again, many people came over to Baba's *chabootra*.

"*Ree,* Shaidan!" Hirni saw her neighbour walking ahead of her and walked hastily to catch up with her. "Were you also coming towards Baba's *maqbara*? You should have called out to me as well."

"Dust be in your mouth! Why *maqbara*? Call it Baba's *chabootra*," she paused and looked at the *chabootra*, "though it does look like a tomb."

"I tell you, Shaidan, you know, these fakirs—they are really people from another world." Hirni's husband often said, "My wife wins one's heart by talking so jubilantly."

"Even after they die, they get up shaking the dust off their clothes. And if they wish to die, they go in whatever direction they desire and start breathing their last—what?"

As they reached Khodu Baba, they stood still and astonished.

Innumerable hornets formed a flying roof hovering over Baba's head. "Don't be scared, Khodus, they don't sting," Baba smiled peacefully. "Like you and me, they are happy while they are buzzing away."

In a short while, the hornets' canopy moved further, flying ahead from above Baba's head. And people slowly settled below the inclining *chabootra* near the edge of the graveyard. Khodu Baba recognised many of the corpses. "*Arre*, why are you all sitting stuffed at this end? Some can make space over there and sit with those people."

Baba and Choudhuri's eyes met each other, "Why, Choudhuri? Are you doing well?" Without waiting for his response, he added, "How can you be doing well when you live alone under such a huge roof? What alternative do you have? Tossing and turning in the grave, he keeps moving his body everywhere!"

"We sleep so well in our graves, totally oblivious of the world."

Baba looked at the fellow who spoke up. "But I was talking to Choudhuri, you don't have any space to turn sides."

"I have decided, Baba," Choudhuri began saying, "I shall get married next month."

"Only such a person can marry you, Choudhuri, who is willing to drown in the music of your nose."

"There may be no luck here as well," it occurred to Choudhuri. Tomorrow, as soon as the sun rises, he decides, he'll reach Bashiran's *jhuggi* with hot *jalebis* in his hands. She's sure to melt with a little sweet talk! As for her widowed daughter, Sitara, poor thing, she's gentle as a cow. It won't matter to her, how he speaks, through the nose, or left or right ear! After their marriage, he'll bring Bebe Bashiran to his own dwelling. What'll she do alone in her *jhuggi*—he thought—it's such an inopportune *jhuggi*. He'll sell it along with all the things in it—when he estimated the cost of that *jhuggi*, he forgot all about the widowed daughter—fifty over five hundred, not less than fifty over two—suddenly his eyes collided with Khodu Baba's and he felt that Baba had seen through him. And he immediately decided that whatever he got from the sale of Bebe Bashiran's *jhuggi*, he'd spend every paisa in building Baba's first-class tomb on this very *chabootra*. He'll use marble as the pillow over the grave on which he'll engrave flattering verses on Baba, written by his poet-friend Suraj Narayan Zakhmi—he smiled as he made this plan, and Baba who observed him throughout, smiled too as though both of them had thought the same thing simultaneously.

Pandit Muralidhar too had come to pay his homage to Khodu Baba that day. The Pandit had grabbed three *jhuggi*s; he had combined two *jhuggi*s into one and ran his business of preaching there, and in the third *jhuggi*, he himself lived. By his side sat a man with a white moustache and a bald head; he had never seen him before. He smiled and asked him, "Why, Bade Bhaiyya! Are you from amongst our *jhuggi*s?" He pointed towards the graveyard, "Are you from there?" Some strange cheerful sounds rose from the throat of the man with the white moustache and the Pandit, surprised, pulled away from him. Khodu Baba had heard the Pandit's question and had sensed his nervousness. He identified him as a Pandit when he saw his *choti* and *tilak*, "Pandit Khodu, when the path of knowledge creates a distance between us and the other, we should get onto the path of blind faith. What do you say?"

"Yes, Baba!" Baba's charisma started capturing the mind and soul of the Pandit. As though announcing his faith in Baba, loosening his tight *choti* and folding his hands, he said, "I feel so pleased to hear you."

"Hak...!" Khodu Baba sat up straight and alert, "Do you take me to be an entertainer, Khodu? I am not speaking to please you. Try and understand me and feel me."

The Pandit's face fell.

"Open your folded hands, Pandit Khodu, all right, tell me," he began asking him, "is your simple mother who gave you birth greater or are you, with your long *choti*, superior?"

"My mother, compassionate one."

"In the same way, your simple straightforward talk is superior than the delusion created by your pretentious knowledge as a Pandit. Let me tell you a simple story, just to show how deep are the words that may seem superficial."

"Wahun, wahun!" Choudhuri's chowkidar dog came running this way, "Wait, Baba, let me sit down, then you can start telling the story."

"*Haanh*, come Khodu, sit down and listen carefully. This is the story of your breed." Baba ran his eyes over everybody and paused a little to collect his story together. "Hak—k! Hak—k! Listen. There was a small dog in a very big city, a dog who wandered on the city's roads, lost..."

"Wahun!" Bandhu began to bark, "Who told you this story of mine, Baba?"

"*Arre*, quiet!" The Pandit was getting angry and his hand moved involuntarily to tighten his *choti*, "If you want to hear the story, be peaceful."

"Hak!" Khodu Baba gave a push to his story which was getting interrupted, "The poor dog was a stray dog. Had he been a pet, he would have been catching the ball thrown by his master again and again and he'd be having bread, butter and meat every day. Not just this, in case of a quarrel between the master and his wife, he'd get a place in the wife's bed for kissing and petting..."

"Wahun!" Bandhu could not control himself, "You are absolutely right, Baba."

"*Arre*, again? If you care for your life, Bandhu, don't interrupt." This time, the Pandit tightened his *choti* so fiercely that Bandhu could not help releasing a scream.

"Even our own Bade Maulvi is overawed by the Pandit's *choti*!"

"Hak—k! Listen. One who has no name gets many names, or then there is this one Khodu. So that stray dog acquired whatever name that was given to him by whoever. In the butcher's street, Khodu was called Dulla. Here, he'd keep an eye on the crows and vultures sometimes for this shop and at times, for the other. In return, the butchers threw at him some bones and some useless shreds of meat. But once he detected in the eyes of the butchers how they measured his neck so that his meat could be mixed with that of the goats to be passed over to the customers. Indeed, after that, he felt too scared to go that side. Hak!" Khodu Baba paused for a moment before he went ahead with the story. "And then? Then in one of the residential areas, he struck a deal with a pet bitch..."

Shaidan and Hirni were surprised and happy, and they helplessly rang out like copper bells.

"That bitch called our Khodu 'Wahun' with such style and love!"

"Wahun?" Bandhu interrupted him again. "That's no name!"

"My dear Bhai," Khodu Baba answered, "after all, the bitch did not know any English to call him Tommy or Tiger. She would address him straight and direct, in her own authentic language. She belonged to a cloth merchant and like her master, she ate only roti, vegetables and fruit, and she drank plain and clean water; in fact, she even participated in the *Hari-kirtan* of *kothi-wallahs*!"

"This is really very strange, Baba," the Pandit was very pleased.

"Listen, here Khodu Wahun was in the seventh heaven. As soon as the evening deepened, he'd steal his way to the *kothi*, jump over the wall and reach his beloved in a very sly manner. Nobody knows who cast an evil eye over them and the bitch suddenly passed away without any cause...!"

"Wahun...!" Now, Bandhu had started to think more deeply about the bitch. "This is not possible. There has to be a cause."

"Yes, there must be, but I have no knowledge of it. After losing the name given to him by his beloved, Khodu roamed about aimlessly on the roads of the city. He'd eat if he could find something, or else he'd say 'Allah-Allah' and remain flat on the ground wherever he'd be...!"

Just then, Bandhu sighted a bitch in the graveyard. He sprang in her direction, leaving everything. Everyone's eyes ran after him but just as he reached closer to the bitch, he turned to run back, barking loudly. "Wahun! She's our very own Chhabili," he said, gathering himself together, "the same one who died over three months ago!"

"What's there to be scared about?" Baba laughed, "She may not have found any space to settle. The poor thing has come back."

Bandhu looked at the graveyard. After hesitating a little, he quickly went that side again.

"Your story, Baba?"

"The story goes on. Khodu dragged on for three-four months somehow, but without eating, how could he stand on his four legs? Nobody had any time to even glance at him. He moved around trying to hide himself, because he knew that in big cities, stray dogs are shot dead!"

"And then?"

"Then whatever happened, should have happened much earlier. One day, Wahun..."

"But now Khodu had no name."

"Yes, now Khodu remained a Khodu. That's why when he dropped dead in the market one day; nobody knew who had died. He remained lying there for many days in that crowded market. Nobody could see him. He could be seen only if he had been someone..."

"But, Baba," Bandhu and Chhabili had, during this short while, got together. They sat on the edge of the graveyard, with their legs entangled with each other's. "Aren't the poor dogs human?"

"Yes, Bandhu, if someone thinks about it that way, sure they are." Instead of Baba, it was the Pandit who answered.

"But someone has to make an effort to understand this," said the man with the white moustache from the Pandit's side. "We are humans, but we crave to be considered by someone as their pets."

In the meantime, something strange seemed to have happened internally to Baba suddenly. He became detached from everyone and with his eyes closed, he began to chant, Hak...k, Hak...k! All those present watched him in silence for some time and then they stood up to leave.

Choudhuri shouted at Bandhu when he found him and Chhabili stuck to each other, "*Arre*, get up, is this the time for love-making or *chowkidari*?"

The next day too, at the same time, many people gathered near Khodu Baba's *chabootra*.

"Baba, yesterday's story of yours remained incomplete!" The Pandit was present today as well.

"Stories are always incomplete," Khodu Baba said, "because they belong to the people who say they'll be coming back soon, but never come back. And while we are forever waiting for them, some other people come back..."

"I do not understand, Baba," the speaker was a vegetable vendor and temperamentally rather bitter. That's why he was called *karela*—bitter gourd. "My vegetables begin to stink in a day. Your Wahun's corpse was left in a crowded market for so long. How come nobody got the stink?"

"In a crowded place, hundreds of stinks merge into one another, Khodu. Who knows what stink comes from which source?" Baba sighted Bandhu just as he was completing his conversation. Bandhu sat with a sad face, away from everyone, facing the grave. "Your dead lady has not come today?"

"No, Baba, don't know why."

"Maybe she's not well?"

"You talk very strangely, Baba. All illness is shed after one's death."

"If one can live after death, why can't one be ill after dying?"

As he looked around, Baba spotted a very attractive, rather grubby-looking girl. He paused to look at her goat which was busy moving its jaws in spite of an empty mouth.

"This is my goat Bano, Baba," she said. "She's very naughty. I've brought her along so she becomes wiser after listening to you."

Baba was about to respond to her when a toothless old woman came and stood in front of her. Her dry and brown face was crisscrossed with innumerable wrinkles and appeared like a piece of land hit by an earthquake, cracked and tearing all over.

"I am always suffering from fever."

"Which fever?" Baba asked the old woman and then, as if speaking to himself, he mumbled, "Oh, okay, an all-time fever!"

The old woman opened the knot tied to the *pallu* of her saree. "I managed to get these tablets from Khairati Dawakhana but the *daktar* says you must have good food." She took a small packet out of the opened knot and showed him the tablets.

It was as if the waters of a well rose and spilled over, flowing over the drought-stricken earth. "Do you have anyone of your own, Ma?"

The Pandit told Baba that the poor woman only had herself.

"That too is hardly her own, Khodu."

Baba gestured to the girl with the goat to come closer. She, with her goat behind her, came running towards him.

"Will you agree to what I say, Khodu?"

"Yes, Khodu Baba, whatever you say. Only don't ask me to get married."

"Why?" Baba asked, feeling anxious.

"What do you mean, 'why?' The man will snatch me from myself and also take my goat."

"No, if you can give your goat's milk for this Khodu Ma to drink every day, then our Khuda will send a special nawab bridegroom for you."

"Then please tell your Khuda, Baba, to send not one but two nawabs. If one turns out to be evil, I'll have the other one. Come, Bhaiyya, come and take one *paiyya* milk every day!"

As she stepped aside, the Pandit asked, "Baba, and then your Wahun remained on the street of the city?"

"Yes, but one day, not able to tolerate his own stink, he got up while dead, and moved in the direction outside the city so that he could locate soft earth to dig a pit and lie down in it, and then spread the soil over himself."

Bandhu recalled something and stood up, "Baba, did you dig a pit in the backyard of Choudhuri's *jhuggi*?"

"Yes, Khodu, why? That night when I slept there, I woke up very early in the morning. Outside, I sighted a spade and couldn't restrain myself from digging. One person can lie in that pit very comfortably."

"But which person, Baba?"

"Any…anyone. Even your Khodu Choudhuri. I thought he may wander around needlessly when the time comes. After all, he has obliged me by doing so much; I too needed to do something for him."

Rakha Choudhuri started laughing loudly, out of nervousness.

"Did Wahun succeed in his efforts to get out of the city?" the Pandit asked Baba.

"Initially, in his efforts to get out of the city, Wahun got further into the city; and then later… One day, as he wandered inside the city, he found himself outside it. But of what use was that? Wherever he tried to dig the earth with his paws, the owner of that land would turn up and terrorise him with his stick." After pausing for a while, Baba continued with his narration, "People have put their labels on almost the entire land. There's not even a single foot of land that remains in the name of God."

"What trouble did Khuda get into that he had to sell all his land to heartless people?"

"Don't know. But it must be really pressing, or he would have kept back half, or at least one fourth, in his own name." God knows what got into Baba then. He used his arms as a dog's frontal legs, got on his knees and took a round of the entire platform of the *chabootra*.

"Maaa…aaa…!"

"Quiet!" The beautiful girl slapped the goat on her face—"That's why I don't take you along."

"Wahun, wahun…!" Bandhu addressed Baba, "What drama are you enacting? Complete your story, Baba."

"The rest of the story…" Baba began, "That son of a dog ran from one *basti* to another and in every colony, he would be beaten up. For many a year, he scurried around here and there and completely forgot he was in fact dead, and that he is actually alive only in his forgetfulness." Baba's voice became faint as it drowned in his own inner floods. "But as he wondered from place to place, wherever he got a chance to sit peacefully on raw soft earth, he'd brighten up and he'd start frantically digging up the earth with his paws, not knowing why he was doing so…" Baba rested his hand on a little cavity and gazed at the small nook, which he had created, perhaps by scratching the surface with his nails.

"*Arre*, Baba, you know what?" A young vagabond couldn't keep his mouth shut, "That son of a dog is none other than you!"

"Does Baba look like the son of a dog to you?"

"When you have to face a mountain of suffering, even the son of a dog can look like a man."

"Wahun…wahu…wa…!"

"Maaa…aaa…!"

"Hak…k! Hak…k! Hak! Hak!"

This morning, Kauran Tai was to bring roti for Khodu Baba at the *chabootra*. At the break of dawn, she'd leave her *jhuggi* to sweep and mop in ten different houses. And in some house or the other, she'd fill her stomach with rotis as well as the abuses hurled at her. At the end of the day, after finishing all her work, she returned to her *jhuggi*, lit her little earthen lamp and dropped as if dead on her string cot.

Yesterday, she said to Baba, "I'll leave some roti here before going for work. Eat it whenever you are hungry."

Khodu Baba wondered why Tai was taking so long to come. Should he go himself to her *jhuggi* to find out? Just then, he saw Bandhu running towards the *chabootra*. He had a roti wrapped in a newspaper in his mouth which he dropped in front of Baba and taking a quick breath, he said, "Baba, Tai has *vomited* blood—Wahu—I just chanced to go to her *jhuggi* when she said, 'I have cooked roti for Baba but do not have the strength to walk. Go, give it to him and convey my Ram-Ram to the God's man'."

"God have mercy on her," Khodu Baba took the roti in his hands. Tai had carefully spread some chutney on the roti.

"Hak!"

"Wahun—she's a very good woman, Baba, and very sad." Bandhu wanted to keep barking loudly, "What's the use of your being such a great fakir if you cannot rid her of her suffering? Wahun!"

"Only simple and ordinary people can be of some use," Khodu Baba rolled up the roti, took a mouthful and began to eat. "The rascal of a fakir is worried about himself, you stupid Khodu!"

"Wahun! See, either you call me stupid or just Khodu!"

"Both mean the same, stupid!" Baba laughed out, "Take care of Khodu Tai."

"I take care of everyone. But then how many can I take care of? Each one's life is on tenterhooks!" Bandhu started telling Baba about the other people of the *jhopadpatti*.

"That old man whom you gave Badhwa Chamar's shoes, is hiccupping his end since last night. He's lying down with his shoes on his feet and tells his son repeatedly, 'Send me off with my shoes on or else I'll come back as a ghost." Bandhu was ready with a question for Baba, "Aren't you scared alone at night here in the vacant graveyard, Baba?"

"Scared of whom?"

"Of ghosts, Baba, who else?"

"You too are not scared of ghosts, Khodu.'

"No, Baba, I am very scared."

"Then why..."

Bandhu looked into Baba's eyes and despite himself, he started barking.

"You'll remain stupid, Khodu."

"No, Baba, you are not a ghost, and even if you are, how can one be scared of you? You are our very own Baba! Do you know, Baba..." he suddenly recalled something and said, "Yesterday, Uchat Seth—he's the poorest here, that's why Abdul Chacha calls him Uchat Seth jokingly—he has taken his *jhuggi* on rent from Abdul Chacha but he never pays up the rent. Uchat Seth too was here to listen to you, last evening. When he went back from here, he sat at his *jhuggi*'s door and gulped down the complete half-bottle of *desi* liquor and persuaded me to sit with him. And then he started talking, 'Listen, Khodu, that story Baba was telling—of the son of a dog—do you know who that is? Me...I am that same son of a dog! Look at me.' And Baba, he too, just like you, rested his hands on the ground and started to bark so well that as I attuned my barking with his, I could clearly hear his bark. A dog who is not heard distinctly is no dog." Bandhu began barking loudly to get rid of his own embarrassment. Baba checked him, "Don't be so loud."

"All right. Uchat Singh says, all of us are our own ghosts. Because we cannot tolerate our stench after dying, we stand up on our four legs. You may not believe it, Baba, he pressurised his memory and has actually been able to tell me the date of his death. He's a very sad man. Gets drunk to forget his suffering but after drinking, he seems to recall his suffering all the more intensely." The dog's wahun-wahun became louder again with grief and anger. "Last year, his wife died of—what do you call that disease—syphilis. He was dead drunk when he told me all this. 'How could I weep over my wife's death?', he said, 'I myself died four years ago, the very day when I took my wife to the tourist who had asked for a healthy, well-built woman. I persuaded my wife, dressed her up attractively, took her to him, telling her, *What more do you want, if this gets you money in the house?'* And then, Baba, he started crying, and he asked me 'Do I not look like my ghost?' I looked at him batting my eyelids. At times, all of him appeared clearly before my eyes, but many times, on his entire face, there'd be just his nose, or just the mouth or just eyes. I ran away from there, frightened." To get back in control, Bandhu barked rapidly several times, meaninglessly.

"Wahun! Why do you restrain yourself from eating the *roti*?" he asked Baba. "You don't eat your bellyful, and what you eat is as little as my pretence of *chowkidari*. Shall I confide in you? I am not content with just Rakha Choudhuri's two rotis and am always on the lookout for something to steal from every *jhuggi*. Moreover, now I'll have to work harder for the sake of Chhabili, too. Where has Chhabili disappeared for the last two days, Baba? I think the news about her death was wrong. She must have eloped with some male friend of hers. She probably came here after quarrelling with him and now that she's cooled off, she's probably gone back to him. She uses me merely to get some respectability—that's all. If she is dead, it would have been better for her to remain lying down as dead. Ha…ha...ha." Expressing his anger, Bandhu suddenly broke into laughter. "Wahun, wahun!"

"What's there to laugh about, Khodu?"

"There is, Baba. I just thought of Ramcharan's wife." Bandhu paused to laugh. "Last night, Ramcharan's wife ran away with Janglu, the milkman. Rakha Choudhuri had his eye on her, Baba. When I went to Choudhuri's this morning, he showered abuses and hurled stones at me without any reason. I too reacted and told him off, uninhibitedly. He cooled off then and asked for forgiveness and asked me, 'Am I worse than Janglu, Bandhu? Tell me, truthfully.' What could I tell him? Today, he has gone to Bebe Bashiran, dressed in new clothes and with a basketful of *jalebis*."

"Ha...ha...ha...ha!" Khodu Baba laughed heartily.

"Always laugh heartily like this, Baba," Bandhu wagged his tail rapidly in happiness, "I like you very much this way." Bandhu saw right in front, under the keekar tree, a black cobra, half inside his hole and half out, shaking and hissing with joy, looking at Baba.

"Why do you hold your breath and recoil to see him, Khodu? He's a good friend." Baba stuffed his mouth with the last bit of the *roti* and stood up. "Come, let's go and see Tai. We'll have water there."

Terrified, Bandhu did not give any answer, turned quickly and ran ahead of Baba.

"Slow down, Khodu. Walk along with me."

"Seeing your good friend truly took my life away."

"And yet you are moving around. Hak…!"

Bandhu turned his head and estimated the distance from the keekar tree and halted as he recalled something. "There is a very virtuous Christian lady in our *jhopadpatti*, Baba—Rosy Mother. In the evenings, she runs her business. She'll come to see you sometime in the morning, tomorrow."

"What business does she do?"

"Selling the body."

Bandhu turned his head with the intention of running ahead of Baba.

"Slow…!"

"I can't walk slowly, Baba," Bandhu answered. "You come slowly, I'll go tell Tai."

The next day, Rosy Mother came to Baba's *chabootra*. She took out two apples from her bag and offered them to Baba. Baba took them in his hands and then returned them to her. "Give these apples to Khodu Tai on your way back."

"Who's Khodu Tai?" Mother asked with a laugh. "Oh, all right, our Kauran Tai. No problem…that shall be done." Then, she took a bottle of English wine from her bag, "Kauran Tai will not take this."

"Hak…k..!" Baba's face reddened with anger.

Mother put the bottle back into the bag promptly and despite getting a little scared, she pumped up a sort of anger in her voice and complained, "What do you think…do I like to get into bad business? If I don't do such business, what do I do? You are Khuda's man, Baba, there's nothing to hide from you." She started to speak freely, "Just think, at my age, should I be offering my body to a customer or to God Almighty? Tell me, Baba. At times, while in the arms of a strong young customer, I think of my dead son and start crying." There was both strength and a demand in her tone. "When I myself hate myself, then why do you loathe me, Baba?"

Mother's unhesitant confession melted Baba, "Tell me, what do you want from me?"

"What would I want? I hear that the dead return on your calling," Mother's eyes were flooded with tears. "Please get my Vicky to meet me...just once!"

Khodu Baba felt that the mother's heart throbbed in his own chest, "I'll do so! Hak...! I'll surely do that."

Mother wondered why Khodu Baba will do so, "My Vicky died exactly one year ago, Baba."

"So what, Mother? When a poor man dies, he is not delivered from life."

This evening, almost everyone from the *jhopadpatti* had gathered at Baba's *chabootra*. They came and sat not just on this side of the graveyard but also on the other side, covering the entire edge of the graveyard. Who knows, the dead from the graveyard could very well have made space for themselves to sit there.

As on the first day, Khodu Baba lay reclined, resting his back against the pillow of bricks on his *chabootra*, his eyes wide open, stuck into the skies; it was as if he had come out of his grave and had dropped there itself in the dust and had reached the skies in quest for himself. Everyone sang praises of Baba and they were alert that in a few moments when they hear his usual "Hak," they will turn their attention to him.

To see Baba totally immersed in himself, like this, Pandit Muralidhar opened all the knots of his *choti*, in utter devotion. "I have seen many a mahatma and many a fakir, Choudhuri," he sat beside Rakha Choudhuri, "but our Baba is unbeatable—he has reached the beyond."

"That is why he is taking so long to return." Rakha Choudhuri was restless; why was Khodu Baba not coming back from the skies?

"Listen," the Pandit nudged Choudhuri, "someone laughed."

"So what, Pandit? Should one have you perform puja before laughing?"

"No, Choudhuri," in order to emphasise his point, the Pandit lowered his voice. "I don't mean anyone from this side. Listen again, someone laughed. I'm talking of people from that side," he pointed towards the graveyard.

"How does it matter?" Choudhuri mimicked Baba's style, "Someone from here or from there… Khuda's people are all the same!"

"See, Baba has begun to stir."

Choudhuri looked at Baba immediately, "Oh, that's just a fly moving over Baba's face." He got up from his place and came closer to Baba to whisk the fly away. "Oh, fools!" Surprised, everyone looked at him, "Where is Baba?"

"Who's lying here in front of us?" the Pandit asked.

"Baba has already left us."

"Wahun! Wahun!" Bandhu came and stood close to Choudhuri and barked, "Wahun!"

"Don't be afraid," the Pandit reassured people when they got up, looking scared, "he will come back from wherever he's gone." He thought he heard the laughter of several corpses then. And he was shaken, "Look carefully, Choudhuri, has Baba passed away?"

"Yes, Shaidan," Hirni was telling her neighbour, "pirs and fakirs are not actually present where they are…eh? Who knows where they reach, these God's men, after leaving their bodies..." She was carried away by her words as people got more and more attentive. "I am not comparing myself with Baba. Baba is up there, and I remain a great fool, eh? Many times have I felt, while my life is stuck here in Choudhuri's *jhopadpatti*, I am playing *addi-tappa* in my mother's courtyard, eh? Tell me then, where am I? If I so desire, where do I look for myself...eh?"

"Wahun!" Bandhu was barking with his long face towards everyone, "Keep sitting. Wahun!"

"I tell you, Hirni," Shaidan was saying, "when Baba came here wandering about here and there, who knows, where he was actually lying like this?"

"Wahun!" Bandhu came and stood on the *chabootra* to address everyone, "Earlier, Baba was roaming around in search of a place to settle. Wahun, now where does he have to go—Wahun—now he has settled here forever. Wahun, Wahun!"

"Hak—k!"

(Translated from the Urdu by Sukrita Paul Kumar)

MANNEQUINS

Gauri Shankar Raina

It was late evening and time to close the showroom. The lights were in the process of being switched off. Vinod Pandita, a trusted employee who was responsible for turning off the switches, was engaged in this closing ritual. With him turning off one switch after another, the patches covered by the respective lamps all over the showroom were turning grey if not entirely dark. The shelves stocking *zari, banarsi*, silk and other types and sub-types of sarees were turning grey in succession, almost in a staccato rhythm. The strategically placed row of lamps over the full-size mirror, in front of which the customers—mostly females, dressed in their favourite sarees, would preen around before buying them up—had been put out, making the mirror look grey but strangely translucent and mysterious.

During the hectic business hours, it was Ram Kishan, the salesman, who would partially drape himself in a saree, or place the *pallu* of a saree on a woman's shoulders to show her how cool it looked on the wannabe customer. "How good it looks on you, Madam!" he was used to repeating the expression, parrot-like, as he must have used it umpteen times to lure the customer into buying it. That was his 'trade-talk' and he had used it well all these years.

It was the close of day for Ram Kishan now and he had begun his homeward journey on his old, rickety bicycle. The other salesmen too had left for their homes. Only Vinod Pandita, engaged in the process of putting out the lights, was still busy. But, no, Lalaji was there too, looking after this ritual of closure. He was as usual shadowed by his servant-cum-caretaker Babu Lal, whose job was to look after Lalaji's personal needs, like offering him a *paan* with *geeli supari* every two hours, arranging for his lunch, supplying him with glassfuls of tea every now and then, locking the doors and shutters of the establishment and then handing over the bunch of keys to him after the operation was over. Sometimes, he would sit with the driver on the front seat and get off at a spot close to his living quarters from where he would walk home.

But today, Lalaji had not yet left. Babu Lal had just handed him his last glass of sugarless tea. Lalaji did not seem to be in a hurry. He drank the cardamom-flavoured tea sip by sip. Then, as usual, he talked to his son who managed another one of his showrooms at Rajouri Garden and gave him business tips. The driver had driven the car to the gate and was waiting for the master to step out.

Besides other duties in this showroom-cum-office, Vinod Pandita was given the task of 'window dressing.' This meant that he had to drape the mannequins in bridal dresses, complete with fine trousseaus and matching jewellery, and then place them comfortably in the show windows facing the street. This was done to lure stray shoppers into buying the exhibited products. Mannequins, mute but communicative, lifeless and yet exuding angelic charm, did attract lots of customers.

"You must come early tomorrow," Lalaji ordered. Lolling on a heavily-padded cushion, he was used to keeping a sharp eye on the goings-on.

"Yes...Sir," Vinod Pandita mumbled.

"You have to go to Karol Bagh tomorrow and buy a new mannequin. Due to the heat, the earlier ones have shed their colours. It's your task to get a new one and exhibit it in the appropriate show window."

Vinod Pandita, who had by now mastered the task of dressing up life-sized female frames made of clay and plaster and putting them up as seductive mannequins, wondered whether these exhibits really attracted customers. But he never raised this indiscreet question. He never countered Lalaji even when he thought that Lalaji was not right. In his heart of hearts, he respected Lalaji. For, when he had migrated from Jammu to Delhi, impelled by a host of unfavourable circumstances, it was Lalaji who had looked after him in Delhi. He gave him a job in the showroom and arranged a room for him to live in. He offered him the same salary he used to give his old and experienced *munshi* whom he had replaced. Without Lalaji's generosity, what could he have done in an alien and inhospitable city like Delhi?

Had Vinod Pandita's wife Prabha received proper treatment in Jammu, he would not have left that city. He would have continued to live there in some rented accommodation or shifted to his brother's small tenement in the migrant's colony at Muthi. But Prabha's illness had forced him to wander from city to city. From Jammu, he had to shift to Chandigarh to get her treated at PGI and from there, to Delhi to seek refuge at AIIMS. Thus, he had reached Delhi step by step, almost crossing a string of hurdles, to land up at the place of his final tryst with destiny. He had to take her to AIIMS every month for a check-up. And by God's grace, she was alive and recuperating.

"Lalaji, I'll come early tomorrow. After finishing the pending work here, I'll rush to Karol Bagh. Even otherwise, shops don't open before eleven at Karol Bagh."

"That'll be fine," Lalaji said. He was shutting his briefcase, which signified that the day had finally come to a close for him. Vinod Pandita then paid respectful obeisance to Lalaji and walked towards Ring Road to head home.

Ring Road, the long, unending, girdle-like road sliced the city somewhere in the middle. Late evening was merging with the darkness of the night. The heavy daytime traffic had slowed down and ghost-like trucks had emerged on the roads. At night, the trucks with their glaring headlights looked like ogres moving around the city.

The fruit sellers at the edge of Lajpat Nagar were downing their shutters. Only stray vendors seemed willing to dispose off the remaining stock at throwaway prices. Vinod Pandita saw one such fruit seller hawking apples on a wheelbarrow and decided to buy some for his ailing wife. At this instant, he could not help visualise his own small apple orchard at Harwan, which produced the Ambri variety of apples. When they had cultivated the orchard themselves, Prabha never ate apples. Even later, when they gave out the orchard on contract and the contractor sent them a couple of boxes containing apples as a friendly gesture, Prabha never displayed keenness for taking those apples. So why this liking for apples now?

Vinod Pandita took an apple in his hand and, connoisseur-like, examined it. Then, he asked the seller, "What price?"

"Sixty rupees a kilo. But you can take it for fifty."

"Are these from Kashmir?"

"Yes. Very sweet."

Vinod Pandita knew these were not from Kashmir—neither from Harwan.

"*Arre bhai*, these are Himachali apples. How about forty rupees a kilo?"

"Babuji, pay only hundred rupees for the whole lot," the fruit seller offered.

"This is hardly two kilos. Eighty rupees will be enough for them."

"*Theek hai*," the fruit seller made the final gesture of bargain.

Carrying the apples in a polythene bag, Vinod crossed Ring Road and entered the lane leading to Amar Colony. From a distance, he could see a string of pale-looking two-storey houses symmetrically arranged in a row. These were given to refugee families after Partition and these families had later on made their additions and alterations to extend the living space in them. It was in a single *barsati* room on the roof of one of these houses where Vinod Pandita had set up his home. It was a small room with an attached kitchen and some open space in front of it. When Prabha was free from household chores, she would sit in this balcony-like patch of space and daydream.

Vinod Pandita pressed the locally improvised doorbell hanging from a wire. Prabha opened the door.

"Are you fine? Did you take your medicines on time?" Vinod asked.

"Yes," Prabha replied. "Did you ring up Rakesh?"

"I plain forgot. I was too busy in the showroom," Vinod replied apologetically. "I promise I'll ring up Rakesh tomorrow."

"This is why I've been insisting that we should have a phone at home."

"For that, we need lots of identification papers—identity card, residence proof and what not," Vinod said.

"After all, Rakesh is our only child," Prabha was tearful. "He is studying so far away in Pune. If we don't keep track of his welfare, then who will?"

"I've talked to Lalaji about it," Vinod replied. "He has promised to get me a mobile."

"Poor boy, in the summer he had to be with us for three months to look after me during my illness. When will he complete his course?"

"He's a bright boy," Vinod assured her. "He won't lag behind. He will complete his course and become a good engineer. Don't worry. You take care of your health."

Both were lost in thought about their son and his future prospects.

"Freshen up. I'll bring some food for you," Prabha said, snapping out of her reverie.

"Don't bother," Vinod said. "You shouldn't exert yourself much. I'll get the food from the kitchen myself... Yes, wake me up early in the morning. I have to be at the showroom rather early and then go to Karol Bagh for work."

"You never take me to Karol Bagh," Prabha remonstrated. "I'm told one gets good stuff there and at reasonable prices."

"You get well. I promise I'll take you there for shopping."

Vinod brought them food from the kitchen in two *thalis*. He ate from one *thali* and helped Prabha to eat from the other. Then he helped her to take her medicine and the two retired for the day.

Karol Bagh was unusually crowded that day. When Vinod Pandita went there the next morning on Lalaji's errand, it took him a considerable time to find the establishment. It was for the first time that he had been sent for this work. He went in and introduced himself. He was a bit nonplussed when the owner of the establishment asked him, "Specification?" He did not understand what it meant.

"What kind of mannequins?" the owner repeated the query.

"The same kind that we have in our showroom," Vinod replied playing safe.

"What kind of mannequins do you have?"

"They are good...but their colour has faded," he said.

"Then go on down. Have a look at what we have in there and decide."

An employee of the establishment led Vinod Pandita to the basement where many mannequins were stored. These were of different sizes and shapes, colours and textures. They were fair, grey and dark, with rosy cheeks and darkish eyebrows, with cleft chins and demure faces. Since most of these human-sized, lifeless figures were kept in standing position, they looked like they were staring at the visitors. If someone could just breathe life into them, they would speak, laugh, display a gamut of ideas and feelings spontaneously. They might have the temerity to ask why they had been confined to this dark, airless basement. Why? Some of the mannequins even looked like human embodiments of divine goddesses like Nishumbhmardini or Tribhuvansundari.

Vinod Pandita recalled that in Harwan's Bhuvaneshwari Temple, when the image of the Goddess was to be installed, the image was brought from Jaipur. Draped in azure vestments, it looked divinely beneficent. At that time, a jet-black snake had appeared on the scene. The snake circumambulated the installed image, drank the offered milk and disappeared. When the villagers, who were witness to the miracle, asked the reason for the divine manifestation, they were given a long discourse by the white-bearded Swamiji, highlighting the sacred nature of Satisar or Kashmir and how it had been the abode of innumerable gods and goddesses in days gone by.

"Which one of these would you like to be packed?" the attendant asked him.

"Oh," Vinod came out of the reverie and tried to re-establish his links with the here-and-now. In this world of lifeless and yet strangely alive mannequins, he looked clueless and crestfallen.

"Which one of these have you selected?" the attendant politely reminded him of the task at hand.

"I'm not able to decide which one will suit our purpose," Vinod replied, wistfully.

"I'll help you, Sir," the attendant said. Then he started listing out the features of some of the mannequins displayed there. "Look here, Sir. This one wearing a dark-coloured saree is made of plaster of Paris. It will suit a jewellery showroom. It's a bit expensive too. You need one for your saree showroom, don't you?"

"Yes."

"Then take this one. It is light in weight and reasonably priced too," the attendant suggested.

"All right. But first let's move out of here."

Vinod Pandita was feeling dizzy in this world of mannequins. He felt as if these lifeless forms would alternatively laugh or cry—all in unison. The cry would pierce the basement roof and reach the heavens. Then the sky would burst out in thunderous lightning. The universe would collapse like a pack of cards. Everything would get buried in the fallen debris. Mannequins, workers, masters, salesmen, passersby, car-owners, rickshaw-pullers, Lalaji, Vinod Pandita—all. The attendant quickly led him out of the basement. He offered him a chair and gave him a glass of water to drink.

"What happened?" the owner of the establishment asked, a bit concerned.

"He felt out of sorts in the basement. So, I brought him upstairs," the attendant explained.

"Must be very hot downstairs," the owner said.

"Sir, you ought to get your BP checked," the attendant suggested out of concern.

"Yes...yes..." Vinod emptied the glass of water and kept it on the counter.

On Vinod Pandita's suggestion, the owner ordered the chosen mannequin to be packed. Two workers held the mannequin in a supine position—one holding its head and another holding its feets—and brought it up from the basement. It was kept on the floor and covered with polythene. Then it was again enveloped in a white, shroud-like cloth. Years ago, the dead body of Vinod's mother was bathed and dressed in white after she died of kidney failure. Spotless white, lucent white. She was also covered in a shroud-like cloth and put on a makeshift stretcher made of bamboo and tied with ropes. That was how her journey to another world had begun.

"How will you carry the mannequin?" the attendant asked after the packing process was finished.

"In an ambulance."

"W...what?" the bewildered attendant asked.

"I mean...in some vehicle," Vinod fumbled for the right answer.

"Hey, load the mannequin in an auto. This gentleman will travel by the same auto and support it if necessary," the owner instructed his staff.

"That will be fine."

"*Jenab,* please pay the auto-driver at your end," the owner made the bargain clear. "It is the customer who has to pay for the carriage."

"Yes..." Vinod nodded his head in agreement.

Vinod saw how the mannequin was loaded into a waiting auto. It was resting in a face-down position, cushioned and then tied with ropes to prevent breakage during the journey. Finally, Vinod was given the relevant papers and the auto-driver was signalled to leave.

There was hectic activity in the showroom when the auto arrived. It turned out that an NRI household had descended on it and was making purchases of sarees for a family wedding that was to take place soon. Ram Kishan, the saree salesman, was displaying sarees of all makes, hues and textures and talking them into buying a large quantity. Groups of corpulently-built and heavily-painted women were haggling for the right prices for their favourite items.

"Didi, this one is very cute," the salesman chortled. "You must buy it."

"No...no...not this one."

"Then that one will be ideal. Look, it suits you perfectly well."

"No, that one...with the greenish embroidery work."

"What choice you have, indeed!" the salesman praised the lady for her impeccable taste in a mock-heroic tone. "But you must have at least half a dozen in your wardrobe. After all, you must wear a new one on every wedding function... You just have to select your favourite ones. I'll send them packed to your Greater Kailash address."

When the buying spree was still on, Vinod returned with the mannequin. It was with some difficulty that he got a worker to accompany him to the auto and unload the cargo. Once the mannequin was brought in and safely ensconced on a pedestal, he sat on a stool relieved and reasonably satisfied.

Soon, Vinod got up to decorate and drape the mannequin which at the time was just a dull, lifeless female figure made of a combination of white clay and plaster of Paris. His job was to transform it into an attractive woman draped in an attractive saree—enticing enough to lure customers into buying it. He set about his work diligently. First, he painted the mannequin's face using appropriate colours for its cheeks, lips, hair and eyelashes. Then he gracefully wrapped a saree around its body. Finally, he embellished it with items of artificial jewellery to make it look like a bride. He knew that when put into the glass-showcase, the mannequin would look so glamorous that customers would find it difficult to resist. Yes, Vinod was capable of breathing life into lifeless mannequins.

Vinod had hardly finished when a fellow worker came and informed him that his wife's condition had suddenly deteriorated, and he must rush home. When he looked out of the glass pane, he saw one of his neighbours—Chopraji—waiting to take him home.

"Vinod Bhai, leave the mannequin and think about your own mannequin at home," Babu Lal told him, sympathising with his plight. A shocked Vinod took prompt permission from Lalaji and rushed home with Chopraji.

A clutch of neighbours and sundry well-wishers had already assembled at the gate of the small two-storey house where the couple lived in a *barsati*. A concerned neighbour was talking to the ambulance services on the phone and instructing its driver to reach the spot promptly. Soon, a black Scorpio stopped in front of the house and out jumped Vinod accompanied by fellow employee Babu Lal and Chopraji, his neighbour. Babu Lal asked the gentleman talking to the ambulance to cancel the order as they had a jeep (provided by Lalaji) to take the patient to the hospital.

Prabha was breathing fitfully and her face had turned wan. Lifting her in their arms, Vinod and Babu Lal brought her down, negotiating the old and narrow stairs deftly. They laid her comfortably on the back seat. While Vinod sat with Prabha, gently holding and massaging her hands, Babu Lal sat with the driver. Leaving the concerned-looking clutch of people, the vehicle sped towards AIIMS.

While a grieving Vinod rubbed Prabha's forehead, Babu Lal tried to console him, "Don't worry, Vinod. Have trust in God. Everything will be all right."

"No, Babu Lal, she may not survive this time," Vinod became overwhelmed with grief. "I've just come from our supplier's establishment where I saw lots of mannequins. I've heard their anguished voices, their frantic calls for liberation. Prabha has not been much different from them. Time has come for her to be released from this bondage of pain and suffering. She will be happier where she is going now—to the land of mannequins. How much she has suffered here! First, she was displaced from her native place. She had to move to Jammu, carrying whatever little of the household, its goods, its ambience, its aroma she could carry with her in those dreadful times. Then in Jammu, where she was struggling to settle down, she broke her leg. And then the bypass surgery happened. Do you think hell has more suffering in store for its inmates? No, I don't think so. We waste a lot of time and money in keeping our lifeless bodies moving. But to what avail? To prolong our miseries?"

"You are talking like a crazy person," Babu Lal admonished Vinod. "Don't lose heart. Bhabhi will get well and soon enough."

Vinod did not care to respond. He kept looking out of the glass window of the jeep, at the fleeting trees, the palatial buildings and the glittering showrooms lined up on both sides of the wide road. He remembered a parable his mother Kakni would often narrate to him. The parable of Dharmaraj. Of Chitragupta. Does the Lord of Death really exist? If he does, what does he look like? Is he capable of relieving people of the hellish suffering they have been going through with not a speck of relief in sight? Vinod kept grappling with these abstruse questions troubling his distraught mind. Meanwhile, the vehicle kept speeding towards its desired destination.

(Translated from the Kashmiri by Pankaj Bhan)

ACROSS THE SHORES

Tarannum Riyaz

Sherry put aside the newspaper and looked outside the window. Beside the window was a picture of her parents from the happy days in which her father stood with his arm around the waist of his wife, fifteen years older to him, with his salt and pepper hair and a rather plump face. He was forty, but did not look younger than his bottle-blonde, slim and smart, fifty-five-year-old wife.

"I had married to have you…or…otherwise…"

After divorcing Papa, her mother had given this answer to all her questions and shook her head in a manner which suggested that Sherry was the one to blame.

"You could have adopted a child, Mamma?" She too would shake her head like her mother.

"No…" Mamma would reply firmly.

"Yeah, or you could have had a test-tube baby…" a recently turned out-of-teenage Sherry would say.

"You mind your own business, okay?" Mamma would reply with a quick, stern look and stiffen her lips in such a manner that Sherry would understand that she no longer wanted to be spoken to.

None of this occurred in a tense way, nor did it ever create any ill will. It took place like a healthy, informative discussion.

Sherry's gaze drifted from the frame outside the window. "Poor Papa, a victim of feminism…and if there were a possibility of a discovery or whatever…then this…oh, my hard-core feminist mother!"

Sherry again looked towards the newspaper that had been lying in front of her for some time.

"There was a possibility. Who knows how many times in the past billions of years the world had been destroyed and recreated at various times? What if I were born centuries later? The world could be like that in the future, where I'd not belong to Papa and remain Mamma's. Then I'd start a new civilisation which would actually be like the old one. In return for that great achievement, I would get…my achievements tattooed on my arms…and my fossils would be preserved in a glacier to be discovered centuries later. Which meant that I, Mamma's daughter, granny's granddaughter, and great-granny's…whatever, were to be lost during a glacier expedition and be discovered much later to have my achievements known. That was a possibility."

Sherry got up and walked towards the window and touched her father's face in the photo, but in a way that her fingers did not come near her mother's face.

"I wonder if I would be allowed to do that in the first place, or…or…it may be deemed a crime…a revolt…or a sin…and… I…no, no… When Papa visited me in the hostel last month, he had asked me to keep away from any disruptive thoughts. But, it is not wrong Papa…if your adventurous daughter is given an opportunity, then you know what she would do."

It happened exactly as Sherry had imagined. Several years passed and nobody noticed the passage of time.

Human beings measure time in terms of decades, centuries and millennia and become content with that. But these units mean no more than the blink of an eye in terms of the universe. A thousand years could pass in the blink of an eye.

A thousand years did pass in the blink of an eye.

Sherry had never thought that the reality would come so close to her imagination.

She opened her eyes at the sound of a bird chirping. A speck of dust went into her eye so she began to rub her eyes with both her hands. After having continued doing that for a while, she completely opened her eyes. There was a duck-like bird flying in the bluish grey sky; it had a beak which was bent at the tip but not as broad as that of a duck. Even the sky looked strange, like everything was under a cloudy shadow yet beautiful and radiant. The bird did not even sound like a duck—like the sound of wood being sawed—but more like a melodious plastic whistle made for children. A smile spread over Sherry's face and she sat up straight. She had never seen such a large bird in flight for a long time. The bird disappeared into tall dense trees at her left and Sherry suddenly looked around. As far as she could see there was a stretch of sand in front of her and the vast blue ocean on her left seemed to be peacefully flowing away somewhere. She looked down at herself; her dress was tattered and her body was covered with sand and mud. This happened in a fraction of a second and a scream escaped her mouth. She remembered that she had been flying over the ocean when some technical problem had occurred in her aircraft. She had to make a crash landing. The shore was far off but she was a good swimmer. She confidently decided to turn her plane towards the shore and jump into the water before it touched down, and did that within seconds. The shore she stood on was not the one she had flown towards nor could she see the aircraft's wreckage anywhere.

She quickly glanced at her wrist, it had a deep wound. The communication device planted beneath her golden-coloured skin was out of function because of her wound. No transmitter on her clothes or body was in working condition. She could hear strange sounds in her head though. Maybe some device implanted in her brain was still working and it would serve her mother to know about her crash and location and she would find her.

She had thought all this in a second and the next second her glance fell on a creature that made her choke in her cry of horror. She covered her mouth with both her hands and stared with eyes wide open. After having visited all countries of the world, she had not come across such a creature in the entire twenty years of her life. Her heart throbbed really fast and tears trickled down her eyes. She sobbed with her hands still on her mouth. She intensely missed home then.

"Mamma, where am I...where are you, Mamma...what is this, Mamma?" she cringed. At that thought the sounds in her brain stopped and she could hear her mother's voice in her head. "We are looking for you, dear...and will soon find you."

"Where am I? I've lost all direction...cannot see you, no video in my brain is in operation...and what is this in front of me?" Sherry winced again and opened her eyes to carefully look at the creature in front of her.

"Till some time back, the micro cameras planted in your eyelids were blurrily projecting the scenes in front of you...but you rubbed your eyes like a little girl and the already water-logged and damaged cameras got completely spoilt. You had landed in the north, both you and the craft fell into water... but, thankfully you are safe. I would have arrived, but cannot figure out your direction. There was a shore in front of you... so far, we have covered every place in the direction you were in, yet do not see any shore...but you don't worry, we'll find you. I'm surprised that we have marked all places on the earth in our paper and virtual maps yet can't find the one you are at... Anyway, don't stress or think too much, we might lose contact if your brain radar gets too loud because there are no artificial magnetic fields at your location...there is no detection of radio waves either, and recharging might become difficult. Don't overburden yourself. We are trying to locate you. Eat some fish for nourishment...you have to survive...and remember you're a brave person...catch fish and stay alive...we will soon..."

"Mamma!?" Tears drained into Sherry's voice. The device in her brain caught sorrow waves and used its reserved energy, so her mother's voice was heard again. "No baby, no...you..."

Mamma's grief-laden voice arose but the conversation broke. The sounds in Sherry's brain came to an end. "Why did this happen? I did not even think anything...how did the battery go off?" She thought, looking at the creature in front of her. "Oh, but I've been constantly thinking...what, what do I do now?"

After losing contact with her mother Sherry became even more scared and felt like shouting with fear. However the shock attack did not let her do that, thinking about how the creature in front would react to it.

The strange creature in front of her did not do anything, just stood and stared at Sherry. It was bizarrely similar to her and strangely different. What was it?

She had seen something like it somewhere. She couldn't remember where. Perhaps she did, yes; she had seen it in a museum that was established three hundred years back. The museum contained specimen of creatures which were extinct since that time and before. That is where she had seen this creature and its lifeless appearance. There was a statue of the mummified creature placed next to it on a pedestal of white stone with two steps. The statue was almost the same height as the specimen; it had two eyes, arms and legs which had prominent muscles. It had thick, long hair on its head and dense, shorter hair grew under its nose. There was longer hair on its chin as well. Its body was covered with thin hair. One foot was placed on the first step while the other was on the second with just toes touching. The script under the statue used to send chills running down Sherry's spine.

"This specimen is no longer in existence. It has gone extinct almost a hundred and fifty years before. The creature was a mortal enemy of the current humankind due to intense jealousy. It created various hurdles in the progress of the community and inflicted atrocities. The creature believed in warfare and fighting which it took pride in. It would go to any length to fulfill its desires."

This story is about a time when the world was surprised by the discovery of science. Sherry had read about it somewhere. Even though it was not a part of her syllabus the subject was considered as important as research, criticism and economics and made compulsory till the last year of her school education.

The strange discovery was that women could conceive children without the intervention of men, through a cell of their own bodies. However, male participation was required to bear male children. This discovery led to the development of a secret mission by feminist organisations. They created an organisation in which every member was required to possess an experience which they could use in times of need and achieve the accomplishment of their mission. This organisation was made up of some very prominent names, which were remembered for centuries to come.

The first name was of Qaara Taaz. She had spent all her life hating men and left no stone unturned in proving them fools through her books. At the age of fifty-five she fell in love with a man twenty years her junior and married him. She became a social recluse after discovering his love for a young girl. An embarrassed Qaara Taaz immediately agreed to join the organisation.

The second name was of Kamma Saati. At one point of time, she was emerging as an active feminist when she fell in love and got married. Her husband had an artificial leg about which he had not told Kamma Saati. She then left him and rejoined the feminist group, accepting its ideals as atonement of her error.

Doctor Budnee was the third prominent member to join the organisation. She was never married, yet was such a strong supporter of women's rights that she was known as a strong hater of "man" kind. She always looked for opportunities to prove that men were happiest being involved in mutual love relationships; which is why such cases were coming up frequently, rather, these cases had become so common that they always were in front of one's eyes. She also propagated that men intensely hated women. Though Doctor Budnee looked very much like a man herself, there was no male employee in her Maternity and Fertility Hospital. She was easily able to find a group of women with similar thoughts.

The fourth member, Advocate Zaazi Ridd, had married her classmate from school with the same profession as hers.

He loved her a lot. However he developed a sense of insecurity on the grounds of her professional competence and began to look for excuses to beat her. Zaazi Ridd broke up with him. She then started a media campaign against domestic violence and violence to women.

Social scientist Reza Beir was the fifth member of the organisation. Through her research by means of media she put all her energies in proving that men were solely responsible for all the bloodshed and warfare; they could bomb any country to feed their greed and ego; and that boys grew up to be violent because they enjoyed violent games from childhood. By chance, if one among them would be born with a woman's kind heart, then he would become a victim of social conditioning and grow up to be like the rest of the men. Keeping in view the situation of this category, it had become necessary to take action in order to protect the future of humankind as men were committed to destroying the world in a number of ways. At times they were looking for ways to blow up an entire continent with a single bomb and at other times they wanted to recreate the conditions of the Big Bang Theory in order to understand how the universe came into being. This crazy idea had greater possibility of leading to the destruction of the universe rather than the desired result. Now they were working on developing a hybrid of man and animals in the name of science and attempting to create new kinds of creatures.

Men considered all others to be their prey and their means of entertainment. They had been playing with lives in the name of science, and would continue to do so. In some places, they would make feelings grow over temperament and in others, make bodies smaller than the original. These dramatists were now going to make a playhouse of the world, from which a lot of industrialists, politicians and scientists would be exempted while the other beings would be an object of their experiments and they would decide their lifestyles and the causes of their death.

These speeches were circulated all over the world through the electronic media. They appealed to people's thoughts and ignited the sparks of rebellion in the minds of the masses. This eased the task of extremist feminists.

These women individually took up the task of campaigning against men all over the world. Once they held a live press conference and urged females to boycott men as they were not essentially required in the world. Unless they became extinct, men would destroy the world, and womankind even before that. In the light of the fact that women were naturally selected as reproducers, men might come up with an alternative to produce offspring, in order to eliminate their rights over the child. Hence, it was important that men be brought to an end.

The impact of these concepts was clearly visible on the conscience of women in the results of public opinion polls and live media debates. Newspapers discussed the conference in depth. A lot of women supported the proposals made at the conference and promoted them, because there were many in different spheres who were of the same opinion.

Time passed and ideas changed. However, during the lifetimes of these five members of the organisation, there was no noticeable change in the proportion of men and women in the census. Thousands of their followers emerged in various parts of the world; over the century the population of their followers grew into millions. There was a sharp decline in the male population of the planet while the female population grew proportionately greater. Keeping this in view, some scientists preserved samples of Y chromosomes and left behind them preparations for the future after having lived their lives. However, the opposition was so strong that by the end of the century, the whole population was exclusively female and there was no trace of a male anywhere. The archives were cleared of everything about them—from descriptions of wars to love stories. Personal pictures and keepsakes were lost with time as emotional attachment and inclination grows weaker and does not last beyond the third or fourth generation. Apart from this, countries no longer fought as they were independent of each other's resources due to technological advancements. Thus, the world moved on towards an undefined and unpredictable future at its usual pace.

Sherry's grandmother had heard it from her grandmother, who was told by her grandmother—interesting stories of the horrendous past that were passed on from one generation to another. These scared the little girls, who would gather courage and curiously ask, "What happened then, Grandma?" Sherry too would ask, and then her grandmother would recount what she had heard being passed from a great-great-grandmother.

"They appeared very much like us, but were larger in size, always restricting our thoughts and ready to devour our bodies. They considered it their right to trouble us," Grandma said as she yawned at the TV screen.

Grandma looked young and healthy with the use of the latest devices and technologies, but was nothing like the traditional grandmother, except for the traditional maternal love she gave which could not be altered by any technological advancement.

"Then?" Sherry would ask turning Grandma's face towards her with soft little fingers and ask, "What else did they do?"

"They would hurt us in all possible ways—mentally and physically. They had hair growing below their noses, which they grew and styled with pride…these would come into their mouths while eating or drinking."

"Eew! Gross…" Sherry said rubbing her nose in disgust.

"Their voices were very different. Like a lion's roar…and their laughter was like the sound of a sea storm. You can say that they were nothing like humans, though they very much looked like them."

That day Grandma was lost in watching TV and Sherry was lost in wonder.

At this moment, standing with stunned eyes and hands clasped over her mouth on an unknown shore, Sherry felt herself shiver. She had just been standing there watching, and then she took a step back as she observed the creature in front of her.

It did have hair below the nose. It was taller than Sherry and had broader shoulders. There was dense dark hair on its jaw line, as well. It had deep, dark eyes that shone bright (Grandma had never mentioned that). Its lips were curved into a soft, slight smile that looked charming (which was strange as it was contrary to its nature). None of Sherry's friends had a smile like that, nor did anyone in her family—so this was a man! Who knew if its strange charm and behaviour were indicators of an attack?

Sherry lost balance and fell into the mud and sand as she thought so, but her eyes remained fixed on the man. He would roar like a lion and torture her now, Sherry thought and considered running away—anywhere, maybe back into the water.

Sherry stared into his eyes to predict his intentions of attack. He looked back at her and smiled. He stepped forward and bent over with an extended arm towards Sherry for her to hold and stand. She did not take his hand but kept on staring at him with her head tilted back. After being bent for a few moments, when Sherry showed no signs of holding his hand or getting up, he held her by the arm and pulled her up on her feet. Sherry let out a stifled shriek. The man said something with a smile. To Sherry's surprise he did not sound like a roaring lion, but like heavy raindrops on earth. His grip was not snare-like, rather firm but friendly—the way Grandma and Mama held her and the way her friends at the institute did. His grip was not like her bulky friend Sata's, whose thin fingers dug into Sherry's flesh when she held her. Sherry had felt no pain while being lifted by the strength of the man's fingers. He led wonderstruck Sherry by her shoulders for a distance and then moved in front of her. Sherry stood for a few moments and observed the light around her; it was neither bright nor dull but very prominent. The sky did not appear to be very distantly high, but as if they were under a low canopy of colour. Sherry shook her head and followed the man looking at the ground. She did so because he seemed to intend no harm and also because she had no other option. They were headed towards the jungle; the man increased his pace after a while. Sherry ran behind him as he did. There was no trace of another being around them.

The jungle was located on a cliff. After having walked a distance, they were on a path that received sunlight only from the sides. It was as if a world existed under the forest roof, which was completely lit yet hidden by a slanted rock. The slanted rock was covered with numerous trees. It was not possible to even see the shore without climbing over the rock. Even then the place was well lit with sun rays bouncing over everything.

They were treading over a muddy track, surrounded by trees from which birds flew across chirping and twittering. Sherry had never seen some of the birds; others she had seen as stuffed models at the museum in the section of extinct species. All the birds had melodious sounds. The paths which emerged from the one that they had been walking on were lined with fruit and flower blossoms. They had come into a valley now. Next, they came across golden fields of ripe grain. There were wooden houses with sloping or flat and round or square roofs with gardens around them. Sherry noticed beasts of burden but there were no vehicles of any sort.

The man walking in front of her kept turning back to ensure that she followed. He would make way for her on narrow or water-logged tracks and move forward after making her cross comfortably.

After a while, they reached an orchard where Sherry saw men and women of all ages. The faces of women here appeared more peaceful from the ones Sherry had seen all her life. The man spoke to another one of his age in a hushed voice. He sounded like the lower tones of a guitar. The second man guffawed at what he was told. Sherry looked at him with amazement. His guffaw was throaty and sounded like a cascading stream of water and appeared to come from the Adam's apple of his well-built neck. Over his toned pelvis—which was covered with animal hide—his bare chest swelled up further. A girl of their age, who was bundling up straw nearby came over to the laughing male and joined his laughter when he said something to her in a strange language. This surprised Sherry further as her ears were not accustomed to listening to the sound of male and female laughter combined, they sounded like a nightingale singing during the rumble of clouds before rain. Observing Sherry's surprise the girl looked into the male's eyes with a smile and said something leaning close to him. He smiled back and spoke looking back into her eyes.

Sherry had never seen anything like this before. Birds neither smiled nor laughed. Neither did males and females in animals talk while looking into each other's eyes. Nature had only gifted the human race with an ability to speak, smile and use eyes as an intermediate medium to the heart. Among all the couples that Sherry had seen so far, the human couple was the most different and superior to them all. It seemed the complete whole as it had the capability to convey feelings through words. Sherry closely observed everything and tried to understand it (and succeeding eventually) because it was all new to her. A lot of new things awaited her.

The man looked at Sherry and said something to the girl that drained colour off her face. She looked at Sherry and then back at her partner with large, hurt eyes, and then turned to go towards her work. The man called her back with a smile and followed her to the haystack when she did not look back. She pretended to be busy in work with a lowered head. He went and sat next to her speaking with a smile and laughing. She turned her head away, so he moved in front of her. She continued to ignore him as if she had sworn not to talk to him. At this, the man became serious for a while, and then suddenly picked her up in his arms and began turning in circles. The girl tried to push him away with a stern face but then laughed and put her arms around his neck and continued laughing, cradled in his arms as he carried her around, laughing along. After the man got tired of carrying her, he flung her on the haystack and ran away laughing. The girl let out a shriek and ran laughing after him till they were out of sight.

A broad smile had crept over Sherry's lips. She had forgotten that she was away from home, lost in a strange world. She had never witnessed or imagined such a scene. When they were out of sight, Sherry realised that she had been smiling and the man who she had met at the shore was looking at her with a stretch on the left corner of his mouth as if about to smile. She looked at him and he smiled, looking at her the way the girl's partner had looked at her a while ago. Sherry continued looking into his gaze helplessly. She could not look away from his eyes; however, she felt no remorse at her helplessness.

What strange sort of helplessness was this? Why did she feel comfort in it? Why was music playing in her heart? Why did her soul feel at peace? Why did this life appear easy? Most of all, this life felt so much better than the one she had lived. This was so real and natural.

Sherry could not break away from the strange trance created between her eyes and the man's...and when Sata looked into her eyes...

Sherry's expression grew dark at the thought of Sata's gaze; it made her feel almost sick. Then she quickly focused on the man's eyes and let its feelings take over her with a smile. She felt really fortunate to have seen the real way of life. She went on looking at him, spellbound.

The spell broke on the arrival of some children near them followed by a middle-aged woman. The woman looked at Sherry with interest and said something to the children. A bearded old man came next, carrying a little child on his shoulders. Then came a young couple. The children ran about playing, and out of them a naked toddler came running towards Sherry, stopped midway and smiled at her shyly. This made her laugh; as she thought that male children, like their female counterparts, are truly innocent and responsive to the exchange of love.

All that she had read, heard and understood during her life was a lie. It was unnatural and wrong, Sherry thought as her face grew tense. She jerked her head and looked away. It was also sickening, she thought, as she felt Sata's image come into her mind with a feeling of disgust.

There were rare examples of such unnatural behaviour in birds, animals or other beings where one sex became involved with another of the same physical construct in such a way. The past centuries were spent exploiting innocence through the sick ambitions of certain individuals who were drowned in selfish pride while justifying and enforcing their wrong ideas upon others. Their mental muddle was proved natural as like-minded individuals were involved in propagating and protecting such ideas. While the fact remained that nature had created humans as halves of a whole, like all other beings – with logic of its own.

The middle-aged woman came closer as she found Sherry lost in thoughts and signalled her to come along with her. Sherry looked at the man from the shore, so the woman spoke to him.

Sherry was taken to a cottage to freshen up where she had a meal of fruits and juice with the man. It was a pleasant and peaceful place. Sherry did not feel the loss of having crashed her craft. She was satisfied as though she was not lost away from home at all. She felt happy as never before. She was silent as though there was nothing else to achieve in life and that life meant being with this man forever.

So, she settled herself there—away from the civilised world, in this more civil and natural world, where machines and mechanics had not taken over humans and their environment. This island was saved from destruction by being hidden from the world. Sherry had learnt their language and customs to become a part of them.

Months later, when her partner's (the man from the shore) child was making its presence felt with movement in Sherry's womb, she held her partner's hand and walked to the spot on the shore where they had first met.

It was a pleasant evening when she saw that her craft had been washed up on the shore from the sea. The fact that this would enable her to contact her family made her sad instead of happy. Her partner hugged her as he saw her talking to herself out of worry.

Sherry shivered and turned pale as she thought that her happiness could be taken away and this place could be robbed of its innocence. Her world would be in chaos. If she took her partner along with her, then he would be maltreated…it might even be a threat to his life.

Sherry let out a cry and passed out. Her partner placed her head in his lap and stroked her forehead. Sherry opened her eyes and turned her head towards her craft. Moments later, she got up and walked over to it. The craft was not much damaged; she knew how to repair the minor defects. She knew how to contact home which only required pressing a few buttons. Sherry also knew how the signals could be permanently turned off.

She turned back to look at her partner. There was a shadow of fear in his eyes. He knew nothing about technology. He just knew that the mother of his child was with him, but could also go away. He placed his hands on Sherry's shoulders. She felt the security of her future in his arms and saw promises in the depth of his eyes. His face spoke of being together in times of happiness and sorrow. The hair blowing over his forehead (drawn into a worried frown) made him appear more handsome. His long-fingered hands were made to hold her shoulders. The toned muscles of his arms were meant to support her waist.

Sherry's eyes welled with tears as she stroked his stubble covered cheeks with soft fingers.

These sources of happiness could be taken away from her and she would never be able to explain their pleasure to anyone. More females who thought like her would be deprived of these pleasures forever. Forever.

Sherry turned to look back at the crashed craft. If she could somehow make Mama see her point of view, then it would lay the foundation of a new world. The future generations would be born complete. For the sake of those future generations, she would have to bring two worlds together and risk leaving him behind...only to miss his beautiful forehead that was lost in concern with matters of both the worlds.

Sherry looked away from the craft, back into her partner's eyes. She took both his hands and placed them around her belly. Then she leaned her head against his chest and cried hysterically. She did not realise how long she had been crying, when she felt that she heard Mama's voice.

"This is good; you won't require some Tom, Dick or Harry to make me a granny. You alone can make me one. You can become a mother on your own, baby..." Sherry was startled to hear that. She would not bear a child against the rules of nature. Never! She tried to shout as she saw her mother reading from the science page of the day's newspaper, which Sherry had read some time back. It was dated June 2007, and not June 2507. She stroked her belly with her fingers. There was no unborn child in it nor were a handsome youth's arms around her waist. This discovery brought a quick smile on her face. She turned to look at the picture hanging beside the window.

"I love you, Papa," she said aloud, walking over to the frame.

"I hate him, okay? Hate him a lot..." Mama said in an equally loud voice.

"Why, Mama?"

"That is none of your business."

"No, Mom…it sure is my business."

"You have no idea of how much womankind has suffered for centuries…"

"Men might have suffered before that…or might have to suffer in the future, undeservedly."

"Nonsense! Don't argue. You don't know what we had to endure. Even after claims of civilisation, we were deprived of so much. It took almost a century to gain voting rights. The earliest voices that rose in Europe and America had to appeal for decades. Then the movement spread all over the world. It continues to work and spread in a number of ways, and…"

"Okay, and Papa…"

"Your Papa, my foot! He too was like them all, a typical male chauvinist…"

"Okay, Mama…now, when women have secured all their rights and can legally demand them, then I…" Sherry paused to hug her mother and then walked towards the window. "I will also start a movement, Mama. An anti-feminist movement… because I love both of you."

She spoke as she slid her soft fingers over the glass touching both her parents' faces on the photo and turned to look at her mother with a smile.

(Translated from the Urdu by Miraan Punjabi)

STRANGE INTIMACY

Manmohan Saral

Everybody had gone. What remained was a corpse and two dead souls. A body from which the spirit had disappeared into infinity some hours ago while the souls remained in the stranded bodies.

One was himself and the other was Chander's wife whose name he did not remember. And this was no occasion to ask her identity.

It may sound strange but he did not know Chander's wife's name, even though they had been friends for long. However strong the ties may be, it wasn't necessary in big cities to have a level of informality with each other's family as well.

They met every second day, but the distance between the respective families was as far apart as Meerut is from New Delhi, though they lived in the same metropolis. Musings aside, these elemental distances do help in bringing hearts closer.

The accident had taken place in the morning itself. He had met Chander at Dadar, as usual. Dadar was a terminus where trains from two different directions stopped. "Where two hearts meet," Chander would have said. After meeting, they would go out to work together.

The local was crowded as usual. It would be wrong to say the compartment was unusually crowded just because of the accident. It could've happened any day, with Chander, with me, or any of the other commuters. And the possibility of the accident hadn't diminished with Chander's death.

The possibility jolted his entire frame. His eyes would revert to Chander's covered body. The very sight of his crushed head brought the hair on end. It was so badly mutilated that he would have found identification impossible had he not been himself at the site of the tragic accident. After all, we recognise a man by his face; the torso is immaterial.

Identification is not difficult, but the formalities are exhausting. When he thought of that, he felt it would have been better had he himself died and Chander been left behind to undergo the living ordeal. It's a terrible responsibility to be witness to an accident.

But he had to withstand a lot more. He hadn't only been a witness. He had been a friend as well. And in a city like this, the presence of a friend or an acquaintance is a necessity.

A lot of people came—neighbours, office colleagues, acquaintances, God knows who all. But they all came and went. Some offering condolences, some expressing shock, and others enquiring about the funeral. Some gave vent to apprehensions, talked about the arrival of close relatives, presuming everyone had been informed. Some promised to return the next morning, others offered help.

Every time someone came or went, Chander's wife raised her head. Otherwise, it remained glued to the cemented ground. She neither reacted nor responded to the conversation.

He had actually been tense even before Chander's wife knew about the tragedy. He had been into it right from the moment of the accident—from informing people to bringing home the dead body from the railway tracks to the police station to the morgue, to filing the FIR, and what not—torturous exercises, cross-examinations. They had shattered his nervous system.

Darkness had set in by the time the dead body could be brought to its once-abode. And the scene there further aggravated his worries. The death of a friend is shocking, even if it is less than losing a husband. Worse if you have been a witness. You almost see the shadows of death dancing in front of your eyes.

He was totally exhausted. First because of the fatigue since morning, then depression, but mostly hearing the same monotonous talk over and over again. He tried stretching his legs on the chair in front and produced some sound from his parched throat. He had remained quiet for so long that it seemed he had lost his voice.

But Chander's wife couldn't see his movements. She sat there with her head bent, perhaps mentally reliving the time with Chander—good, bad, irritating, lovers' tiffs, love, closeness—intimate moments which she alone knew. And all those dreams, fantasies which will now only remain so and eventually regret not having realised.

He looked at her carefully, perhaps for the first time that day.

She was sitting there on the floor, her head on her knees, motionless. He suddenly remembered a painting by a renowned artist. He mentally started comparing the similarities in the two expressions.

She was shivering now. There's a stirring in her body. She must be crying, though no sound came out. Actually, she had become dumb, crying all the while.

A confrontation with agony is also an experience, a crude, cruel reminder. He felt sorry for her. He should have felt that way much earlier, but then he didn't really have an occasion.

He searched for words to speak to the trembling woman, but did not remember a feminine name. He felt angry at the departed friend's idiocy. While he must have told him a million things about his wife, he had never spelt her name. And now because of that old-fashioned fool, he was at a loss to suitably address her.

Finally, he mustered courage, and said, "Listen..."

Perhaps she did not hear because she did not lift her head. So articulating himself, he said, "Listen, how long will you keep sitting like this?"

She raised her head and looked vacantly at him.

He spoke again, "I mean you've been sitting like this for such a long time. You haven't taken a morsel since morning. Please try to take control of yourself."

She couldn't speak.

"Please, kindly get up and wash your face. I'll make some tea in the meantime."

"No, please don't bother," she finally spoke in a faltering voice.

"How long can you starve like this? Besides, I'll also be able to gulp down a cup."

She lowered her head again. And without uttering a word, started sobbing. He couldn't decide what to do. He had no more words to console her with. He thought he was an amateur. Perhaps this was the first time he was confronting such a situation.

He got up with a start and looked around for an opening to the kitchen. His roving eyes skipped the dead friend's body and spotted the kitchen. He didn't particularly like the idea—his look crossing over the corpse...

His friend was really dead. He looked at the body with a heavy heart and walked across towards the kitchen. It was a small, one-room-kitchen flat. One room. It was no longer a room. It had become a mortuary. His friend's corpse had enveloped everything and everyone in the room.

But he found some relief in the kitchen. As if he had escaped from a mortuary. It was easier to make tea than to console. After a long time, he had been able to shed stains of tension. He lit the gas, put on some water to boil and then looked for the other ingredients.

He made deliberate sounds while searching the various boxes, every time stealing a look into the room. He felt good. Because from that angle, while he could look at Chander's wife, he couldn't see the corpse. Despite those sounds, she continued to sit like a corpse herself.

He wanted to ask her about tea leaves and sugar, but couldn't bring himself round to do that. Instead, he would start exploring the boxes again, making louder sounds. She still did not look back to see whether he had found the stuff. He soon realised his mistake. Everything had been strategically and conveniently placed in the twosome family. He wanted to throw an appreciative look at Chander's wife, but she continued to sit there, sobbing.

He brought in two cups of tea and kept them on the floor, hoping the sound would make her lift her head.

She didn't. He continued to stare at her and she came up with a fresh outburst of tears. He too sat down and after helplessly looking around, put his arm around her shoulders while attempting to say something. But the sobbing increased.

He withdrew his arm, not really knowing what to do next, and eventually saying, "Here, have some tea."

He found his own words awkward. Keeping quiet for a while, he mustered enough courage to repeat whatever he had said earlier, "I don't know how long you've been sitting without eating or drinking anything. Please try to take control of yourself. How long will it last? Come, have some tea."

And he went on and on, as if reading from a book.

Chander's wife tried to feel a little relaxed. She lifted her face, alternated her glance between him and the cup of tea. Then God knows what happened, she clung to him and started sobbing again. This time, he listened. Along with the sobs were some inaudible words. But he failed to grasp the punctuated lines.

Startled, he failed to grasp the situation and quickly sifted through his condolence dictionary. Emerging no wiser, he started patting her back.

The stiffness in her body increased with the sobbing. He caressed her back. She started crying uncontrollably and held him closer, in a tighter grip.

He wanted to console her verbally, but only inanities came out. Holding her face with both his hands, he lifted it up. It was drenched with tears that were scaling down her cheeks, touching her lips. This was the first time he was looking at her face so closely. Even the pain-paralysed, tear-drenched face couldn't hide the softer contours. He opened his lips to speak while still holding her face in his hands. But suddenly, she sealed his open mouth with her own lips.

Startled, he pulled back; his hands slid down from her face but continued to hold her shoulders. Placing his chin on her shoulders, he said, "Listen, please take control of yourself."

Instead, she put her entire weight on him. He looked at her bent head and quivering body and got glued to the whiteness of the covered corpse. "No," he shouted, and clutched onto Chander's wife's body in a tight embrace. "No," she also cried out, tightening her own grip around him. And just four feet in front of them lay Chander's body, sleeping in death. Her sobbing continued.

The floor was cold and bare. Tears fell down and evaporated. She was quivering in agony—bitter, painful, deeply penetrating agony. They all seemed helpless. It was as if she were searching for an asylum. She gripped him and the grip grew tighter.

The floor was cold like Chander's body. He pondered. He closed his eyes as if to overcome the strains of the day. Just ease them out.

Beyond all pain, agony, stress and emotions is a human condition which makes you forget it all. The floor then did not feel cold and Chander's corpse—and him—were surrounded by a self-invited darkness.

Dawn opened its eyes first. Chander's wife got a hold of herself, cast a distant look at the man sleeping on the floor like a corpse and picked up the dead cups of tea. She then put them in the washbasin, opened the tap and allowed the water to flow full stream.

(Translated from the Hindi by Suresh Kohli)

ONCE THERE WAS A VILLAGE

Mohinder Singh Sarna

The village square lay desolate, darkened by the creeping shadow of the twilight. The tall trees in the distance stood dejected and lifeless. From the dung-heap near the pond, a dog raises a howl like a loud, long dirge that circled that village and died away where it had begun. A vulture rose from the branches of the trees and, barely able to carry its heavy, well-fed body, slowly wheeled away into the darkening sky. From the direction of the mosque, an owl hooted its invitation into the night.

In an instant, the twilight deepened into the night and fell upon the village like a canopy of death. A weak, pale moon began to stagger across the sky, like a maiden in the grip of a wayward spirit.

A shadow stirred under the banyan tree and took on the outline of a human silhouette in the moonlight. A hoary head lifted from hunched shoulders and looked up in the sky. The pale moonlight touched his henna-dyed beard and the web of sprinkles that covered his swarthy face. Then the head fell back on to the man's chest as if his neck had suddenly snapped. The old man cast a yearning look at the village. He jerked away the tears that filled his eyes and sighed.

Yes, it was all over. But, he, Khuda Baksh Varaich, the old Choudhury of the village, the caretaker of the village, was still alive.

What good care he had taken!

How well he had lived up to the responsibilities of a Choudhury!

His village, the village settled by his forefathers on the metalled road from Hafizabad to Pindi Bhatian, the village called Ladewallah Varaich had become a cremation ground! And he was still alive like a stubborn piece of wood that refused to burn. He squeezed his head with both hands and sighed again.

All his desperate efforts had failed. He had dragged himself through the neighbouring villages, begged and beseeched the headmen to listen to him for the sake of their God, for the sake of the grey beard, for the honour of his ancestors. But they had all turned him away, the Kazis of Kazi da Kot, the Maans of Maani, the Gujjars of Kila Mian Singh, the Dogras of Kotli, the Gondals of Godianwala. They had called him an enemy of Pakistan and a murderer of believers.

A young man of Godianwala had grabbed his beard: "Why are you bent on dying, old man? Come to your senses, or else..." The young man had threateningly raised his axe.

"Finish him off," another man had shouted.

"Get rid of him. Why are you dragging this on?"

"That's right!" An old Gondal screamed. "If he doesn't feel the pain of his brothers, we don't need him. The Khatris of Amritsar are chopping up Muslims like cotton buds. Our sisters and daughters who have never been out of purdah are being raped in the bazaars. And this man is behaving like an uncle of the infidels."

He had not understood all that they had said, but his head had been seized by a sudden trembling and his few remaining dark hairs had instantly turned grey. Dragging his weary legs, he had returned to the village. In all his years, he had never felt so worn out.

He had gotten wind of the plan. They would come on Friday night. The Bahts, Chinmis, Maans, Gondals and Dogras had all got together. They had mopped off the smaller villages. And on Friday night, after the evening prayers, they would beat the drums and descend on this village from all directions.

Desperately, he had rushed from house to house, telling everyone he could of the planned attack. He explained to the villagers his helplessness and begged them to leave before Friday night. He helped them tie up their bundles, dismantle their cots and pack them up, and stitch up sacks full of kitchen utensils. He negotiated with the potters to sell assets at reasonable prices to those who did not have mares to carry their things. Then, he blessed the women of the families, bolstered up the spirits of the young men, and holding back his tears, bade farewell to the old men, apologising for not being able to help them. But one of his own people, a Varaich from his village, had let the word out, and it had all come to naught.

Now, it was all over. Vultures were circling over his village, and he was alive.

The dog got up from the dung-heap and walking up to him, began to roll at his feet. The Choudhury ignored him, and letting out another long howl, the dog ran away towards the fields.

The old man turned his head and sighed again.

Yes, even the dog knew. Even the dog was scared of going towards the village where happy homes had been burnt to ashes, where painted cots, spinning wheels and carved stools were still smouldering, where half-burnt human bodies lay rotting, where the corners of the houses and in the ditches in the lanes lay pathetic piles of old bones and where, in the doorway of the Thakurdwar, a handsome young man lay on the side, his intestines pulled out by some sharp, hooked weapon.

It seemed to the old man that the shrieks and wails of the dying had dissolved along with the slogans of 'Pakistan Zindabad' into the night air. By Allah's grace, Pakistan had been formed in his village too. Here too, the believers and Qaid-e-Azam had taken over.

Gripped by a deep fear, he began to follow the dog towards the field. His beard trembled under the pale, sickly moon, and fresh tears stained his cheeks. He did not know where he was going.

At the edge of the first field, he stumbled against a heavy object and fell forward on his face.

It was a corpse lying face down. He turned it over, and pressing down on the elbows and knees, straightened the rigid limits. It was the body of a young boy, no more than ten or eleven. He peered closely at the face. It was the son of Chanda Singh Jat. With his fair skin, round face and light hair that now shone like gold in the moonlight, the boy has been called Sahib by the villagers. To celebrate his birth, his father had arranged dances in the village and had gifted everyone twenty-one rupees and a pot of *halwa*.

And now, the only son of that proud father was lying dead at the edge of the field. His turban lay where it had fallen, covered with grime, and across his forehead was a long cut from an axe. Dried blood glued his light hair to his temples.

The Choudhury tied the boy's turban around his own waist. Then, he locked his hands under the boy, and with a strong heave, threw him over his shoulder. He began to walk across the fields, circling the village towards the brick house that Chanda Singh Jat had built behind the *madrasa,* a little apart from the village.

For a long while, he stood outside the house, dispirited. The place was enveloped in deathly silence. He had been wrong. Even the isolated house had not escaped the blood-crazed mob. Still, he knocked on the door. A faint whisper could be heard inside the house. A thin hope lit up his face. There was someone still alive. He put his lips to the crack in the door, and said in a loud whisper:

"Unlatch the door, daughter. It's only me, Khuda Baksh."

There was a long sigh of relief. Someone raised the flame in the lantern and the light filtered through the cracks in the door. But the hand on the latch still hesitated.

"It's only me, girl. There is no one with me."

The door opened. The light from the lantern hit him in the face.

A bewildered Nand Kaur, Chanda Singh Jat's widow, quickly shut the door behind him and followed him into the house. Her fifteen-year-old daughter, Jagiro, stood in the kitchen door, her dusky face turned to the wall.

The light fell on the face of the dead body. Sobs tore through Jagiro. Nand Kaur wailed and beat her breast.

"Courage, my daughters, courage. I feel your pain. Crying is of no use. You are not alone in your suffering. Not one of our people has survived here. Somehow, you two have escaped their notice. That is why you are still alive. Why was this boy out of doors, anyway?"

"A curse came on me; it was I who sent him to the well to bring back the cattle. If only I had known, my son. I had felt it in my guts since yesterday, since I heard the sound of the gunfire. Death on me, my son! Why did I ever send you?"

The old man bit his lip and swallowed his tears.

"Now, don't make too much noise," he said roughly, "or they'll be here, and you know them well. Even these walls have ears; you can't trust anyone. Otherwise, we would not have come to such a pass."

The old man's tears had taken the edge off his voice.

"Look, I'm telling you that it is no use wailing and crying. No good will come of it. You must leave this house now, before they come charging down here. I would take you to my house, but they'll definitely find out, and then you would meet the same fate as all the others."

The old man fell silent, thinking. He could hear his heart beating loudly in the chest. He opened the door and peeped out. The night was dark and desolate. From somewhere near the mosque, the owl's hoots still pierced the silence.

Relieved, he latched the door and returned to the room. The woman was looking at him, wide-eyed. Her daughter was still sobbing uncontrollably, head bent over her knees. He put a trembling hand on Jagiro's head and raised her face. Then quickly, blinking back his tears, he sat down. His tone turned rough again.

"Why don't you listen instead of just staring at me? Listen to me, and pack up whatever you need. I'll take you to a Sikh village during the night. I can't think of anywhere else. Let's not waste anymore time." He continued to speak as if he were talking to himself in a dream, his eyes fixed on the floor.

"That's it, what else? I can't think of anything else. I'm just an old man and they are running all over me. The riff-raff of my own class, those whom I have brought up with my own hands, stare at me with murder in their eyes. See, one of them went and squealed to the Gondals... As I was saying, from there you can join a caravan. You'll find room in a camp in Amritsar. And who knows, by then these people may have come back to their senses and you could come back and live in your own house again."

He stopped. The woman was staring at her dead son, as if she had heard nothing. Khuda Baksh sat silently, his head hunched over his shoulders, until she turned to him. Then, he spoke again.

"We'll take the boy with us. We won't leave him here. On our way, there is a well that belongs to the Varaichs. There is no one there; they're all awry, killing and looting. We'll cremate him there."

His tone was sleepy now, and the same drowsiness seemed to envelope his whole being as they left the village. His unsteady steps seemed to sway across the path. Every few minutes, Nand Kaur would start, fearing that her dead son would fall to the ground.

But the old man's grip on the dead boy was firm, and he walked slowly and cautiously. At the slightest sound, he would freeze and they would move into the shadow of a tree, holding their breath. And then they would move hurriedly from the shadow of one tree to another, always trying to escape the moon.

Khuda Baksh stopped suddenly near the grave of Bonga *pir.* Not more than ten steps away from them, against the side of the grave, some men were lying on the ground. They were facing the other way, and had not seen them. The three of them sat down right there, at the edge of the field. Their path passed by the side of the grave; the open fields glistening under the moon offered no cover. A cold sweat broke out on the Choudhury's brow. He could feel the eyes of the woman and her daughter searching his face for an answer.

Then his face relaxed and he felt he could breathe again. Wiping his forehead, he spoke.

"They are our own people and they are dead. See, they don't move, they don't speak or turn."

As they passed the corpses, Jagiro screamed and clung to her mother.

"Save your screams, girl," the old man said sharply. "There are enough ears to hear you. Just follow me quietly, and don't look left or right."

They had left the village behind, and had even crossed the wall of the Cheema clan. The fields around them had been ploughed and tilled. The furrows waited to receive the seeds, but their masters had forgotten all about them. At the edges, patches of water shone like silver in the new grass. The sugarcane stood knee-high. In another month or so, it would be ready for the harvest. Then the air would be sweet with the fragrance of fresh jaggery and on every hearth, sweet pots of rice would be cooked in sugarcane juice and eaten joyfully. A few cotton buds had already flowered. The following month, groups of slim, young girls would have been all over, teasing each other, dancing and singing. The sweetness of their songs would entice and enchant, and play havoc with the hearts of men.

But this year, the month of *sawan* had been strange. It had frightened life into silence. And now, in *bhadon*, someone had gone and murdered the songs with axes.

The sound of laughter rose from the well of the Varaich clan. Then someone began to sing tunelessly in a wavering voice. At the edge of the well, a few men were drinking and gossiping. The old man and his companions left the path and stepped into the sugarcane, bending low.

The singing stopped.

"Stop staring out there. There isn't a soul there."

"No bother. I saw the sugarcane move. I think I saw a violet *dupatta*."

"Ha! You see *dupattas* even in your dreams! Hand me the pan. This is what I call Pakistan brand. I swear by the Qaid-e-Azam, you'll forget all your foreign bottles."

"I'll be back, brother. Just let me check out these girls first. They may be of use to us, and help us pass the night well."

Their lives hung by the thinnest of threads as they lay down in the cane field. The approaching heavy footfalls fell like hammer blows on their hearts. Someone caught Jagiro's *dupatta* and dragged her out. Old Khuda Baksh leapt to his feet.

"Old man, you too? And who are these girls?"

"They are ours, young man. My daughters."

"Well done, old geezer! Trying to fool me? This young lass is of the Khatris; that old crone may well be your daughter. Why don't you speak, sweetie? What's your name? And you, old man, what are you doing fooling around with young girls in the fields at night?"

Choudhury Khuda Baksh took off his turban and put it at the young man's feet. The sight of his white hair seemed to touch off some memory in the young man's mind.

"Aren't you the one who came to our village? I should have finished you off then. You haven't mended your ways, I see."

Khuda Baksh recognised the young Gondal who had caught him by the beard and threatened him with his axe.

"Let's be on our way, my sweetie. If your mother wants to mess around with this old man, let her. You're crying? No, no, my darling, come with me. I'll get you some candy."

Jagiro screamed and shrunk back in terror.

"I'm with you, my young thing. Move on now." With that, the young man shoved his knee high into Jagiro's stomach.

Nand Kaur was at his throat in an instant.

"You want to come along, old woman? I'm not interested. I think I should finish you off right here, or you could become a problem."

He pushed the woman to the ground and raised his axe with both hands. Khuda Baksh ran towards him. The axe caught the old man at the hip and he fell.

When he came to his senses, a faint light had just touched the sky in the east. A cool breeze caressed his bare head. The soft fragrance of the sugarcane comforted him. If only he did not have this red-hot iron stuck in his side ...And why was he face down in the cane? Was there a thick keekar branch hanging low over him, or was it the arm of Death himself?

He was burning with thirst, dying for a sip of water. The well was not far away. It was not his own well. Only last month, he had fixed a new wheel and changed all the cans that brought up the water. Where were his servants now? He, the owner of the well was lying thirsty, and they could not even get him a cupful of water? Lazy, ungrateful wretches.

And on that pole, was hanging the *salwar* of his granddaughter little Salma...how many times had he told the wretch not to wash her clothes at the well, but she just could not understand... No, but this was the *salwar* of Jagiro, the daughter of Chanda Singh Jat... Yes, of course, Jagiro was Salma...they looked so alike; it was difficult to tell them apart.

The little *salwar*, the *salwar* of a fifteen year old, was beginning to bloat in his vision. The little green plants embroidered on it became huge, brooding trees. Countless *salwar*s were hanging all around him. In the fields, on the parapets, on the hedges and even on the keekar above his head. They swayed to the wind, they got caught in the thorns and were torn to shreds.

His own children had destroyed him. They had trampled on his old bones and rubbed his grey beard into the dust. His disgrace was visible everywhere. There was a time when people had not dared to look him in the eye. And now, his sons and grandsons had raised axes against him. There was no point in living anymore.

Barely conscious, he held his waist and staggered to his feet. He tossed one end of his turban over the keekar branch. With tight knots he fashioned a noose and jumping up, put it around his neck.

The sun came up. The birds began to chirp in the trees. A corpse hung from the keekar tree in the sugarcane field. Its pupils were fixed on a village in the distance which the dead man's ancestors had built on the paved road that ran from Hafizabad to Pindi Bhatian. A village called Ladewallah Varaich.

(Translated from the Punjabi by Navtej Sarna)

A SEALED BOTTLE OF WINE

Sukhbir

"It's heady…absolutely fresh…a sealed bottle of wine… ready for inauguration today," said the tout to Santokh Singh standing near the lane beside Congress House.

Santokh Singh looked rather sternly at the tout, then, smiled softly. His curled moustache was in the clock position of twenty past ten. He gave a twist to his left moustache to bring it to the ten past ten position, put his hand on the tout's shoulder and said, "Okay, let's go."

They passed through a few lanes and then the tout stopped at a house and knocked softly. Santokh Singh pressed down his hand-woven long jacket, put a finger through the fold of his blue turban to sharpen its angle and then curled his lip upwards to admire his moustache.

The door was opened by a tall portly woman. She smiled, her betel-red lips parted and her teeth blackened with tobacco showed through. She welcomed Santokh Singh with courtesy. Santokh Singh stared at her, then cleared his throat, smiled and followed her.

Just then the sealed bottle of wine walked in—the sealed bottle of wine that had a license to provide pleasure to men of this dry city during prohibition times. Santokh Singh stared at her, smiled and continued gazing at her beauty draped in a virgin white dress. He could already feel the warmth of her young body spread to his inner core. She was really beautiful. Her eyes and body had not yet matured from youth to adulthood. Even childhood had not vanished completely. She was at that point and place where childhood innocence and vulnerable adulthood overlapped briefly before final separation. Santokh Singh was pleased that he had really got a fresh, sealed, virgin bottle of wine and that he was destined to inaugurate it.

The tall portly woman returned and sat next to Santokh Singh. They smiled at each other and a deal for ten rupees was suggested. But Santokh Singh took out four notes of ten rupees from his wallet and said, "No, not ten—I will make it forty, and this night will be all mine."

Santokh Singh was in no hurry as he had the whole night for himself He slowly took off his long jacket, half a bottle of whiskey from its pocket and put it on the table in front of him. The sealed bottle of wine, 'Malati,' wearing a virgin white dress, came and sat next to him. Santokh Singh looked around. It was a small, neat and clean room. On one side, was a window dressed with a curtain of small floral design. On the other wall was a picture of Saraswati, the Goddess of Knowledge, seated on a peacock chariot playing the *veena*, a musical instrument. Just below that, two incense sticks had been lit and their sweet fragrance was spreading. There was one more picture, probably of Shivaji, which seemed to have been cut out from a calendar. There was a calendar on the wall stuck on seventh April, which had the picture of a half-naked girl sitting beside the edge of a pond, lost in her own thoughts. Santokh Singh looked at it fixedly for a while, then took a large shot from his whiskey bottle, gave another upward twist to his moustache and moved towards Malati. Her slim and tender body trembled at first, then engulfed by his huge arms, her discomfort increased.

The calendar was frozen at seventh April, the darkest hour of the night was upon them and Malati was lying on the bed like a helpless pigeon in the clutches of its predator. She was frightened of Santokh Singh's bulky paunch, the heavy smell of his drunken breath and the movement of his taut muscles. Compared to her slim and small body, she felt his was like a huge mountain and she was scared how the night would turn out.

But as Santokh Singh had the entire night to himself, he showed great patience. Stuck close to his hairy chest, Malati answered his questions timidly and softly.

Today's spend of forty rupees did not seem much to Santokh Singh as he never before had such intoxicating virgin wine. In the last eight years, he had experienced intoxication from a variety of wines, but never felt satisfied. His lusty encounters ended with him spouting out his bitterness and hatred. But today, he felt the worth of the forty rupees which he had earned at some weddings by singing blessings for the bridegroom.

Santokh Singh was a poet. But he would often write articles and essays on religious and social issues. He was well-known in literary circles as well as in religious gatherings. His audience was always impressed by his well-built six-foot body, white pyjamas, long black jacket and stylised blue turban. He looked so regal that his audience was more impressed by his personality than his poetry! When he would recite his poetry on stage, there would be pin-drop silence in the audience and only his voice would roar. However, the audience was more floored by his presentation style than content. He had a way of luring his audience and they would generously shower currency notes on him. It was said that his poems about riots during Partition in Punjab, would charge the youth to pick up swords for action. His long eulogy on the plight of women of India was very popular among women. His emotionally charged sermons at weddings would move the listeners to tears. His oration was his only source of income. Though his earnings were not much, and in fact rather erratic, he did not feel a lack of money. Santokh Singh earned little but spent it lavishly on drinks in gatherings of poets and whatever was left was spent seeking intoxication from bottles of wine. If he had less money, he would make a deal of two rupees and sometimes even twenty rupees was not too much for him.

Santokh Singh's face had a raw and scary look. He had large red eyes, as if always drunk. He used to boast that no woman could escape his probing eyes. He had not got married, or maybe he could not bring himself to marry a second time. Eight years ago during the terror-driven Partition times in Punjab, his wife was kidnapped while she had gone to purchase groceries, and was never heard from again. He had struggled to take his four children safely to India and had left them with their maternal grandparents...and thereafter, never bothered to find out about their well-being. Every two-three months, he would money-order ten to twenty rupees to them, but he never wrote them a letter.

He had changed a lot during the last eight years. He used to write poems and articles even when he had his land to till, but writing was not his source of income then. Having left the land behind, he was now dependent on writing as his only source of income. He had no haunting memory of his late wife, as he had never cared much for her and had never liked her looks or physique. But whenever a craving for her body arose in him, he would dig into his pocket for money and go looking for a bottle of wine that he could afford. It had become a habit and a daily routine. He would say that a poet could not be at his creative best without women and wine. Even tonight with Malati, he was looking for inspiration for a poem.

Santokh Singh had the entire night for himself, so he was patiently talking with Malati and sympathetically asking her about her past life, as was his habit. He would say that this helped him find new ideas for his poems.

As Malati was narrating her past, Santokh Singh was feeling an upsurge of anger and hatred towards the society that compels its women to join this profession and sell their bodies. While speaking about her life, Malati's fear of him slowly melted and she kept talking to him, as if she was at home talking to a family member. She kept rolling her fingers on his densely hairy chest and shared her childhood memories.

Hers was a small home, in a small village and she used to play with her friends in the small courtyard. One day, she had celebrated the wedding of her doll and all her friends had enjoyed the wedding feast in her house. Her father used to love her a lot, but she could not bear her stepmother's overbearing presence. Whenever her stepmother scolded her, she would tremble, cry and withdraw into herself. At such times, she would remember her own mother who had died two years earlier and she would burst into tears. If her father saw her crying, he would hug her close to his chest and pacify her.

Santokh Singh could feel her misery and felt as if an eight-year-old Malati was crying on his chest. He moved her gently away and wiped her tears. Suddenly, he felt a wave run through him and he thought of Deepo, his small daughter, whom he had left eight years ago with her grandparents. He remembered how at night, rather than sleeping with her mother, she would sleep close to him and he would feel the rhythm of her small breaths on his chest. Deepo must have grown up by now...

His reverie was broken when he involuntarily let out a loud burp, laden with the horrid smell of liquor and raw onions and he turned towards Malati, who was then talking about her school. Her sixth class schoolbook had lovely stories and poems which she had learnt to recite. It had a picture of Shivaji and a lesson on him that narrated his deeds of bravery and valour. She was also very fond of dancing. Her father would tell her that he would get her admitted in a dance training school after she completed two more classes. But that was not to be...

One day, when she was returning home, she was kidnapped by two men who carried her away, screaming and crying. A boy from her village had similarly been kidnapped earlier and was released after the family had paid a ransom of three hundred rupees. Such incidents took place frequently in nearby villages. She could not make out where and how far her kidnappers had taken her from her own village. She stayed in that hell for several days. She was assaulted, mauled and abused every day and lived in constant pain and fear, with no hope of escape in sight. Then her feet got swollen and pains started in her stomach and sometimes she felt as if something was pushing and pulling inside her body.

In this state, she kept remembering her father and her village and wished she could go back there. Then one night, she escaped from that hell running through vast stretches of open fields and on to the main road. But when she turned around, she saw the man from that hell coming after her. Her legs gave way with fright and she became breathless. She then saw the headlights of a truck coming towards her. As the man tried to drag her back, the truck stopped and the driver freed her from the man, put her in the truck and drove off...

She felt scared and apprehensive, as she thought she could be moving into a different hell. Timidly, she looked at the driver's flowing beard and turban and she felt he somewhat resembled the picture of Shivaji that she had in her sixth class school book—similar type of beard and a turban. She spent the night at the truck driver's home. His wife assured her that she was safe now and that her husband would return her to her village.

In the morning, when the truck driver had changed into clean clothes and dressed his beard, he looked even more like Shivaji and she felt assured. Shivaji had also saved women like her in distress. She looked forward to going back home to her village. She just wanted to put her head on her father's chest, hug him and cry away the nightmare she had suffered for so long.

And she did cry a lot that day. Her stepmother, her helpless father and the entire village refused to take her back, looking at her swollen stomach and accept her in her condition. She felt surrounded by an intense darkness and feared that she would sink into the earth and be gone forever.

This had happened six months ago. She had left her village and home and was wandering around, till fate brought her to this place.

Malati looked at Santokh Singh. He seemed absorbed in his own thoughts. She ran her fingers through his beard and started telling him about the truck driver. No one in the village believed his story about rescuing her and instead, blamed him for her shame, abused him and even came out to attack him. He somehow managed to get away from the village. No one would ever know of his kindness towards her and his having saved her from hell! The villagers kept saying that these truck drivers are hooligans. But his beard was like Shivaji's and he had been her saviour. Why are those with beards called Sikhs?... Shivaji was a Maratha.

Santokh Singh was looking fixedly at Shivaji's picture on the wall. He saw a fleeting image of the truck driver and then his own image. He kept gazing at the wall for a long time.

Santokh Singh had the entire night and he was in no hurry. It was the last hour of the night, darkest before the dawn. A blue lamp was softly lighting the room. Santokh Singh looked at Malati and smiled softly. He gently moved the little curl on her forehead and kissed her forehead lightly.

Wearing his long jacket, he curled up his upper lip to look at his moustache which had returned to the clock position of twenty past ten. He left it at that. He looked again at Shivaji's photo. Then he stared at Malati, smiled, and took out the last note of ten rupees from his wallet, handed it over to her, opened the door and left.

(Translated from the Punjabi by Kamal Singh)

CONTRIBUTORS

Varsha Adalja (b. 1940) is a prolific feminist novelist and playwright who has written several stage plays, screenplays and radio dramas. She won the Sahitya Akademi Award in 1995, the Soviet Land Nehru Award in 1976, the Gujarati Sahitya Akademi Award thrice and the Gujarati Sahitya Parishad Award twice.

Chandrika Balan (b. 1954) is a bilingual fiction writer, critic and translator who has published books in English, and in Malayalam under the pen name, Chandramathi. Her published work includes 12 collections of short stories, a novelette, an anthology of medieval Malayalam poetry, two collections of essays, two memoirs and five books translated from English. She is the recipient of the Thoppil Ravi Foundation Award (1995), Katha National Award for fiction and translation (1997) and the Kerala Sahitya Akademi Award for Best Fiction, 1996–1998. (1999)

Ajeet Cour (b. 1934) has written novels and short stories in the Punjabi language on social-realist themes such as the experience of women in relationships and their position in society. She received the Sahitya Akademi Award in 1985 and the Padma Shri in 2006.

Keki N. Daruwalla (b. 1937) is a poet and short story writer in the English language. He received the Sahitya Akademi Award in 1984 for his poetry collection, *The Keeper of the Dead*. He was awarded the Padma Shri in 2014. Daruwalla lives in Delhi. His latest novel is *Ancestral Affairs* and his latest short story collection is *Daniel Comes to Judgement*.

Jagannath Prasad Das (b. 1936) is an Odia poet, playwright, fiction writer and art historian. He has published eleven volumes of poetry, eight collections of short stories, a novel, two collections of essays and five plays besides a number of books of children's verses. A Ph.D. in Art History, he has to his credit several books on Odishan Art. His works have been widely translated into English and various Indian languages and his plays have been staged in many languages all over India. He is a recipient of the Sahitya Akademi Award, the Saraswati Samman and the Nandikar Theatre Award.

Kamala Das (1934–2009) was one of the most prominent feminist voices in the postcolonial era. She wrote in her mother tongue, Malayalam, as well as in English. To her Malayalam readers, she was Madhavi Kutty and to her English patrons, she was Kamala Das. On account of her extensive contribution to poetry in India, she is known as The Mother of Modern Indian English Poetry. She has been likened to literary greats like Sylvia Plath because of the confessional style of her writing.

Vijaydan Detha (1926–2013) was a noted writer from Rajasthan. Detha has more than 800 short stories to his credit, which have been translated into English and other languages. With Komal Kothari, he founded Rupayan Sansthan, an institute that documents Rajasthani folklore, art and music. His literary works include *Bataan ri Phulwari*, a 14-volume collection of stories that draws on folklore in the spoken dialects of Rajasthan. Many of his stories and novels have been adapted for the stage and the screen, including *Charandas Chor* by Habib Tanvir, *Parinati* by Prakash Jha, *Duvidha* by Mani Kaul, and *Paheli* by Amol Palekar. He received the Sahitya Akademi Award (1974) and the Padma Shri (2007).

Arvind Gokhale (1919–1992) was one of the pioneers of the modern Marathi short story. He has over 300 short stories in Marathi, collected in 20 books to his credit. His stories have been translated into many Indian and European languages. He was the Editor of *Pick of the Year*, a Marathi annual of short stories.

Gulzar (b. 1934) is one of India's leading poets. He has published a number of volumes of poetry and short stories, several of which are available in translation. He is also regarded as one of the country's finest writers for children. A greatly respected scriptwriter and film director, he has been one of the most popular lyricists in mainstream Hindi cinema, gaining international fame when he won an Oscar and a Grammy for the song 'Jai Ho.' Gulzar received the Sahitya Akademi Award in 2002 and the Padma Bhushan in 2004. In 2014, he was awarded the prestigious Dadasaheb Phalke Award. He lives and works in Mumbai.

Thomas Joseph (b. 1954) was born in Eloor, Kochi. A recipient of the Kerala Sahitya Akademi Award (2013) for fiction, he has held sway over Malayalam literature for nearly four decades. He specialises in short stories which are a blend of lyrical-fantasy, magical realism and allegories which hold key to the meaning of life and death. He has six short story collections and one novel. He has also won the Mrigaya Award (decided by readers' votes) in 1980 for the story 'Adbhuda Samasya' (A Wondrous Riddle), the Katha Award, Delhi (1996), SBT Sahitya Puraskaram (1997), for the story 'Chitrashalabhangalude Kappal' (The Ship of Butterflies), K.A. Kodungallur Smaraka Puraskaram for the story 'Lokavasanam' (The End of the World), V.P. Sivakumar Smaraka 'Keli' Award (2003) for the story 'Manushavaahanam' (The Human Vehicle), The Kerala Samsthana Balasahitya Institute Award (2009) for the short story collection *Deivathinte Pianovile Pakshikal* (The Birds of God's Piano) amongst others.

Suresh Joshi (1921–1986) was a novelist, short story writer, literary critic, poet, translator, editor and academic in the Gujarati language. While pursuing his teaching career, he led the modernist movement in Gujarati literature. He was a prolific writer who transformed the field of literary criticism.

Mamta Kalia (b. 1940) is a prolific wordsmith who has published several short stories, plays, novels, essays and poems. Proficient in both Hindi and English, this bilingual writer was awarded the Vyas Samman for 2017 for her novel, *Dukkham Sukham.* She has four novels, ten collections of short stories and two volumes of poetry to her credit.

Amin Kamil (1924–2014) excelled at creating an intimate tone in his poetry by blending Persian and Kashmiri words and expressions, aphoristic comments on life, satire and pathos, and through the use of musically potent meters and Persian and Indian mythological allusions. He received several prestigious awards and honours including the Padma Shri (2005) and the Lifetime State Literary Award (2006).

Lakshmi Kannan (b. 1947), also known by her Tamil pen name Kaaveri, is a poet, novelist and short story writer. Writing in Tamil, she translates her works into English herself. She is particularly celebrated for her sharp, brief verses concerned with a woman's search for identity, the place of nature in human experience and cultural identity.

Shiv K. Kumar (1921–2017) was a poet, playwright, novelist and short story writer. His poems have appeared in leading newspapers and magazines including *New York Times, Poetry Review* (London) and *Western Humanities Review* among others. They have also been broadcast on the BBC. In 1978, he was elected a Fellow of the Royal Society of Literature (London). He received the Sahitya Akademi Award in 1987 for his collection of poems, *Trapfalls in the Sky.* In 2001, he was awarded the Padma Bhushan for his contribution to literature.

Kuvempu/Kuppali Venkatappa Puttappa (1904–1994), popularly known by his pen name, Kuvempu, K.V. Puttappa was a renowned Kannada novelist, poet, playwright, critic and thinker. He has over 70 works to his credit. Widely regarded as the greatest Kannada poet of the 20th century, he won the Jnanpith Award for the year 1967 for his magnum opus, *Sri*

Ramayana Darshanam. He is the first among the eight recipients of the Jnanpith for Kannada.

Prabhakar Machwe (1917–1991) wrote more than 100 books in Marathi, Hindi and English. His range of writing included translations, novels, poetry, short stories, biographies, children's books, travelogues, satire, criticism and edited volumes and reviews. Dr. Machwe was a linguist and an authority on Indian literature. He taught Indian literature, religion and culture, philosophy and Gandhian thought in many universities in the United States. He was invited by former Indian Prime Minister Jawaharlal Nehru and former President Dr. Radhakrishnan to establish the Sahitya Akademi in 1954. He contributed immensely to the development of the institution.

Indu Menon (b. 1980) writes both poetry and fiction. Her work grapples with contemporary themes such as communalism and the regressive tendencies creeping into Kerala society. She is the winner of various honours including the Kendra Sahitya Akademi Yuva Puraskar (2014), the Uroob Award (2002) and the Mathrubhoomi Katha Award (2009).

Prabhat Kumar Mukhopadhyay (1873–1932) was a renowned Bengali writer. His short stories are mainly based on real-life situations and his characters belong to middle-class families. Their hopes, dreams, disappointments and joys are finely woven into his stories.

Pritish Nandy (b. 1951) is one of India's best-known poets. Widely published and internationally acclaimed, Nandy's work has been translated into many languages across the world. He has nearly 30 books of poetry and translation in print. He has won several awards and distinctions including the Padma Shri (1977). Mulk Raj Anand in his introduction to *The Poetry of Pritish Nandy*, hailed him as "the harbinger of the new Indian consciousness."

Joginder Paul (1925–2016) was born in Sialkot of present-day Pakistan and migrated to India at the time of Partition, after which he lived in Kenya for nearly 15 years. With a Master's in English, he taught literature until he retired as the principal of a post-graduate college in Maharashtra. He chose to write in Urdu, with the conviction that Urdu is "not a language but a culture." While he was seen as part of the Progressive Urdu Writers' Movement, his creative writing also reflected a strong modern sensibility. Paul's 20 works of fiction exposed social ills sensitively. He was honoured with several awardss including the SAARC Lifetime Achievement Award, Iqbal Samman and the Ghalib Award. His fiction has been translated into many languages.

Gauri Shankar Raina is a Kashmiri playwright, translator, theatre director and television producer. He is the author of a collection of plays titled *Ek Wohi Main*. His plays, *Lalla Main Toh Prem Diwani* and *Nagar Udaas Hain* have been staged to much acclaim. He received the National Human Rights Commission's Biennial Award for Translation in 2011.

Tarannum Riyaz is a noted Urdu fiction writer, critic, poet, essayist and translator. She holds a Master's in Education and Urdu and a doctorate in Education. This former senior fellow of the Ministry of Culture, Government of India, has written over 20 works of fiction, criticism, poetry and translation. Riyaz won the Delhi Urdu Academy Fiction Award for 2006 and the best book award twice for her short story collections, *Yimverzal* and *Mera Rakht e Safar*. She has also received the Uttar Pradesh Urdu Academy Fiction Award and the Sahir Ludhyanvi Adeeb International Award for her contribution to poetry and prose. Her work has been included in several anthologies and translated into Indian and foreign languages. Her edited work, *20th Century Urdu Literature of Women*, published by the Sahitya Akademi was widely acclaimed. She was a SAARC Literature Awardee for 2014.

Manmohan Saral (b. 1934) is a veteran Hindi fiction writer and journalist. His oeuvre includes the short story collections, *Ek Achanak Shyaam* and *Pyaas Ek, Roop Do*. He is the recipient of the Premchand Katha Award (Maharashtra State Hindi Sahitya Akademi), Akhil Bharatiya Muktibodh Award (Madhya Pradesh Sahitya Akademi) and National Varnapat Samman (Kalavart Nyas, Ujjain).

Mohinder Singh Sarna (1923–2001) started writing at the age of twenty. His first collection of short stories *Pather de Admi*, was published in 1949. This renowned Punjabi writer has several short stories, four novels, four epics in verse on the lives of Sikh Gurus and heroes and a literary autobiography to his credit. He received several honours and awards, including the Sahitya Akademi Award (1994) for his short story collection, *Nawen Yug de Waris*.

Sukhbir (1925–2012) was a well-known poet, storyteller, playwright, essayist and thinker. During his six-decade long creative career, he published eight books of poetry, 15 collections of short stories and seven novels. He wrote in both Punjabi and Hindi. His contribution to children's literature includes the novel *Kutch da Shahar* (Town of Glass). A prolific translator, he translated Leo Tolstoy's epic novel, *War and Peace* into Punjabi. He was honoured with many awards but was reluctant to accept such recognition. Hence he is often called the 'martyr' of Punjabi literature.

TRANSLATORS

Masooma Ali is a former lecturer in the English Department of Miranda House, University of Delhi. She has contributed extensively to literary magazines and has several translations of literary works by eminent writers to her credit.

Pankaj Bhan is an educator, writer, translator and the editor of *Miraas,* a quarterly journal for the promotion of Kashmiri culture and heritage.

Yasmin Dhorda has an Master's in Clinical Psychology and a diploma in Human Resources Management. She retired as Assistant General Manager, HRD from Bank of Baroda after 32 years of service.

Bal Gadgil was a prolific and multi-faceted writer with several novels, travelogues, plays, literary criticism, children's stories and short stories to his credit. His works have been translated into a number of languages including Hindi, Gujarati, Urdu, Kannada, Malay and Turkish.

Madan Mohan Mathur was a well-known short story writer and dramatist and former Chairperson of the Sangeet Natak Akademi.

Sukrita Paul Kumar is a well-known poet, critic, and academician. A recipient of several prestigious grants, as well as national and international fellowships and residencies, she has published several collections of poems in English.

Lila Ray/Majumdar was a teacher and pioneering children's writer in Bengali. A recipient of the Sangeet Natak Akademi Award (1963) and the Rabindra Puraskar (1968), she wrote over 125 books, including a collection of short stories, five co-authored titles, nine translated books and 19 edited books.

Sindhu V. Nair is a post-graduate in Literature from the University of Kerala. Her translations from Malayalam into English have been published by Oxford University Press, International Collective in Support of Fishworkers and D.C. Books.

Gieve Patel is a poet, playwright, painter and a practising physician. His poems, included in various anthologies, speak of his deep concerns for nature and expose man's cruelty to it. His collection, *Mister Behram and Other Plays* was published by Seagull Books in 2007 and his *Collected Poems* was published by Poetrywala, Mumbai, in 2017. He has worked as a medical practitioner in rural and urban India.

Premjish is a curator, writer and translator based in Delhi. His translations have appeared in *Indian Literature* published by the

Sahitya Akademi. He has initiated an independent curatorial platform called Future Collaborations, aiming at theoretically and politically informed curation.

Miraan Punjabi is a translator, freelance photographer, traveller and an entrepreneur. His translations have appeared in several literary journals including *Indian Literature* published by the Sahitya Akademi. His deep insight into culture and languages makes his translations highly authentic. Punjabi lives in Delhi.

Navtej Sarna is the author of the novels, *The Exile* and *We Weren't Lovers Like That*, the short story collection, *Winter Evenings*, the non-fiction works, *The Book of Nanak, Second Thoughts* and *Indians at Herod's Gate* as well as two translations, *Zafarnama* and *Savage Harvest*. He has been a regular contributor to several Indian publications as well as to the *Times Literary Supplement, Financial Times (UK), London Magazine* and the *BBC*. A career diplomat since 1980, he has served as High Commissioner of India to the UK and Ambassador to Israel. He was India's Ambassador to the United States till December 2018.

Antara Dev Sen is a literary critic, translator, columnist and commentator on the media, society, politics, culture and development. She has edited several books including the *TLM Short Stories from South Asia* series.

Kamal Singh was former head, Governance & Social Justice, British Council, India. She has published many articles and reports and been invited as a resource person at several prestigious national and international events.

Khushwant Singh was an iconic writer, political commentator and columnist. The author of outstanding works such as *Train to Pakistan, I Shall Not Hear the Nightingale, Delhi: A Novel* and *A History of the Sikhs,* he was awarded several honours, including the Padma Bhushan in 1974 (which he later returned in protest) and the Padma Vibhushan (2007).

A.J. Thomas is an Indian-English poet and fiction writer who has translated fiction as well as drama from Malayalam into English over the last two decades. He has several books to his credit. He regularly publishes poetry, short fiction, translations, book reviews and features in publications in India and abroad.

Paul Zacharia is a Malayalam writer with several short stories, novellas, travelogues, screenplays, essays, columns, children's books and a novel in English to his credit. Zacharia is a distinguished fellow of the Kerala Sahitya Akademi and a recipient of the Vallathol Award (2019)